Going Broke

By Trista Russell

Going Broke

By Trista Russell

Urban Books
6 Vanderbilt Parkway
Dix Hills, NY 11746

ISBN 0-7394-5113-8

First Printing February 2005

Acknowledgements

First, I would like to offer up thanks and praises to God for breathing into my body each morning, and continually blessing me with words, a vivid imagination, and the time to do what I love to do most, write. I would like to acknowledge my immediate family: my parents, Reverend Everett & Mrs. Zerlean Russell, my sister, Roslyn Underwood (and Mike), my brother, Minister Phillip Russell (and Stefanie), nieces: Raeshawnda and Philisha, nephews: Phillip Jr., Ray Jr., Mailk, and Javon. Relatives and friends in Bimini, Cat Island, Grand Bahama, Nassau & Abaco Bahamas, Miami, Homestead, Florida City, West Palm Beach & Jacksonville, Florida, Brunswick & Atlanta Georgia, California, Pennsylvania, and Illinois. If you find yourself sucking your teeth (Bahamians know what that means), shaking your head, calling another friend or family member, or saying "Lord have mercy on this child," during the course of reading this book, remember that it's just a story and enjoy it. Steve Burris, where would I be without you? Not here. Thank you for your continued and unconditional love and support and for reading this book over and over each time I made a change. You were there from day one and I appreciate your motivation, thoughtfulness, and patience throughout this process. Loving you has changed my life. Roshunda Slaton, you made me feel like this book is the best thing since the invention of the wheel, which means the world to me. Some people actually think that my creative inspiration comes from some of our weekend trips back in the days—the nerve of them. Erica Calderon, if I didn't believe in myself I know that you're the one person who would. Thank you for not only making time, but also for taking time out to fly on the wings of my dreams. Sha-Shana Crichton, my agent, thank you for taking me under your wings. It's to the top from here. Carl Weber and Urban Books, you came along at a time in my life where the thought of this dream was almost packed away for a while. There are no words to say how grateful I am to you. You are a welcomed blessing. Lisa D'Angelo, my editor, thank you for not only working with my manuscript, but also for working with me and coaching me on the do's and don'ts of this business. You know your stuff, which is why your opinion meant so much. LaTonya Williams, author of Mixed Messages, thank you for your meaningful advice the many times you helped out. To the dedicated few that read Going Broke before the ink dried: Melissa Jones, Ken Hadley, Nikki Samuel, Lori Sanchez, Letanya Brown, Raquel Bogle, Angela Redmon, Steve Hazle, and last but far from least, Joelle Janvier. Thank all of you for your outlook and various opinions on Going Broke. Because of your honesty the finished product will stun, bring tears and put a smile on the faces of many. Your inputs breathe new life into my characters. Many thanks for the accolades you threw my way, even comparing me to some of the industry's finest, thank you.

To you, yes I'm talking to you, I appreciate your support. Thank you for choosing Going Broke amongst the various other books that it sat nearby. Your purchase means a lot to me. I'd like to hear from you. Visit www.TristaBooks.com to write to me.

To Grandpee for Father's Day.

Going Broke

"Money, it turned out, was exactly like sex. You thought of nothing else if you didn't have it and thought of other things if you did."
–James Baldwin, *Nobody Knows My Name*

Bank Statement # 1
Account Balance: $23,567.28

"Someone needs to write a book on how to love a man with a small dick," Natalya was rambling the moment she saw me approaching the bar. "Is it possible to truly love a man with a dick the size of his thumb?"

"Shh." I looked around. "Why are you talking so loud, and who are you talking about?" I slipped onto the barstool next to her.

"I am so disappointed and depressed." She sipped her martini then slammed the glass back down so hard that the bartender shot her a "bitch, you break it you buy it" look.

"What are you talking about?" I giggled off her dramatics.

"There ought to be a law stating that when you meet a man he issues you a card with the exact measurements of his dick before you give him your number, or before he gives you his." She sighed. "I've wasted the last six months of my life."

"Nick?" My jaw dropped.

"Yes." She rolled her eyes. "Now known as two-inch dick Nick."

Going Broke

I laughed but quickly sympathized. "What happened?"

"I finally gave in," she said.

"When?" I couldn't believe my ears. Nick had been wining and dining Natalya for six months. He worshipped the ground she walked on, sending her flowers once a week, cutting her lawn bi-weekly, making appointments for her, and picking up the bill for her monthly spa visits. He took her to Jamaica and not only did he respect the fact that she wanted separate rooms. He even paid for both rooms. He seemed to be the end all be all. Damn!

"So, Mr. Nick only has a grand in the bank, huh?"

She looked at me like I missed the point. "I wish." She turned toward me. "The man has insufficient funds in his dicking account." She finished her martini in one large gulp; I grimaced while watching her. "His account is negative thirty-two dollars and seventy-eight cents."

"So, what are you going to do?" I asked.

"Sarai, I really don't know. I'm so confused." She motioned the bartender over. "I truly believe that he cares for me, but . . ."

"But his account is in negative status." I finished her sentence and looked up at the new bartender. I was used to being served by Tammy. It was always two for one on her shift. "I'll have a Chocolatini, please."

"Forget the martini, Jack." She looked at his nametag. "I'll have a double shot of tequila."

"My opinion is if the sex isn't good, everything else will fall out of line," I continued. "Regardless of how good he looks in a suit, how passionate he kisses you, or how well he eats the cooty-coo, he still can't throw down when it really matters, so life would be a constant tease."

"I'm hating life right now."

"I told you to stop believing all of those stupid

myths. Oh, he's tall, he wears a size seventeen shoe, and his fingers are long and fat." I rolled my eyes. "All that shit ain't true. He'll have you wondering where the fuckin' beef is." In the blink of an eye, I thanked God that this wasn't something I had to worry about. I met Damian almost two years ago, and my baby had a whopping ten grand in his account and didn't mind investing it in my bank whenever necessary.

"Damn." She shook her head from side to side as though this was the worst thing that could ever happen to her.

"I think I need to send out an e-mail," I joked. "Too many women are fooled by brothas who know exactly when their accounts are low in funds. That's why they drive those fancy cars and spend their paychecks on cologne, clothing, and expensive shit. All of that is to compensate when they can't penetrate. They want us to fall for the presentation." I found an example. "I bet P. Diddy has a small dick."

"But I'm getting too old for this." She pouted. "I'm less than a week away from my thirtieth birthday and I'm *still* single, with no children and *still* no active sex life. I really thought I had it going on with Nick, thought I had fallen for him, until last night."

She sounded like she wanted to cry. "I mean, am I stupid for freaking out because of this?" She tried to rationalize. "Shouldn't I be looking at more than just the sex when it comes to a relationship?"

"Okay, just calm down." I tried to take her situation seriously, but I couldn't believe that her urgent voicemail on my cellular to meet her at The Clevelander was about Nick's dick. "Did he at least know what to do with his limited access pass?" I tried not to crack the smile hiding beneath. "I mean, did he know how to work

4

it?"

"First of all, it wouldn't even stay hard." She rested her head on the bar like the world was coming to an end. "When he was holding it to put it in, his hand completely covered it. I mean his hand completely swallowed it up like a pig in a blanket."

"Damn!" I frowned at the picture she was painting. What a waste of brown skin. "But he is so fine."

"I know, *and* he loves me," she said. "So, what do I do?"

Why was she asking *me*? I'd be out. See ya! Good sex is like oxygen; if you don't get enough of it, you're bound to do something stupid. "Well, Nat, I think I'd just—"

I was interrupted by an approaching voice. "Sarai and Nat, why in the world am I in a bar in the middle of the week?" For the first time, I was happy to hear India's high-pitched voice. "I hope she hasn't told you what the emergency is yet." She hugged us both, did the cheek-to-cheek kiss, and sat on the other side of the drama queen. "What's with this urgent message business? I couldn't even find a damn parking spot, and you know that I don't like parking my baby just anywhere." She shouted at the bartender like he was her hired servant. "A glass of Moet."

"Forget your puke-colored Benz and its stupid parking spot." Natalya grabbed the shot and swallowed it. "I'm in the midst of a crisis."

I looked at India and playfully smiled behind Nat's back. "The sky is falling," I said.

Natalya looked at me glaringly. "Excuse the hell out of me, Miss Dick-for-Days."

I joked, "Don't get mad at me because I'm gett'ng it good."

India held up her hands. "Whoa, will one of you please tell me what the heck is going on?"

I shut up and let Natalya tell her story. She reminded us of how she met Nick, (a financial advisor at her bank), and how he had just been picture perfect up until last night. She fell hard for him and all but wore out the batteries in her bedroom toy trying to play hard to get. Now look at what she got. A financial advisor, who drives a Jaguar, owns a three-bedroom home in Coconut Grove, a speedboat, and a dick like Mini Me.

I chuckled as I listened to the gory details of Nat's night. After four Chocolatinis, the story got more and more hilarious. My side was hurting like it did when I was watching Martin Lawrence's *Runteldat*.

As you've already heard, my name is Sarai, pronounced Sa-*rye*, Emery. I'm twenty-seven years young and work as a radio personality, disc jockey, hostess, or whatever you choose to call it. I pay my bills by talking between songs from 12:00 midnight to 5:00 in the morning at WBIG, also known as BIG COUNTRY 104.5 in Miami, Florida. Why? Like I said, it pays the bills while I'm waiting for Tamara G., Supa Cindy, or Cheryl Mizell to slip up, then I'd be able to submit my resume to 99 Jamz. I'd love the opportunity to dance to hip-hop, rap, and reggae during my sets. Along with my job at BIG COUNTRY, I also own two very small Internet based businesses, youplanmytrip.com and picnictogo.com.

I moved to Miami eight years ago to attend Florida International University and would not ever move back to Dover, Delaware to save my life. There was nothing that I missed about Dover, nothing that I liked about Dover. The only reason I still had ties to the town was because I still had a father.

Going Broke

I met Natalya during my second year at FIU, where she and I had a psychology class together. I always thought she needed to do the studies on herself, but if you asked her, she had all the sense in the world and then some.

Nat was smart, ultra-sensitive, and generous enough to give you the bra off of her back if she wasn't worried about her breasts sagging. At twenty-nine years old, she valued our friendship and loved teaching math at Northern Dade Middle School. Her dream was to be married and have two children before the age of thirty-five. However, because of her many failed relationships, her heart was naïve and fragile. She had forgotten what having fun, love, and sex at the same time was like.

Though she drifted off from time to time, Natalya was my dearest friend. When I met her, she had an idiot named Joseph. She let him run her around like a chicken with its head cut off. He didn't have a job, but he didn't need one. She paid for everything, including his monthly car note. Error! Boy, did Joseph hate me! In just three months, I revolutionized Nat and she kicked him to the curb. Joseph began looking for his own apartment and a nine to five, but he didn't find one in time because his car was repossessed. Over the years, I've seen Nat grow a backbone, but she's still not where I'd like her to be.

India was a new friend to both Nat and me. We met her in a book club we joined a little less than two years ago. India was a sight for sore eyes. At six feet one inch, she weighed a whopping 120-pounds with a wet mink coat on her back, and her flawless, professional weave job rivaled Toni Braxton's and Lil' Kim's. She claimed that she didn't get as many modeling jobs as she'd like because of her dark brown complexion, but I suspected it had a lot to do with her mind-set. Nobody wanted to work with a model with diva attitude and no experience. She didn't have the name or credentials to prove that she was worthy. However, she did have the money.

Days after learning of her pregnancy, her boyfriend of just ten months, police officer Andrew Covington, took out not one but two life insurance policies listing her as the sole beneficiary. When she was three and a half months pregnant, he was killed when a gunfight broke out at a Carol City nightclub where he was working overtime as security. Two weeks after the funeral, she had an abortion, stating that having the child would be too painful. I guess having $3 million was worth the haunting memories of that day in the doctor's office. Ever since, she's been living out her dreams: new cars, a house, trips, clothing, and parties. You name it, she had the money for it. Unfortunately, money couldn't buy her love. Since Andrew's death, love was still the one thing she'd been lacking.

"You know what, Nat?" India got more talkative after a few drinks. "I say, fuck a big dick."

"That's what I do, and I like it," I joked.

"No, you idiot." She explained. "I don't mean it that way. Okay, maybe fuck was the wrong word. Forget looking for a man with a big dick. If he has a big heart, then everything else is gravy." She pretended to be sentimental. "Life is too short to worry about simple things."

"Thanks, India." Nat smiled. She was very pleased with the fake answer.

"That's real, girl. True love is worth more than any amount of dick or money in the world." A tear was frozen on the edge of her eyelid. I wasn't buying her sob story.

I'd bet anything that she'd choose the $3 million rather than a resurrection of Andrew.

I allowed the alcohol to speak through me like an evil spirit. "Are you really buying that?" I asked. "One of three things will happen. One, you'll spend the rest of your life wondering what another man would've been like. Two, you'll cheat on him and end up hurting both yourself and him. Or three, you'll be one of those miserable old women that can't stop fussing at everybody because you spent too damn long with a gentleman with a petite prick instead of a Mandingo brotha with da magic stick."

"It is not all about that, Sarai," India said.

"It *is* all about that. Who wants a man that can't cause any pain?" The liquor spoke up again. "Well, you ain't getting none, so maybe she should take your advice."

Her eyes grew wide. "Don't worry about me. I gets mine."

"From who?" Nat asked as she slapped her on the shoulder.

"Wow, this is a shocker," I added. India made a promise to Andrew's ghost that she wouldn't sleep with anyone for at least five years.

"It's a guy friend of mine, no one special." Feeling the need to explain, she said, "It was something that just happened. I feel terrible about it."

"Has it *happened* more than once?" I asked.

"Yeah." She blushed.

"Oh hell," Nat said. "Well, that didn't just happen."

"Congratulations." I held up my glass. "I knew that five-year shit wasn't gonna hold up."

"Oh, ye of no faith." She rolled her eyes. "I did go a year and eight months, thank you."

"That's still not five years." I was sarcastic. "So, who is this guy?"

She seemed nervous. "I don't want to jinx anything."

"So, how long have you been seeing him?" Nat asked.

"We've been seeing each other over the past two months."

I was in shock. "And you've been keeping him a secret?"

"I just don't want to start talking about him yet. Maybe it won't turn out to be anything."

"Tell us something." Nat was the nosiest. "Where did you meet him? How old is he? What does he do?"

"Do you really care about that or do you want to know about his dick?" She smiled.

I didn't allow Nat a chance to answer. "Tell us about the dick account. Is it overdrawn, barely opened, does he have direct deposit, is he in the hundreds, thousands, or is the man a millionaire?"

"Definitely in the thousands," she blushed.

We slapped hands. "I'm happy for you, girl."

"I'm jealous of you, ya slut." Nat smiled.

India pushed her playfully. "Whatever."

"So, tell us. What's his name? Where did you meet him?"

"We ran into each other and got better acquainted the night of Randy's birthday party."

Nat tried to recall. "But I didn't see you with anyone."

"It's all about what you didn't see," India joked.

"You would pick a party that I wasn't in town to attend, huh?"

She turned to me. "Oh, that's right. You weren't

there."

"No, I was in country-ass Nashville at a Tim McGraw concert." Working for BIG COUNTRY had its perks. I traveled a lot, but it was always to attend country music concerts, parties, and clubs. Then I had to come back and hit the airwaves with a smile as I reported on how great it was. After those events were done, I also found a hip-hop club or concert and used my media pass to get my groove on properly. "Well, is this guy going to be at the party on Saturday?" I asked.

"He might be there. We'll see."

"That's right. Let's talk about my party," Nat said.

We spent the next hour and a half ironing out the details for Nat's party. Being the balla she was, India was picking up the tab. She gave us a $10,000 check and permission to do whatever we wanted. Of course, we didn't need that much, so we pocketed $2,500 each right off the top and used the rest to throw a party that no one would soon forget. My share wasn't actually pocketed. It was already spent. I used it to pay for my all-inclusive vacation next month. I needed a break not just from everything, but also from everyone. I pretended not to pick up on Damian's subtle clues to be invited. In fifteen days, I'd be aboard a Bahmasair flight to Paradise Island in Nassau, Bahamas where I'd be staying at the world-renowned Atlantis Hotel.

India, Natalya, and I parted ways around nine, leaving me with only three hours free before work. I cruised down Ocean Drive; the beach wasn't nearly as busy or live as it would be on Friday night because of the Memorial Day Hip-Hop weekend. My apartment was right across the Rickenbauker Causeway in Downtown Miami, so getting home from South Beach was never more than a ten-minute ride. I searched my parking garage for a space and couldn't help but get excited when I saw Damian's Hummer. I'm not sure if it was because he had been out of town or because I'd been talking about penises for hours, but chills ran through my body. I was so anxious that I nearly got electrocuted pressing the button for the eleventh floor so hard.

I unlocked my apartment door with a Kool-Aid grin, but found the living room area empty. Miles Davis was blasting from the stereo, which meant that my man was in a good mood, the best mood—a sexual mood. I dropped my purse on the couch, watered my plants, kicked off my shoes, and lit a jarred candle. We had a large, three-bedroom penthouse-style apartment. One of the spare bedrooms was my home office, and the other was his. I tiptoed past both and continued down the hallway leading to our bedroom. I slowly opened the door and saw him lying in the king-sized bed with our black satin sheets pulled up to his chest. Without him seeing me, I quickly slid my hand down the wall to turn off the light.

Startled, he sat up when the darkness hit him. When he saw me approaching with the candle, his surprised look turned into a smile. He waved me over. He was on the phone. "Well, thanks for calling. I'll definitely know something by tomorrow afternoon." He continued to speak into the phone while he held his left hand out to me. "I'll have all the details at the meeting." I rested the candle on the nightstand and placed my hand in his warm hand. "Right, right." He was trying to get rid of the caller. "Yeah, that's right." He paused. "Tomorrow. All right, have a good night."

I sat on the bed next to him. "Hi."

"Hi back at you." He moved close to my face. "I

missed you."

"I missed you more." I squeezed his hand.

He kissed me and I realized just how much I did miss him. Damian was my lover, my best friend and roommate for the past year. He was also an architect working on opening his own architectural firm. He stood at five eleven and weighed around 180 pounds. He kept himself tight, and my favorite thing to see him in was his skin. "How was your trip?"

"It was productive. I think we may have landed the deal to design the shopping center, but I'm not certain about the hospital." He leaned back against the headboard.

I removed my shirt and he smiled, but I wondered why he wasn't helping. "So, when will you know?"

"By next Thursday. They're still meeting with other firms." He leaned over to the other side of the bed and placed the phone on the charger. I stood up and watched him not watch me as I pulled down my pants. Removing them slowly, I hoped it would interest him. He looked, but I could tell that he wasn't into it. "Hey! What's wrong?" I asked.

He grimaced. "I'm sorry. I'm just a little tired."

I slid under the sheets next to him. "I'll fix that." I allowed my fingers to glide down his chest as I kissed him softly again and again on the lips then smiled. "I'll give you something to be tired about." My fingers moved from the smooth surface of his chest to sliding around his abs like they were wrapped in lotion.

I was confused. "What's that?" I yanked the covers and saw the transparent fluid plastered like glue to his lower abdominal area. "Thanks a lot." I rolled my eyes.

"I'm sorry, baby," he said. "I didn't know you were coming home right now. I thought you'd be gone until it was time for work. I couldn't wait."

I blew out the candle. "Why couldn't you wait?" I pulled away from him. "You've been out of town for a week. Why would you wait until you're home to jack off?" I jumped up from the bed and headed toward the bathroom.

"Sarai, I missed you. I came home and you weren't here, but I smelled your perfume, saw your pictures and couldn't wait. I got hard so I stroked," he shouted as I walked away, "What's the fuckin' problem?"

"You." I turned and looked at him before I closed the bathroom door.

"Yeah?" he yelled. "Well, fuck you too, then." I bet the guys at the firm never heard him talk that way.

Dwayne Cart was born and raised in the Bronx, New York. His dad was currently serving life in prison for the murder of his mother, a murder that happened right in front of him at the tender age of nine. From then until he was eighteen, Dwayne was placed in a total of twelve different foster homes. An unruly, violent and troubled soul, he found comfort in joining a gang. After numerous run-ins with the New York City juvenile crime system he used the streets to his advantage, selling enough drugs in high school to pay his own college tuition and have his name legally changed to Damian Carter.

Though he traded in the streets of New York for the Sunshine State, Damian was *still* very much what I considered a thug. He moved south not only because of a job offer from The Steinbach Group, but also to be closer to the Jamaican and Colombian drug dealers he befriended and started conducting business with. Yes, it was safe to say that he lived a double life; it might even be safe to assume that he had multiple personalities at times. The president of the firm, William Steinbach, cherished him as a devoted, brilliant, young and extremely skilled architect. But when he left the office, he became Dwayne Cart, drowning in Sean Jean gear and strapped with a 9-millimeter pistol, roaming the Miami streets in his white H2. The best thing about it was that Damian was sexy in a suit and even more attractive when he threw on his Tims and baggie jeans.

Seconds after I turned off the shower, I watched the bathroom door open through the fogged-up shower door. "Why in the hell do you put me through this, Sarai?" he asked.

I faced him through the door. "Can I have some privacy, please?"

"No." He reached for the door.

"Damian, I'm being serious." I held the door shut and tried not to smile. "Get out of here."

"No." He sounded angry.

"Why not?"

He pushed the door open and grabbed my hands. "Not until you ride this dick." Damn, he knew how I liked it. He sat on the toilet pulled me out of the tub and onto his lap. "Why do you put me through this, huh?"

He smacked my butt. "One of these days I'm gonna hurt your ass with that playing hard to get shit." My man knew me well. I rose and fell onto his thick nine inches in between his sentences. "You know I just take this pussy when I want it."

I was melting. I loved to hear him talk that way, and he knew it. "I don't have to ask for this, I don't have to ask for shit. I take it." I loved him. "You missed me?"

"Yes," I whimpered.

"No, you didn't." He smacked my wet ass again.

"Yeah, yes I did."

"Then fuck me like you haven't had dick in a

15

week." He took my breast into his mouth.

I did exactly what he asked. After it was all said and done, I had to take another shower, and he joined me. Damian knew that I liked dramatic sex, so at least twice a week I brought out the Dwayne in him to hit me with some thug passion. I like that New York gangsta to handle me like I stole some money from him or was giving away his drugs for free. He could read my moods and decipher when to present me Dwayne or Damian. Tonight was definitely the night that I had out an APB on Dwayne Cart.

Later that night, I hopped around, putting on my jeans, boots and a shirt, I checked my messages on my office line. I wrote down a few names and numbers, grabbed my keys and the cordless phone on the way to kiss him goodbye. "Baby, I'm leaving." I entered his office.

"Here is the phone." I quickly went through the caller ID to see who called while I was out or while we were busy. "India called?" I noticed her cellular number on the display.

"Yeah, she called when I was on the phone with Rick."

"I just left her out on the beach." I was concerned. "Was she all right?"

"She didn't say that anything was wrong. She said that she tried you on your cell but you didn't pick up." He was at his drafting table.

I looked at my cell phone and saw that I did have a missed call. "I'll call her on the way to work." I put the phone on his desk and kissed the back of his bald head. "I love you, boy."

He grabbed my hand and kissed it before I walked away. "I love *you*, girl."

16

"It's midnight," I spoke into the microphone with a sexy bedroom voice. "Is your lover next to you?" I always smiled during my opening. "If they're not, then Sarah is here to give you a little something to hold on to."

The station manager, Richard "Country Ass" Motes, thought that Sarai Emery wasn't "hick" enough for WBIG, so everyone at the station referred to me as Sarah or Sarah E. "I'm here to give you something that you can feel." I giggled when I said it, thinking of Natalya's dilemma. "Let me ease your troubled mind." I had a good ole boy set already lined up: Brooks & Dunn's "Till My Dyin' Day", Trace Adkins' "Help Me Understand," Dwight Yoakam's "The Back of Your Hand," and Kenny Chesney's "On the Coast of Somewhere Beautiful."

By the time I made it home, Damian was heading out the door with his coffee in one hand, briefcase in the other, and a bunch of rolled up plans under his arm. I fixed his tie, gave him a quick smack on the lips then locked the door behind him. I caught up on much needed rest until one in the afternoon, then I mailed out two personalized picnic baskets that were ordered from my site, and responded to the six queries to youplanmytrip.com. I ended the day with a profit of $117; that was a record day.

It was Thursday. I called Nat and discussed the details of her birthday party on Saturday night. Since we were spending India's money, we went all out. We reserved a private room at B.E.D., a nightclub/restaurant on Miami Beach. At B.E.D., all of the tables were actually king-sized beds; draped in clean crisp, white sheets and white fluffy pillows. Patrons ate dinner in beds enclosed by silky sheer material draped from floor to ceiling. Candles helped to provide a sexy and very romantic atmosphere.

The private room that we reserved was designed to comfortably fit eighty people. We were expecting a total of seventy-eight. For $4,000 it included ten beds decorated in our Mardi Gras masquerade theme, an open bar, buffet appetizers, main course and desserts, and our own personal DJ. The "get your freak on" party gift bags ran us $300. We used $200 on the games we decided we weren't too old to play, $200 on prizes, and $200 on decorations.

My favorite color was purple, Nat's yellow, and India's green. We bickered back and forth about the color of the decorations until Nat decided that we put them together. They were the Mardi Gras colors. Purple sheets were set to adorn the beds, and green and yellow sheers would be falling from the ceiling. We asked the guests to wear masks, and even talked the chefs into creating a spicy New-Orleans style feast for the party. We had enough beads to keep the party interesting, and even planned on hanging poster-sized pictures of topless women in the room. This was going to be a real Mardi Gras party. Saturday needed to hop a train to Miami. It was not coming fast enough for me.

Going Broke

"Never invest your money in anything that eats or needs repainting."
–Billy Rose, in *The New York Post*

Bank Statement # 2

Account Balance: $25,027.92

"Hi, Daddy."

"Who is this?"

A tear ran down my cheek just like every other time I talked to him. "This is Sarai."

"Sa . . . what?" he said.

"Sarai." I tried to hold myself together. "Sarai." I repeated it, hoping to jog his memory.

"What kind of name is that?" He sounded upset.

It was the name he had given to the oldest of his twins, Sarai and Savion. It was the name he wrote poems and songs about, a name he used to smile to and scream when I walked through the door. "Daddy, it's me."

Suddenly, I heard a tremendous amount of noise and commotion before I heard the nurse's voice.

"Hi, Miss Emery." She was polite. "I'm sorry. Your father is having a bad day. He refused his medication again. I'm sure if you call tomorrow he'll be a little better." I could hear him in the background telling her to tell that gal never to call back again. Alzheimer's was a bitch.

My father's name was Lawrence Emery. He was just sixteen years old in 1952, when his 14-year-old girlfriend, Esther, turned up pregnant. They were forced to marry and later became the proud parents of not just Lawrence Jr., but also Emerald, James, and Rose. After twenty-eight years of marriage, at age forty-four, Lawrence left his wife and children and relinquished the family grocery store to his wife when he met twenty-one year old Sarah Irene Peterson. Sarah was a nightclub singer traveling through Louisiana with a jazz band called the Bed Bugs.

Joining the band on the road, not only did Lawrence become their manager, but also Sarah's husband. Married only two years, twenty-three year old Sarah became pregnant with twins. She begged Lawrence not to cancel shows, promising him that she'd take it easy. However, Sarah Irene fell ill in the middle of January 1976. Everyone thought it was just exhaustion from her hectic performance schedule, but faith took a tragic turn on January 29th when she died in childbirth. It was rumored that Esther, Lawrence's ex-wife, who had deep Creole roots, conjured up a voodoo spell to put Sarah and the babies to rest and bring her husband back home. Only a portion of the spell was successful.

Lawrence gathered his babies and belongings and moved to Dover, Delaware. He raised me and my brother, Savion, all alone, never remarried and never wanted us to return to New Orleans to meet our half-sisters and brothers. Alzheimer's started plaguing him at the young age of sixty-five. He'd been in a nursing home for a little over a year. The disease was said to be yet another spell cast by Esther before her death from a short battle with cancer.

I sniffled. "Please let me just say goodbye to him." I was begging to speak to my own father.

"Well, he's a bit feisty right now," the nurse said.

"Just give him the damn phone," I snapped. I was

paying $700 a month to have him in that nursing home, and as long as I was paying *her* bills, she'd better give me what I wanted.

"Who is this that keeps calling me?" he screamed.

"Daddy, I love you," I cried.

"Yeah, yeah." He asked, "If I tell you that I love you, will you stop calling here?"

"Yes." I was desperate.

"What's your name again?" he asked.

"Sarah Irene," I said as though there was hope. "That's why you named me Sarah I. Sarai."

"I said what your name was. No time fo' long talk."

"Sa-*rye*." I sounded it out.

"I love, you Sarai." He hung up.

With tears streaming down my face, I ran into the kitchen and poured myself a glass of Kendall Jackson's Syrah. "What's wrong?" Damian walked up to me and took the glass out of my hand.

I tried to speak between my heavy breathing. "I just spoke to Daddy."

"Oh." He cradled me in his arms. "Baby, I'm sorry."

I hated talking to my father. "Why did this have to happen to him?" As if having my mom die in childbirth didn't make me crazy enough. Having a father who didn't remember my name was like dipping me in a pool of alcohol after being clawed by a lion. "Why?" I asked him.

"Sarai, I told you to stop calling him so much."

I stepped out of his embrace. "He's my father, Damian." I looked at him like he was insane. I knew my daddy loved me, but I guessed Damian couldn't understand what the love of a father felt like, since he grew up with a deranged alcoholic rapist for a father. Damian's father was so angered by his wife smiling while

22

talking to a bill collector over the phone that he shot her point blank in the temple.

"You don't know my daddy. He's not like—" Damn, I couldn't throw that in his face. It wasn't his fault. "He's not like this. He loves me."

"But whenever you talk to him, you get so depressed."

"Do you expect me to run around the fuckin' house after speaking to the man that raised me, hearing him tell me that my name is ugly?" I grabbed the glass from the counter and gulped down the wine. I felt faint.

"He named me." I wept. "He named me after her." Damian wrapped his arms around me and held me close for so long that I almost fell asleep standing up.

A few hours later, I was getting ready for the party. That's right, Saturday was finally here and I needed something to get my mind off of Daddy, WBIG, and Lydia Delks in Houston. Lydia, a client from picnictogo.com, ordered a picnic basket with hunter green accessories. I knew she'd love the hunter plates, napkin rings, and tablecloth. So, I arranged a set of small ivory, hunter and mint green silk flowers on the stems of the glasses and thought that mint green linen napkins, place settings and pillar candles would be a perfect match. Yeah right! I received a nasty e-mail from Ms. Thang on how I need to learn to follow instructions. Hunter green means hunter green, she didn't ask for my creative opinion.

The good thing about being my own boss was having a choice. I could've done one of three things. One, laugh and ignore the e-mail. Who would she complain to? Two, reply to her e-mail, notifying her that I'd seen the picture on her AOL homepage and no amount of hunter green accessories would make her any more appealing to any man who might have a pity picnic with her. Three, I could chalk it all up to experience, entertain her with good customer service, call instead of e-mailing and offer to FedEx new napkins, place settings, and candles. I did the latter, and she was so impressed with my professionalism that she apologized and said that now that she spread the arrangement over her living room table, she could see where I was going with it. Whatever!

Damian wasn't ready when I was leaving, so I told him to meet me at B.E.D; I promised Natalya that I'd be there at seven to help add the finishing touches to the room. I checked myself in the mirror before leaving. My cinnamon brown skin was looking nice, pressed out over my 5-foot 7-inch, 147-pound body. My naturally pouting lips were glistening, and the way my fitted, one-sleeved purple shirt hugged my breasts, I was sure a few people would ask me for the name of my surgeon. But I wasn't a nip/tuck victim. It was just pure luck. I turned around and examined my backside, slapping my butt through my black pants a few times to make sure that nothing would be seen jiggling when I walked. I slipped on a pair of three-inch black sandals, put on my purple, green, and yellow-gold feathered butterfly mask and smiled.

"Damian, I'm gone baby," I yelled from the front bathroom.

"Okay. See ya in a few," he shouted from somewhere in the back of the apartment.

I decided not to remove my mask for the drive. Motorists were doing double takes all the way to the beach, trying to be certain that the chick in the black Expedition actually had feathers coming from the sides of her face. I loved the attention. It was wild. I found myself waving and blowing kisses back, something I wouldn't do in plain face. I was hiding, no one knew my name, no one knew my face, and I could do whatever I wanted. If everyone at the party had the same feeling behind their masks, it would surely turn into an interesting night.

If there was a Mardi Gras section in Heaven, it must look just like the room that I walked into. It was an absolute dream. The purple sheets were spread tightly over the beds, and the sexy green and yellow-gold silky material fell from the ceiling as though it was being poured from the skies. There were no lights, just hundreds of candles carefully placed around the room, and the disco ball sent white sparkles circulating on the walls. The party wasn't set to start until 8:00, but Natalya and I wanted to make sure that everything was exactly the way we wanted it. We hung the topless pictures around the room and sat at the bar awaiting our guests, enjoying a few cocktails.

The non-black guests showed up at eight, and the first of the black guests strolled in around nine. I was working the door; I didn't stop anyone. I just assumed that no one was tacky enough to just walk in. With my wineglass in hand, I bounced to 50 Cent. "Go shorty, it's ya birthday. Go shorty, it's ya birthday." Natalya and Li'l Dick Nick were bumping and grinding to the song like they were really going to get it on hot and heavy-style after the party. Error!

I handed out ten strings of beads to every man and also handed them a key. There were locks all around the room, on tables, at the bar and on the walls. Also every woman received a belt with a lock attached. In order for a man to be granted unlimited access to the bar via a stamped hand, he had to approach the bar with not only his key, but also the lock that it belonged to. The women had their hands stamped from the moment they walked in. However, they had to work to get beads from the men. There were no rules, but the three women with the most beads at 12:00 a.m. would win prizes. The man who kept the most beads would also receive a prize, so the women had to really work their stuff to take beads from the men. The games were a way to get people to interact.

I was at the door sipping on something and flowing to Li'l Kim's rap about how she had the magic, when a guy approached me from behind. "Will you turn my key?"

I spun around. Before even checking him out, I looked around the room for Damian. He was at the bar with his three uninvited friends. I glanced up at the man less than two feet away and smiled nervously. He was wearing a white mask that extended from his forehead to mid-cheek, just like the Phantom of the Opera. He wore a black dress shirt and slacks. His curly black hair was cropped neatly against his scalp, and his goatee accentuated his sexy, pinkish lips. They looked as if he had just kissed the surface of the Red Sea. "I'm sorry. What do you need?" I forgot what he asked.

"May I try your lock?" He didn't wait for my answer. He just reached for my waist and grabbed the lock.

"Whoa." I was shocked by his aggression. "You're really trying to get your drink on, huh?"

"I'm trying, but," his key didn't fit, "I think you girls hid the lock to this key in the birthday cake or something." He grinned. "I've tried everybody."

"So, I was your last choice, huh?" In the midst of my flirting, I was wishing that he'd walk away before Damian looked in my direction.

"I saved the best for last." He sighed and gave up. "But it looks like my mission is still incomplete." He gave me a polite smile. "Sorry to bother you." He turned to walk away.

"Hey." I grabbed his arm. "At least thank me for my trouble."

"What trouble?" He stared intensely.

I thought about it and realized that there *was* no trouble. "Okay, at least thank me for my time."

"Thank you." He touched his mask as though he were tipping a hat.

"Who was that masked man?" I asked myself.

I gave up the door around 11:00 and made my way around the room. I spotted India's extravagant rhinestone-studded angel mask. As I approached her, she threw on a smile. I didn't know if it was paranoia or intuition, but sometimes I got bad vibes from her. "So, is he here?" I asked.

"He had to be somewhere else." She looked a little down. "As a matter of fact, I'm leaving in a minute."

"Leaving?" I looked at her seriously. "You just got here."

"There's nothing going on." She rolled her eyes.

"I know you're not leaving because he didn't come." I threw my hand up. "Forget him. Damian has some friends here." I quickly checked them out. "I've never seen the guy in the white jacket before," I said as I studied him from afar. "He's kinda cute."

"Damn, you're checking out his friends now?" She added. "That's just nasty."

"I was checking him out for you." I smiled. "Want me to introduce you?"

She looked over at them at the bar where they were standing. "Naw, I'll be all right."

"Are you drinking?" I asked because she seemed

tense.

"I had a drink, but I'm still not hanging around."

I couldn't believe her. "What's wrong with you?"

"Nothing." She looked at her watch. "I just need to get out of here."

"Aren't you having a good time?" It was *always* hard to please India. If she wasn't the center of attention, then her night was ruined.

She looked around. "I mean . . . it's all right."

Trying to get the party on her mind, I asked, "So, what do you think of the place?"

"It's nice." She looked around. "I wonder what you girls would've done without me."

I said, "We would've gotten the job done somehow."

"Well, I'm sure you'll get the job done in the Bahamas as well."

Her words took me by surprise. Nat and I swore that we'd never tell anyone about the five grand that we split out of the ten that she offered for the party. "What?" I tried to smile, but I was dumbfounded.

"It's cool." She smiled. "You need a vacation, I'm just glad that I was able to assist."

I'm not rich, but I wasn't broke, and I wasn't about to let India treat me like I was.

"Look, I'll write you out a check tomorrow." I was embarrassed.

She laughed. "Don't worry about it, girl." India's mood seemed to be improving as she made me more uncomfortable.

"I have it and it's no problem," I lied.

"Well, if you insist. Or you could just think of it as a gift from me to you." She giggled. "Everybody can't be rolling in cash, ya know?" I didn't know if I should be offended or grateful, but I was damn glad when a dude in an ugly orange mask came over and asked her to dance. She rejected him then told me that she'd call me the next day.

I ran into Nat coming out of the kitchen, giving orders no doubt. "What in the hell is wrong with India?"

"Why?" she asked.

"She just left." I added, "I am so damn tired of her antics."

Nat said, "I guess money doesn't make life easier."

"Well, give me some and I'll tell you." Then I remembered my talk with India earlier. "Did you tell her about my trip?"

"No." She glared at me. "Why?"

"She mentioned it."

"No. I never said anything." She covered her mouth. "So, she knows that I kept my share too?"

"I don't know." I needed another drink. "But I'll write her a check tomorrow. She is way too dramatic for me. I think we need to let her go Nat."

"I think she's just lonely."

"Whatever! She's chasing that dude around." I sighed. "After I give her this check, I'm through dealing. She is really starting to get on my nerves."

"Don't give up on her. I think she's missing Andrew too."

I laughed. "You can't be serious." I had to look into her face. "If she was missing him, she would've kept the baby. The man you're supposed to love gets killed and you have an abortion right after the funeral?" I was getting hot. "I need another drink." Nat looked at me and shrugged her shoulders. "It's your birthday. Go find your man." I began walking toward Damian but ran into Mr. Phantom. "Did you find what you were looking for, sir?" I asked but kept walking.

"Yes, ma'am, but it keeps passing me by," he said to my back.

I reached the bar, grabbed Damian's hand, and pulled him away from his friends. "We haven't danced in a while, baby," I said sexily while licking his earlobe. "Dance with me." He followed me to the floor and gave me just what I was looking for. He had me hurting, sweating, and horny during the thirty minutes we spent out there.

When Mya's "My Love is Like . . . Whoa" blasted through the speakers, I turned my back to his chest and did a provocative grinding number on him as he tried to keep his hands from going where they shouldn't go in public. "Keep doing that and I swear I'll have your ass pinned up in the bathroom after this song," he whispered.

"Is that a promise?" I teased him.

"You damn skippy it is." When I spotted Mr. Phantom watching me from the wall, I felt uncomfortable and turned back to face Damian.

After the song, I gave him a kiss and told him that I surrendered. I couldn't take it any longer and needed to rest. After a little mingling, I found Natalya and Nick resting on one of the beds in the back. He was holding her like there was no tomorrow, and she looked like tomorrow wouldn't matter without him. I guessed Nick only having a half an uncooked Oscar Mayer wiener wasn't an issue anymore. She should've kept that part about him to herself. I'd never see him the same again. Women need to learn that *everything* about their man isn't for their girls to know too.

"Birthday girl, have you been on the dance floor?" As I approached, Nick smiled and excused himself to the bar.

As we watched him walk away, she smiled and said, "Sarai, he is such a good man."

I knew why she was saying it. "I know he is, Nat." She didn't have to sell him to me. If he truly loved her, then I was already sold. I'd just give them a penis pump as a wedding gift. I smiled. "Go with your heart."

"I am." She looked at him until he disappeared. "We can work the other stuff out."

"You better." Hopefully she'd wake up and remember what good dick was like and then we'd have this conversation again. "If you love him, love him."

"Thank you." She leaned on me.

"Question." I looked around the room. "Who is the Phantom of the Opera?"

"Huh?" She looked at me like I was insane. "I think Andrew Lloyd Webber wrote it."

"I don't mean the actual opera, you retard." I giggled. "I mean the guy with the white half-mask." I pointed in the direction I saw him in last. "He was over there."

"I have no clue who half of these people are, and I guess I won't know until they take off the masks," she said. "I barely recognized Nick."

That was easy. Just look for the guy without a bulge. I kept that comment to myself. "I want to know who he is."

"What happened to him?"

"Nothing," I said. "I just thought you would know."

"Well, after the unveiling, I'll see if I know who you're talking about."

As I stood, I saw Damian approaching with a look of urgency on his face and his cell phone glued to his ear. "Baby, something's up and I need to make a run."

"Is our meeting in the ladies' room being

rescheduled, Mr. Carter?" I flirted.

He kissed me on the forehead. "Unfortunately it *has* been rescheduled, Ms. Emery. The location has been changed as well." He smiled. "I'll see you at home."

I was past the stage of whining and asking or begging him to tell me where he was going. When I met him, he was straight-up about his lifestyle, so all I could do was kiss him goodbye and pray that he'd make it home safely.

"Those Bimini boys want to talk business." He kissed me again. "Be ready when I get home." As Damian walked away Nick was returning. I told Nat that I would let them have their cuddle time.

The party was jumping, but the party inside of me died knowing that Damian was gone, India was tripping, and Mr. Phantom was shaking his groove thing with a Latina girl on the dance floor. I walked over to the bar. "Let me have a dirty Beefeater gin martini, please." I thought of writing India a check and quickly regretted my offer. I didn't have $2,500 of my own to spare. Twenty thousand dollars of the money in my bank account belonged to Damian, a large portion was tied up, and the rest was needed for my bills.

Damian had several accounts. He never kept all of his money in one spot; that way if anything ever went down he wouldn't be completely out of commission. He kept his "clean" money in my account. However, he entrusted some other very close friends with a little over $200,000 in accounts scattered throughout Miami, Atlanta, the Bronx, and Detroit.

Damian always told me that while it was in my account, the money was there for the taking. He paid the rent and utilities and bought the food, so without him, the lifestyle that I lived would be almost impossible.

Youplanmytrip.com and picnictogo.com paid for my father's nursing home and Nookie, my Expedition, which I still had three years left to pay on. My job at the radio station was paying back my student loans, credit cards I maxed out when I was younger, weaves, nails, toes, shoes, outfits, and perfume.

"A black woman drinking a martini." I felt someone brush against my back. "Damn, that's sexy."

Before I could look up he sat right next to me. I smiled. "The only thing that makes me sexy is the martini?"

"No." I could only see half a smile through the mask. "*You* actually make the martini sexy."

I had to check myself. I was blushing and I couldn't even see this man's face. "Thank you." I looked at my watch. It was 11:57. In just three minutes, the masks were due to come off. "What are you drinking?"

"Bailey's on the rocks." He held up his glass. "You're a pretty good dancer." Before I could smile or say thanks, he continued. "Your man is all right too."

I wasn't confirming or denying anything without seeing his face. "I saw you out there. I take it that you like arroz con pollo." I was referring to the Latina girl.

"Actually, I prefer collard greens, macaroni and cheese and potato salad, but you were busy." He smiled. "I'd also prefer not to get my skull cracked by your man for talking to you."

"He's gone." I laughed. "You have nothing to worry about."

He extended his hand. "I'm Tremel."

"Hi." I placed my hand in his and he squeezed it gently. "I'm Sarai."

"Pretty name. It suits you well." He was still holding my hand. "It's very nice to meet you."

I eased my fingers from his sweet grip. "So, what's with the Phantom of the Opera thing you have going on?"

"I picked it up at the last minute." He seemed a bit shy about it.

"The phantom was hiding something serious behind his mask." I asked, "What are you hiding?"

"Aren't we all hiding?" He touched my mask. "But what was the guy in the opera hiding?"

I checked my watch and jumped from the stool. "I'll tell you in a few." It was twelve o'clock and I needed to get things moving. "I have to go and wrap things up."

"No problem."

I issued the prizes for the games. The woman with thirty-two beads won the top prize, a $100 gift certificate to Burdines. I didn't know what she did to collect all those beads, but she sure had all the men clapping and carrying on when she won. All in all, the party was great. Although though it was almost over, I got the crowd together to sing "Happy Birthday" to Nat. Then came the part I couldn't wait for, taking off the masks. We had only an hour left in the room, so Natalya and I hurriedly sliced and served the red velvet birthday cake.

"So, where is that phantom guy you were talking about?"

I had forgotten about him. I looked around, but he wasn't in sight. "I don't see him." I joked, "He must've been too ugly to stick around after taking off that mask."

"You're stupid, girl."

"He said that his name was Tremel or something like that."

"Are you talking about Mel?" She stopped slicing. "Tremel Colten?"

"I don't know." I was afraid about what she might say about him. "I don't know his last name."

She laughed. "I didn't think that he would come."

I was curious. "Well, who is he?" I bit my bottom lip.

She smiled. "We work together."

"He's a teacher?" A man with an education, looks, and a tad bit of street in him— just my type. "What does he teach?"

"Cleanliness." She laughed.

I was confused. "Cleanliness?" I asked. "A male home economics teacher? Is he gay?"

"He's a janitor."

"A what?"

"A janitor." She continued, "Tremel is a sweet guy. I didn't think he'd show up."

"He's a janitor?" I was still in shock. I wanted to shout, "Shit!"

"Yes. Everyone can't be a big time architect," she joked.

"True." I frowned. "But everyone can't be a damn janitor either." Nick strolled over and volunteered to help with the cake. "I'll pick up the locks." I grabbed the backpack we brought them in. As the crowd dwindled, I picked up the locks that had fallen to the ground, ones on the table and on the bar, and shook my tail feather with Nelly and P. Diddy. I didn't mind staying to help with the cleaning. The later I got home, the better the chances were of Damian being there.

"Need help?"

"I'm all right." I didn't even bother turning around.

"Well, you can at least thank me for offering."

I turned around and was stood in front of the unmasked Tremel. The first thing that came to me were the words to India Arie's song "Brown Skin." *Apparently, your skin has been kissed by the sun.* Not only was he brassy brown, so were his eyes. His skin looked softer than a swab of cotton, and those lips, Lord those lips. *You make me wanna Hershey's kiss your licorice.* He was more handsome than I expected. I was lost for a moment, until a second wind hit me, whispering, Janitor.

"Thank you for your offer." I looked away. "But I think I can handle it."

He said, "I think that I can handle it too." Of course he could handle picking up things. It's what he does, and he should be good at it. He took the bag from me. "At least let me take a load off."

I guess he wasn't going away. "Thanks." I continued gathering the locks and threw them into the bag without too much to say. When we reached the back of the room and were clearly out of locks, I was glad. "Well, thanks so much for your help." I tried to smile.

"Anytime," he said, handing me the bag. "Would you mind having another drink with me?"

"I really shouldn't have any more. I have to drive," I said as an excuse. Tremel would be to me what Nick was to Nat—just a tease. A man without a promising career couldn't do anything for me. I had bills to pay plus I already had a man. "Thanks for the offer." I smiled and walked away.

"By the way, what was the phantom hiding?" he asked.

I turned back toward him slowly. "Well, he was disfigured and didn't have anything going for himself, so he had to pretend."

He smiled. "Well, I'm nothing like that."

"Is that right?" I really wanted to say, "Yeah right."

He smiled. "Come on, have a drink with me."

"Really, I can't." I kept walking. He was probably only offering because it was free.

"Well, is there a number where I can reach you?"

I decided to be a smart-ass. "Do you have a business card?"

He looked embarrassed. "No."

"Well, maybe we'll see each other around." I couldn't be bothered with a man with no future.

He looked me up and down and finally read what I meant. "Maybe."

"I'm living so far beyond my income that we may almost
be said to be living apart."
–E. E. Cummings

Bank Statement # 3
Account Balance: $22,527.92

"I should tear this check up," India said.

"You better not." It took me a couple of days to build up the financial nerves to write the check out to India. I mailed it instead of going through with the nonchalant yet malicious hand delivery I had planned. "If you tear it up, then I'll just send you cash." I pressed the phone against my ear with my shoulder and threw my toothbrush, toothpaste, soap, and mouthwash into my makeup case.

"I'll tear that up too," she said. "You didn't have to give me the money back."

Running from the bathroom back into my bedroom, I positioned the bag into the suitcase and zipped it close. "It wasn't mine to start with."

"You know what's mine is yours." She giggled. "Because what's yours is mine, right?"

"I guess." I was just talking for her to hear. I wouldn't trust her with a pet rock if I had one.

"So, what time is your flight?" she asked.

"In an hour and a half." I looked at the clock. "I should've been at the airport already."

"What time is the concert?" she asked.

39

"I think it starts at eight." I grabbed my suitcase, purse, and keys and headed out the door. "My plane makes it to Orlando at six. All I'll have time to do is pick up the rental car and head to the site. I won't even be able to check into my hotel until after the concert and interview."

"When do you come back?"

I boarded the elevator. "Tomorrow night." I really didn't want to go, but in order for me to move into a better spot at the station, I had to bite the bullet and do what other people didn't want to do. A new country artist was debuting in Orlando, but Garth Brooks was performing in Miami the same night. Instead of being invited to the American Airlines Arena for the GB concert, I was taking an American Airlines flight to Orlando to interview a no-name crooner. "My flight gets in around six or something."

"Why didn't they just rent you a car to drive from here to there? It's only a little over a three-hour drive."

"Who?" I rolled my eyes. "I'm not driving to Orlando unless I'm going to Disney World. If I'm going to a country-ass concert, I don't want a three-hour drive ahead of me. I'm liable to turn my black ass around or miss the exit and take the highway all the way to ATL," I joked.

"Well, have a safe trip." She added, "The weather is looking a li'l crazy, though."

"I didn't even look at the Weather Channel." I sighed. "What's going on?"

"Well, it's not raining here, but there is a little system moving north."

"Damn." I hated flying. "That's all I need."

"Well, I'm not going to cash this check just yet," India said. "You might need it back."

I couldn't believe her. "Fuck you, India," I said jokingly, though I really meant it.

"No. I'm fucking with you." She giggled again. "Call me when you get in. Let's have drinks."

"I will." I hung up and raced through the parking garage to find my car.

By the time I made it to the American Airlines gate, the passengers were boarding and I was last in line, but I had a first class seat. I would never pay for a flight from Miami to Orlando on my own. It seemed as if as soon as we hit cruising altitude, the pilot announced that we were preparing for landing. The flight couldn't have been longer than an hour. The only problem was the tremulous turbulence due to the storm hovering over the area. When the plane landed, I was one of the first people off because I only had a carry on. Being a Budget FastBreak customer got me in and out of the car rental office in five minutes.

The sky was the darkest shade of gray I'd ever seen without becoming black. Not only was it raining, there was hail and talk of tornadoes in surrounding towns. When I learned that the concert was supposed to be an outside event, I pretty much knew that it was off. I made a few phone calls and learned that I was right. The show was off and not being rescheduled. The artist was already heading to Georgia for his performance the next day, so I couldn't even do the interview.

Without an umbrella, I sat in the parking lot of the Marriott hotel for twenty minutes. The rain wasn't letting up. I jumped each time a lightning bolt flashed across the sky, and trembled when the thunder rumbled. At only eight o'clock, I didn't want to be stuck in my hotel room for the night, but with weather like this, I wouldn't dare go anywhere besides the hotel restaurant.

My cellular phone rang in the midst of the crackling of a thunderclap and frightened me so bad that my foot slammed on the gas pedal. Thankfully the car was still in park. "Hello!" I didn't look at the caller ID.

"Hi, sweetness."

"Hi, Damian." I guess he saw my note. "Sorry about tonight. I tried calling you but I guess you had your phone off."

"Yeah, I was in a meeting." He sighed. "They just told you today?"

"Yep." I was always the last-minute girl. "I found out around noon."

"Well, happy anniversary anyways, baby." He continued, "I guess I'll find something to put these roses in until tomorrow."

"Aw." I smiled. "Thank you, baby."

"Want me to reschedule the dinner reservations?" he asked.

"Yeah." I blushed. "Where were we going?"

"I'm not telling."

"I'm missing you," I said with a pout. It was our second anniversary as a couple, and we weren't going to be together. "And the stupid concert is—"

"Hold a sec," he said then answered his other line. The rain was really coming down by then, and the lightning wasn't joking, lighting up the dark sky like it was trying to write a message. Damian returned. "Baby, I need to take this call." I heard him rustling papers around.

"All right." I frowned.

"Call me after the concert." He sounded a bit disappointed. "I really wish we you were here tonight, though."

"Me too." I got the message the lights in the sky were giving me and smiled. "Me too." I hung up and shifted the gear into reverse. I was on my way back to Miami. Forget checking into a cold, lonely hotel room on my anniversary and flying back tomorrow. I was driving back to Miami to celebrate with my man tonight.

Forty minutes south of Orlando, the weather was perfect. I took advantage of the dry asphalt, put the pedal to the metal and was in Downtown Miami and exiting I-95 at 10:40 p.m. I called the apartment to be certain that I wasn't rushing home to an empty bed. "Hello." Damian sounded like he was already asleep.

"What are you wearing?" I asked in a sexy, sultry voice.

He groaned a little. "Nothing."

"I was hoping that you weren't." I smiled.

"Really? Why?" he asked.

I was in a naughty mood. "'Cause I want to lick you."

He chuckled. "You do?"

"Yes."

"Lick me then." He was in a wicked frame of mind too.

"You gonna touch it?" I asked.

"What do you think?" he said. "Don't worry about what I'm doing. You're supposed to have your mouth full right now." I smiled and started to make sucking noises, using my finger as the object of my affection. "That feels real good, baby. Don't stop."

"You like that?" I asked, but he didn't answer. I heard him moaning softly, and imagined him biting his bottom lip the way he did when I was kneeling in front of him. I continued my slurping and sucking sounds until I heard him say, "Suck that dick, girl. You know how I like it."

My panties were drenched like I had them on the antenna of my car while I drove through the rain earlier. "Are you hard?"

"Of course."

"Damn, I want that dick, baby." Damian and I always had phone sex when one of us was away on business. "I'm so wet."

He groaned. "Shit." He was breathing heavy. "I want you on this dick."

"I want to give you this anniversary pussy." I pulled into the garage and found a parking spot right next to the elevator.

"Come here and ride me."

I'd get the suitcase in the morning. I grabbed my purse and sprinted to the elevator. "Damian, you got me open, baby."

"Slide down on it," he spoke in a whisper. "Take it all."

"I can't take it unless you give it to me," I said as the elevator started moving up.

He asked. "Can you take it?"

"You know I can." I began unbuttoning my shirt. "Just shut up and give me what you got."

"Here you go," he said. "Take it. Oh take it take it, baby." I imagined his brown fingers wrapped around his swollen chocolate bar. I could almost hear his strokes. "Now jump off and suck it again," he said as the elevator doors opened.

"That's what you want?" I asked

"That's what I said, so suck all the pussy juice off my dick," he said.

I sucked my finger again, giving him desirable sound effects. "Fuck my mouth." He knew that meant me on my back and him over me, just as we were when we made love. The difference was him in my mouth with the same style aggression. "Fuck my mouth, baby."

"Yes." His voice trembled. "Oh yeah."

I couldn't wait to get inside and jump on him for real. We needed this excitement. "I'm finished sucking it, and I want to get back on."

"All right," he said. "Get back on it." I let him talk while I quietly opened the apartment door, rested my purse on the kitchen counter, and threw my shirt to the floor. "Your pussy is so good, baby," he said in my ear. "I love it when you ride me, your hair in my face and your tits in my mouth." He was breathing heavy. "Damn, your pussy is so good."

I moaned softly to encourage him as I removed my pants and underwear. "Fuck me, baby." I continued moaning as I led my naked body down the hall. I was hoping to catch him before he started spitting.

"You want this pussy?" I asked as my hand touched the doorknob.

"Hell yeah," he groaned.

I turned the knob with the biggest smile. "Well, I'm here to give it to you." I walked into the dark room and saw Damian lying in bed. He wasn't stroking himself as I imagined. Instead, he was lying back and his hands were wrapped around the waist of a woman bouncing wildly atop him. "Ride my dick, girl," he said into the phone he had wedged between his shoulder and his ear, then leaned forward, taking her breast into his mouth while groaning into the phone. "You like it when I suck your tits?"

My heart was pounding too hard to have my brain

make sense of what I was seeing. I felt the wall for the light switch and couldn't find it. "What the fuck is going on here?"

It really wasn't a question, and to show them that I didn't want an answer, I threw my cell phone across the room, hitting the woman on her side. "I don't believe this shit." I was frozen.

He threw her off of him and reached toward the floor for his boxers. I continually slammed my hand against the wall in search of the switch but kept coming up with nothing.

"What in the hell are you doing here?" he asked.

"This is where I live." Forget the lights. I sprinted toward his silhouette and wailed at him. "How could you do this to me?" Again, it really wasn't a question.

He was ducking my blows so I tried to get at his friend, but he held me back. In the darkness, I saw her run into the bathroom and I screamed after her. "You better jump out of the window, bitch, cause if you come out, 'm gonna kill you." I was crying. "Damian, what in the hell are you doing to me?" I screeched and punched him over and over on his back.

"Why didn't you tell me that you were coming home?" he screamed at me as if he had just walked in and met me riding his daddy.

"Why didn't you tell me that you were fuckin' in our home?" I jumped up and finally found the light switch. I wanted to see his face. This had to be a joke, but he wasn't smiling. I yelled, "I can't believe this shit." He stood up and walked toward me. "Get away from me." He tried to grab my hands and I slapped him.

He was shocked. "You fuckin' bitch." I flinched as he stopped himself halfway down the road to hitting me back. "You hit me again and I'll ..." The fire in his eyes told me that he wasn't just talking.

"What, you're gonna kill me like your crazy-ass daddy did to your mom?" I was dead wrong, and I paid for it against the side of my face. When he pulled his hand back, my face was numb. I stepped back from him with my mouth wide opened and screamed, "Get the fuck out of my house!"

"I pay the damn bills here. You get out," he yelled and walked over to the closet and started throwing my clothes out onto the floor. "Get *your* ass out."

I picked up the phone. "*My* name is on the damn lease. If you don't leave, I'll call the police and have them help your ass out." It wasn't until then I remembered that I was naked. "I can't fuckin' believe you did this shit in our house, in our room, and in our bed," I cried. "You think I didn't know that you had somebody else?" I pointed and screamed. "I knew! But why would you bring her here? Doesn't she have a fuckin' bed?" I had forgotten about the woman until then. I ran over to the bathroom door and he tried to block me. "Move out of my way." I wanted to see this woman's face. I wanted to spit on her, scratch her, and put my foot deep into her backside. "You better jump out of the window," I yelled at her through the door as I pounded his chest with my fists. "Cause it's over when I get my fuckin' hands on you."

"Look," he said, trying to block the door and put on his pants at the same time. "This is between you and me. Just leave her alone."

"You're hitting me but protecting the whore you brought here?" I looked at him and wished that just for a minute murder wasn't a crime. "Fuck you." I built up the strength to push him away. I didn't care if he slapped me again; I wanted to see her. I reached for the knob before he could grab my hand. The door swung open and slammed against the tile. I fell into the dark room and almost hit my head on the sink, but I quickly assessed the situation and flipped on the light. I was confused when I looked around and saw no one, but I heard whimpering coming from behind the shower door. I rushed towards the sound, pulled the door back, and saw her thin body rolled up in a fetal position in the far corner of the tub.

"Who in the hell are you?" I cried. Her head was face down into her knees and her hands were covering her head against the blows she knew to expect. "Look at me," I screamed at her. "Look . . . at . . . me."

In extreme fear, India looked up at me. "I'm sorry, Sarai." Tears streamed down her face, snot drained from her nose, and she could barely speak. "I'm sorry. Please don't . . ."

I couldn't hear anything else. I couldn't breathe, I couldn't talk, I couldn't even cry anymore. It all suddenly made sense. This "new guy" that India met at Randy's birthday party, when I was out of town, was my guy. I walked in on Damian right after he masturbated, with cum all over his chest. He was on the phone with India, but said that she called while he was talking business. *They* were having phone sex. India left Nat's party because she was jealous when my man and I were having a good time together. She found out about my trip to the Bahamas through him. All the questions she asked me about my trip to Orlando were so that she and *my* man could plan their booty call.

"I can't believe you." I was trembling, but I didn't see "our" man coming to her rescue now. "You nasty, fake-ass bitch." I reached down toward her and came up with a handful of expensive weave.

I grabbed her again. "Come here!" I shouted. This time I grabbed the hair that she was born with.

"Sarai, I'm sorry." She continued covering her face as she moved across the tub at my command. "Please, please forgive me. I didn't mean to—"

"Is this what you meant when you said that what's mine is yours?"

"Sarai, I didn't—"

"Shut the fuck up." Before I could pull her to her feet, my rage took control and I yanked her head up and punched her in the face. Immediately, blood splattered from her mouth to the wall, and she let out a sound as though her life was through. She fell back into the tub. I had no remorse. As her body slid down the wall, I climbed into the tub and yelled, "Look at me." I bent down and slapped her like I had wanted to for the past three months. "Look at me." I turned on the hot water and held her still between my legs. She begged, pleaded, and even tried to fight back when the scalding water began to burn her skin. While she was pinned beneath me, I hit her repeatedly before Damian pulled me off kicking and wailing.

He carried me back into the bedroom, threw me on the bed, and yelled to India to get out. He informed her that her clothing was already out the door. She never looked at me, but I threatened her over and over. "I know where you live, bitch. I know where you fuckin' live." I watched her narrow ass run out and heard the front door slam behind her.

My rage turned back to Damian. "Get out!" I shouted and tried to bite him. "Get your ass out of here." I bucked like a wild horse until I was free from under him then ran to the kitchen. I raced into the bedroom with a meat cleaver, but what I met him with was no match.

"Sit your stupid ass down." He cocked the 9 millimeter three feet from my head. "Sit your ass down," he yelled. I walked toward the bed and did just what he asked. "I'll be out of here in ten minutes, but if you say another goddamn word, I'll be out in twenty and I'll be dragging your wannabe *bad* ass behind me in a garbage bag." He approached me, and with every step he took, the gun got closer to my forehead until I felt the frosty steel kiss my temple. He snatched the knife from my hand and threw it into the closet.

"All this excitement has my dick hard again." He dragged the gun down my face and stopped at my neck. With his other hand, he reached down to remove his boxers and this maniac really did have an erection. "Suck my dick like you said you wanted to." He pressed the gun into my neck. I was paralyzed with fear. I forgot how to move, talk, or feel. I just sat there waiting for something to happen.

"Suck it." He laughed maniacally. "You know you want to." He began beating his hardened stick up against my mouth. When I started to cry, he moved it over my cheeks to wipe the tears away. "Open your muthafuckin' mouth, Sarai." He positioned the gun to my ear and my mouth flew open. He fell into the gap, moving his body back and forth. Tears fell in abundance as I smelled India's juices on him, but I couldn't stop. I was careful about my teeth and continually moistened my mouth so things would be over with faster. He moaned, grabbed the back of my head, and stabbed me deeply with his body. "You know you like this."

He pushed my body back on the bed until I was lying flat. "Didn't you tell me to fuck your mouth earlier?" I kept my lips fastened tightly around him. I had to suck him like there was no tomorrow because if I didn't, that might be the case. Plunging in and out of my mouth, he pounced and pounded wildly like I had no face. Seconds later, he spat his thick, evil liquor down into my throat. For the first time in my life, I swallowed, but I welcomed it. It meant that the torture was done.

With his 9 millimeter still in hand, he rolled off me and walked into the bathroom. I heard the water falling into the sink and watched him toweling his privates. I continued lying on the bed like a helpless blanket. Without a word, he grabbed his suitcase, tossed some things into it, threw on some jeans, sneakers, and a shirt, tucked his gun into his waistband and smiled. "We're going to the bank on Monday. I want *all* of my money out of your account. All twenty Gs." He began walking out, then stopped. "If any of my money is missing, or if you even dream of getting lost with my shit, I will fuck you up so bad that dentist records won't help them identify you."

When I heard the apartment door shut, I scurried out of the room to put the two extra bolts on. My face was hurting, the corners of my mouth felt ripped, and I was petrified to say the least. I barely made it into the bedroom, and I couldn't for the life of me figure out why I even wanted to go back there. The phone was making that off-the-hook noise, the water was still running into the sink, and I was still naked. I grabbed my cell phone and dialed 9-1- then paused for a moment before hitting the last number. Damian was no joke! Reporting this crime could mean paying a bigger price in the end. I never wanted to see him this way again and I wanted no retaliation. I left well enough alone and dialed another number. I couldn't remember whom I called or what was said, but Nat and Nick were there in forty minutes.

Nick stayed in the living room while Nat and I

cried together in my room. I told her the entire story while she held me, rubbed my back, and wiped my nose and my mouth. Realizing that she couldn't leave me in my current state, Nat told Nick that he could leave because she'd be spending the night. However, Nick didn't want to leave either one of us alone, fearing the return of Damian, so he made himself comfortable on the sofa. I never fell asleep. I was shaking, throwing up, and crying uncontrollably throughout the night. Thanks to India and Damian, I was too uncomfortable to lay my head down at night, in too much pain both emotionally and physically to make it through the day, and suddenly too confused about everything in my life to think that it had any meaning.

The next morning, not only did Nick make breakfast and serve it to us both in bed, he had already gone to both his house and Nat's for a change of clothes. He was all right again in my book. He even helped me box and bag up everything that belonged to Damian then bring it to the living room. This was so he wouldn't have a reason to pass the kitchen counter if he ever came back.

"So, what about tomorrow?" Nat asked.

"What about tomorrow?" I plopped down on the couch after dragging the last garbage bag of clothing to the front.

"How are you guys going to work out the money situation?"

I hadn't even thought of it since I first told her the story. "I've used so much of his money." I rolled my eyes.

"So, it's short?" Nick asked, full of concern.

"No, there is more than twenty in the account, but over the months I spent more than I should have because he told me that it was mine as long as it was there." I sighed. "So, he really only has about thirteen. But whatever, I can't keep it."

"Well, just give him the thirteen."

I didn't tell them about his threat. "Naw, he can have it all." That bastard was crazy and I wanted him out of my life.

"So, how much will you be left with?"

"I know that heifer will cash that check now." I grabbed my checkbook from my purse and did some quick math. "Two thousand, five hundred, twenty-seven dollars and ninety-two cents." I tried to smile. "Rent is three weeks away, so I'll make it."

"How much is that?" Nat asked.

"Fourteen hundred." I continued to smile because I was too proud to do anything else. "I do have a job, guys, and the websites."

"What about your father in the nursing home?" she asked.

"Savvy is going to have to start helping." Since my brother moved to Atlanta five months ago, he still acted brand new. I hadn't seen him in over a year, and hadn't heard from him in about a month. "He'll be getting a phone call from me this evening. I can't do everything all by myself."

"And your student loans, credit cards, and other bills?" Nat was starting to stress me out.

"Damn, Nat. I know what I owe. Fuck the student loan people." I sighed. "And Chase Manhattan, Sears, and Discover can kiss my ass." We all laughed.

"Just promise me that if you need anything you'll ask me," she said.

"Nat, it's not that serious." I giggled.

"I didn't say that it was." She smiled at me. "Just promise me."

"Okay." I gave her a crazy stare. "I cross my heart."

"Well, at least you'll be in the Bahamas this weekend."

I had totally forgotten. "That's right."

Nick joined in. "When are you leaving?"

"Friday morning." Now I did have something to smile about.

"Good for you," he said. "For how long?"

"I'll be back *next* Friday." This vacation was coming right in the nick of time.

I was grateful for Nick and Natalya. They were too sweet, spending not only the entire day at my place on Sunday, but also another night. My best girl had already gotten me through my first day, so I took two sleeping pills and vowed that tomorrow would be the second day of the rest of my life.

Going Broke

"No one can earn a million dollars honestly."
–William Jennings Bryan

Bank Statement # 4
Account Balance: $2,027.92

I woke up around 6:00 to lock up after Nat and Nick left for work. It was Monday, and that meant Friday was only four days away, so I stayed up and started packing. I didn't care if it was hurricane season. I could almost hear the Bahamas calling my name, and I was answering, "Hey, mon."

I called the landlord about changing my lock then double-checked my checkbook, but the balance wasn't changing. After Damian wiped out my account I'd be left with just a thousand dollars. I checked my orders for both websites and there were only three picnic basket orders and seven trip queries. This wasn't bad, but with things going the way they were, it wasn't enough. "I have to start advertising," I said to myself. My ghetto style of advertising was paying a few crack addicts a hundred dollars apiece to stand on various street corners and hand out a thousand flyers each. I couldn't even afford to advertise at my own radio station. Mr. Motes wasn't letting anybody get away with anything close to free.

Around noon my phone rang. I said, "Hello?"

"What's up, sexy?" I didn't recognize the voice, and the caller ID wasn't telling me enough.

I hit the mute button and made Oprah's guest be quiet. "Hello?"

"What's up, sexy?"

"Who is this?" I was nervous.

"This is a very damn sexy man." He laughed. "You know how I know that you're sexy?" He didn't wait for my answer. "'Cause I'm your sexy-ass twin brother."

I was able to breathe again. "Don't scare me like that."

"I wasn't trying to scare you. I thought you'd be flattered."

"Maybe last week, but not today," I said and turned the television back up.

I didn't feel like telling the story again. "Damian and I aren't together anymore."

"Thank God." He laughed. "Is Tupac really dead this time, though?" He was referring to the one other time we split.

I sighed. "Thanks for the comfort."

He informed me, "You know I could never stand him." Yes, I did. Savion made that known, and Damian didn't like him either. "I think you can do a lot better than someone like him."

"Well, apparently he thought that he could do a lot better than me."

He sounded confused. "What do you mean?"

"He was cheating on me." I blew a bit of steam. "I walked into *our* bedroom to find a woman on top of him."

"Shut the hell up, Sarai."

"I'm serious."

"You're not serious."

"I'm very serious, Savvy." He could hear it in my voice. "Wanna hear the worst part of it?"

"Anything worse and I'll be flying down there," he

joked.

"I guess I'll start planning your trip." I sighed. "The woman was India."

"India?"

"India," I repeated.

He was quiet for a while. "Damn."

"What?"

"Nothing."

"What?" I asked again.

"India *is* fine as hell, though." He went on. "That's a sexy bitch."

"Thanks for your continued support." I rolled my eyes. "I was thinking about calling you last night. I'm going to need your help."

"With what?" he asked.

"Daddy."

"Sarai, I haven't even found any real clients here yet."

"Nobody told you to move from Houston." I was serious. "You had clients coming out of your ears there. You still haven't told me why you moved to Atlanta." A personal trainer, Savion's good looks, seductive speech, and charm brought him more clientele than he was ready to handle. It wasn't a surprise to anyone when he started mixing business with pleasure and was in and out of bed with his female clients.

"I couldn't stay there anymore," he said.

"What, one of those ladies' husbands finally found out how his wife was really losing weight?" I joked.

"I wish it was that simple." He sounded serious.

His new tone concerned me. "I haven't seen you in over a year. Come and see me."

"We'll see." His voice saddened.

"What's wrong?" Being twins, I felt emotional pain

that confused me. Something was going on with my clone soul. "Talk to me, Savion."

He didn't speak right away. "I'm in a little bit of a fix."

"What's wrong?"

"I can't burden you with my problems."

"Shut up," I said, "and tell me right now."

He sighed. "Trina died a few months ago."

"What?" I shrieked. "What?" Trina was his old girlfriend back in Dover. They were together until he went to Houston. She didn't move because of her promising career as a stripper. She was a good girl who took the wrong road. She started dancing to pay for college, and all of a sudden she forgot higher education and was buying a car, a house, then along came the silicone, and that was all she wrote.

"My life," it sounded like he was crying, "my life has been a downhill plunge since then."

"Savvy, I'm sorry." I was crying now too. "Why didn't you call me?"

"Sarai, I couldn't." He barely got it out. "There is so much going on in my life, I had to just pack up and leave everything and everybody. I just needed time."

"I'm so sorry, Savvy," I said. "Did you go to the funeral?"

"No," he said quickly.

"What happened?"

There was a long pause. "Somebody killed her."

I was in shock. "Jesus."

"Shot her dead," he repeated.

I wish I had him in my arms. "Savvy, it'll be all right."

"You don't understand, Sarai," he said.

"Understand what?" I asked.

He said, "It's just like they killed me too."

"Why?" Why was he trippin'? He and Trina had broken up months after he moved to Texas, and he was in Houston for at least three years. To my knowledge, there wasn't anything still going on between them. "What's going on?"

"I had to move to get my mind together." He sniffled. "I had to start a new life."

I didn't understand what he meant, but I guessed he'd explain later. "I'm sorry. I wish you would've called me. We could've gone back home to the funeral together."

He said, "Naw, I couldn't go to the funeral. I just couldn't go."

I didn't know what else to say. "Have you talked to Daddy lately?" I changed the subject.

"I called him yesterday."

"Oh yeah?" I tried to stay upbeat. "How is he?"

"Terrible," he said. "It's so damn sad."

I wanted to cry again. "I hate it."

"What are we going to do?" he asked. "It pisses me off to talk to him."

We were feeling the same way. "Somewhere inside he still loves us."

He giggled. "Yeah, I can hear it in his voice sometimes. It's like the old him wants to scream my name, but his mind is too confused to do it." Savion's thoughts were mine. "He's in there; I just wish I was lucky enough to talk to who he used to be for at least a minute again."

"Me too." Over the next hour, Savion and I melted into being two happy people again. When he learned of my trip to the Bahamas, he told me to be like Stella and get my groove back. With him not working, I knew that I would have to keep pulling the weight of Daddy's nursing home cost. I saw the signs. I was going to be struggling for a while. I told him to use his big mouth to spread the word out about my sites. "Bye, Savvy."

"See ya, sexy," he said.

"It's midnight." I hoped that no one could tell that I was crying. "Is your lover next to you?" For the first time, I hated my opening line. "If they're not, then Sarah is here to give you a little something to hold on to." All I was holding was the microphone. "I'm here to give you something that you can feel." All I felt was pain. "Let me ease your troubled mind." Who was going to ease mine? The first song in my set was Leanne Rimes' "How Do I Live Without You." I played it especially for me, but I was hoping that no one knew.

Around three in the morning, my cell phone rang. It was Damian. I didn't know if I should throw the phone, turn it off, or answer it. Tommy, the segment producer, was in the bathroom, so I flipped some switches to play one more song rather than me having a talk spot after the Reba McIntire song was over.

I took off my headset and grabbed my phone. "Hello?"

"Are you purposely trying to piss me off?" he asked.

I decided to be a smart-ass. "Good morning to you too."

"Good morning, Miss Emery," he said. "How is your mouth?"

"Fuck you." I wasn't afraid of him over the phone. "What do you want?" I went on, "Oh, I know what you want. How could I forget? You wanna fuck my friends."

"I have no time for your drama," he said. "Why didn't you show up at the bank?"

61

"You never called."

He spoke as though nothing was wrong. "I called the apartment all day."

I remembered that I had the ringer off. "Well, I didn't know."

"You knew." He added, "You were probably hoping that I would show up and make you suck my dick again."

"You know what, Damian? You're a real sick muthafucka." I stood up. "You are an exact replica of the man you've hated since you were a boy." I wasn't regretting anything I said. "You *are* your father. Holding a gun to my head and doing what you did to me. I guess you think that made you a man, but that just made you a fuckin' rapist. Next you'll be killing somebody, and then what?" I felt empowered. "You'll be somebody's bitch in prison just like your sorry-ass daddy."

"That'll be a hell of a lot better than being like yours," he shouted. "At least my pops knows my damn name."

After two years of pretending that he cared about my father's condition, the truth was finally out. "Fuck you," I blared. "You are a sorry-ass excuse of a man, Damian."

"I was your sorry-ass excuse of a man for two years, though, so shut the fuck up. All I want is my money."

"You're gonna get what's coming to you."

"Tell me something I don't know." He repeated, "All I want is my money."

"You're going to regret fuckin' with me," I cried. "You'll pay for this, you and India. You'll both burn in hell."

"You're probably right." He pretended to yawn. "All I want is my money."

"Fuck you, Damian."

"Meet me at the bank at noon," he said nonchalantly.

"You're an evil muthafucka. You don't deserve anything," I said. "You don't deserve to breathe. One day you'll be so sorry for doing this to me. Just watch and see."

He laughed loudly. "What, are you putting a curse on me like that Esther lady did to your home-wrecking mother?" He continued, "That's what she got. She is the one who didn't deserve to breathe, and oops— she's not. If you wanna be a witch, don't take lessons from Esther, because her weak-ass spell obviously wasn't enough since you and your sissy fuckin' brother are still alive." I was speechless, but I guessed this was what I got for telling him too much of my family's business. My newfound strength was a thing of the past. "Just meet me at the bank at noon, Sarai."

"You can have your money, Damian, and it's the last thing you'll ever get from me. After tomorrow, I don't want to see your damn face again. Do you hear me?" I yelled. "Fuck you and the fuckin' pit bull you rode in on."

"Fuck you too," he said peacefully, almost in the same tone he used to say he loved me. "Fuck...you... too."

I was screaming like a lunatic. "You're a fuckin' lunatic," I cried. "I hate you."

Tommy ran into the booth with a look on his face like he had just heard that there was a bomb in the building. He didn't say a word. He just pointed upward and when my eyes followed his fingertip, my mouth dropped open and the cellular phone dropped from my hands. I had been on the air. Whoever was tuned in to BIG COUNTRY got an earful. My stomach balled up into a knot the size of Tommy's fingertip.

Within ten minutes, Mr. Motes was on the phone demanding not only an explanation, but also that I stay at the station until he arrived at 9:00. I drank a lot of coffee, got a bunch of evil looks from the morning crew, and boxed up my belongings. I wasn't stupid. I knew what was coming. I had to work three times harder than the others just to earn my place in the country radio industry, but I knew that all I had to do was make one mistake for all of my work not to mean a thing. I had given them exactly what they wanted—a welcomed reason to send me packing.

Richard "Country Ass" Motes walked into his office at quarter to ten. "Well, Sarah," he said almost with a smile. "I listened to the tapes three or four times, and each time it sounds a little worse." He sat down behind his desk and shook his head from side to side. "We're going to have to suspend you."

"For how long?" I asked.

"Well, when you come to pick up your next check, you'll know something definite."

Lord, please don't let my ghetto spirit show. "I'm not coming in here to pick up my check and learn that I no longer have a job."

"Well, I really can't say anything until then, Sarah."

"Of course you can say something." I was still suppressing the Chiquita within. "I've worked here long enough to know that when folks are suspended, that just means they're really fired but given a chance to cool off. I don't need two weeks to think." I fought the urge to roll my eyes. "You don't have to worry about me coming back to shoot you. If I was going to do that, I'd have done it by now."

"No one said anything about anybody shooting,"

he said nervously. "When you pick up your next check, we'll talk."

"No, let's talk now." My neck started to roll. *Oh no. Here she comes, y'all.* "I have direct deposit, so you tell me what you have to say right now. I don't need to come back to be told *not* to come back again." He looked shocked. "I already know the deal, so let's get down to business and talk severance."

Within an hour, I was no longer an employee of WBIG and would be receiving a $5,000 severance package. The money would give me two months' rent and two more months of Daddy's continued medical assistance. So basically, I had two months to find a job somewhere before I was evicted and Daddy was denied further care.

I didn't hug anyone on the way out. I opened Mr. Mote's door, put on my shades, jumped into my S.U.V., then drove to the parking lot of Rockwell Mutual and waited until I saw Damian's H2 pull up. I had just lost my job because of him, and I realized that I would probably be losing my truck and other things as well. I didn't wait for him. I just walked into the bank. Two minutes later he was by my side. I hated him enough to make a scene, but he wasn't worth it. Under my breath I said, "Don't say any fuckin' thing to me."

He looked at his watch. It was two minutes to twelve. "Good morning to you as well."

"After we leave here, let this be the last time I see you." I still hadn't looked at him.

"I still have stuff at the apartment," he said.

"Your things are by the door," I said. "The locks are being changed as we speak, so don't come up without a security guard." I signed my name so that we could see one of the bank representatives. He sat down first. I selected a seat that faced his but was two people down. One would assume we were complete strangers. From a distance you'd think that Damian was an upstanding guy. Sitting there in a suit and tie, he was looking as good as he could look. He almost seemed like an honest, hardworking family man, but evil comes in all shapes and sizes.

When we finished our transaction, the money was transferred from my account to one in his name. I signed the necessary paperwork and left the desk without saying another word to the devil or the banker.

I walked through the door of my apartment and finally realized how much I had lost. I was without a man, a friend, a job, money, and my mind all in just three days. There wasn't much else that I could lose. In the comfort of my own hiding place, I did what I wanted to do all day but was too much of a woman for Tommy, Mr. Motes, Damian or the banker to see—I cried. Mr. Velázquez, the handyman, came and changed the locks. I wished he could've done the same thing to my heart. I couldn't afford to have any intruders inside messing things up more than they already were.

The only time I answered my house or cellular phone was when Nat or Savion called. Every other call went straight to my voicemail, which I vowed not to check until I returned from the Bahamas. I didn't want to hear what anyone had to say about what they heard on the air, or what they heard someone else say about what they heard.

I kept my hair appointment at Bob & Weave on Thursday afternoon. I didn't dare say too much in that place; it was gossip headquarters. Although the sign on the door read *Nothing goes back outside except you,* I didn't buy it. Not only Bob, but all those nosy heifers bought, sold, and traded secrets. I've heard them. "You tell me about Latrice's man and I'll tell you who Mimi is pregnant from." Hell no. If they didn't already know my business, they weren't going to hear it from me. I kept my head buried in an *Essence* magazine the entire time.

I treated myself to a $300 weave job, a manicure and pedicure, a facial, and five new outfits. I returned home a little after 9:00 and enjoyed a warm shower. I couldn't wait until 1:12 the following afternoon when I'd be on my way to a week away from my "American problems." I finalized my packing and called Nat a little before midnight, promising her that I'd have fun, be free, and return rested.

As my head touched the pillow, the phone rang. "Hey, sexy," I answered, thinking it was Savion returning my call.

"Damn, what a greeting," Damian said. "Open the door. I'm outside."

"Outside?" I sat up in bed.

"Yeah," he said. "I'm glad to know that you're happy to hear from me."

"I thought you were someone else, actually." I added, "I'm not opening the door unless you have a police officer or the security guard from downstairs with you."

"Are you serious, Sarai?" he asked. "I'm just here to get my stuff."

I was scared. "I don't trust you." I jumped out of bed to make sure the latches were on. I looked out of the peephole, and there he was. "I don't want you in here unless you have the security guard."

"Come on," he said. "I just need my stuff, Sarai. I don't want any drama."

I didn't want to let him in. "Hold on." I ran back to my bedroom, grabbed my cellular and called the security office. "I need one of you up to eleven twenty-seven right away." I went back to the door. "I don't want any problems, Damian." I tried to stall.

"I promise you." He sounded like the man I used to know.

I sighed. "Damian, don't fuck with me."

"Sarai, I'm only here for my stuff," he said. "There are things from my office that I need."

I thought for a minute before I unlatched the locks and opened the door. He stepped in and offered me his hand. I didn't take it. I just opened the door wide enough for him to walk in and I didn't close it all the way. "This is all your stuff." I pointed at the boxes and bags stacked neatly in the corner.

"Damn." He smiled as he saw his things then looked at me. "I fucked up, huh?"

I couldn't say anything. This man was a totally new creature from the one I had been dealing with the past few days. He was insane. One could say that he was sampling the very goods he had young boys hustling for him.

"I'm sorry, Sarai." He took a quick step toward me and I flinched. He hung his head. "I didn't mean to do all those things to you that night." He grabbed for my hand. "I'm so sorry." He kissed my hand and I was close to begging him to stop all the talking. "I love you. Will you forgive me?"

I stared at him. The eyes that used to stare me down and undress me, the lips that heated my nights from head to toe, the ears that listened to my problems, the shoulders that held me up when I couldn't stand. "You're sleeping with my friend, Damian," I said in a whisper. "You can't love me."

"Sarai, this has nothing to do with not loving you," he said.

I still couldn't believe this. "What does it have to do with then?"

"You won't understand." He continued to hold my hand. "Just know that I still love you."

"The fact that you can't even explain why you did it makes it even worse." I snatched my hand away.

"Don't do this." He placed my hand back into his. "I don't care about India."

I was in disbelief. "Obviously you don't care about me either."

"I'm sorry, baby." He added, "I had my reasons."

"I bet you did," I said. "And I hope that they were worth it."

"Please forgive me, Sarai."

"Is everything all right in here?" The security guard pushed the door and walked in. "Everything okay?"

Damian looked at me. "Everything is fine."

The man turned to me. "Is everything all right, ma'am?"

"No." My words hurt my soul. "He needs help taking his things downstairs." He dropped my hand.

"Not a problem," the guard said. "Are you ready?"

He was still staring at me. "I guess so."

I couldn't sway, falter, or lean. I wasn't falling back into the trap. For whatever reason, this man was cheating on me, and I did nothing to deserve that. I looked at the guard. "Can you guys put everything in the hall and take it from there?" I smiled. "I was already in bed."

"No problem at all," the guard said and pointed.

"Let's start with these things first."

"Sarai." Damian turned to me. "Why are you doing this?"

"For the same reasons you did what you did," I said. "I'm tired of you."

He actually looked moved. "Damn. So, I'm really out?"

"Where have you been these last couple of fuckin' days?" I joked. "I caught you screwing my friend, you've drained my bank account dry, and called me everything but a child of God," I cried. "Yes, you're really out."

I looked at the guard. "You might want to take his access pass. He doesn't live here anymore, and if he ever makes it to this door again, I'll see that you'll be looking for work just as I am."

I looked back over at Damian. "That's right. Because of you, I'm on the unemployment line now. Our conversation was broadcast live on the air the other night, so I have nothing." I faked a smile. "Nothing including your sorry black ass." I grabbed a bag full of clothing and threw it in the hallway. "Get your ass out of my face." I crossed my arms over my chest and watched them drag things into the hallway for the next five minutes, then I slammed the door and locked it behind me.

Damn, that felt good. I looked in the mirror and saw a new attitude growing already. "You go, girl." I turned off my ringers and drank a glass of red wine to celebrate my new "bad-ass attitude" and calm my nerves enough to fall asleep.

"There ain't no such thing as a free lunch."
–Robert A. Heinlein

Bank Statement # 5

Severance Deposit: $5,000
Check Pending (rent): $2,800
Check Pending (daddy): $1,400
Check Pending (Car): $1,100
Checks Pending (misc.): $659.39
Available Balance: $1,068.53

"Ladies and gentlemen, I'd like to welcome you to the Bahamas," the pilot announced. The way the other passengers and I clapped after his words, you'd think that we just witnessed the capture of someone who was trying to hijack the plane. Everything happened for a reason, so I was ready for whatever was destined to become reality. The commercial says, "It's better in the Bahamas," so I was planning to live by those words.

Pulling my luggage behind me, I was approached by a man walking into the airport. "Way you tink you goin' wit' all a dem bags?" He all but snatched the pull-cart from me. "Way you stayin'?" I realized that I wasn't being mugged. He was a taxi cab driver.

"At the Atlantis." I tried to keep up with him.

"I shoulda know dat." He looked me up and down. "You look like an Atlantis-type gal." He was old enough to be somebody's grandfather. He had better not even think about trying to turn on his rap.

"What does an Atlantis girl look like?" I asked.

"Jus' like you." He smiled and winked at me. "Sweet like suga', sassy, and sexy."

"How far is the hotel?" I was concerned about the fare. "How much will the ride be?"

"Man, don' worry 'bout dat," he said. "You suppose ta be on vacation."

I checked my account balance before I boarded the plane; I had a little something to play with, but not much. My severance money was already spent. I wrote a check for $2,800 for two month's rent, $1,400 for the next two months of Daddy's nursing home care, and $1,100 to have my expedition for two months. I also took care of a host of other things that Damian used to: cable, lights, Internet, phone, all of the utilities. I wanted him back just for these things and nothing more. I had two months to get it together and find another job, or Daddy and I would be living under the Rickenbacker Causeway taking turns watching my repossessed Nookie drive by.

I was stressing. However, when the airport sliding doors opened, I almost forgot everything. "Wow." I was awestruck when I stepped into the Bahamian atmosphere. The blue sky was sprinkled with milk-white fluffy clouds, and the sunbeams were accompanied by welcoming dark brown faces and the scent of the not too distant ocean "This is paradise."

"This isn't paradise yet," he said as he loaded my bags into his van. "Your hotel is on Paradise Island."

He was right. I flew into Nassau, but was told that Paradise Island was across a bridge that connected the two. During the thirty-minute ride, the taxi driver introduced himself as Ian Ambrister. He was sixty-six years old and had volunteered his services at discount rates or even free if I'd meet him for drinks later that night. I didn't want to hurt the old man, so I let him down by saying that my husband and kids were here since yesterday. It was nice that the friendliness continued after my confession, but the fifty dollars he charged told me that he wasn't mixing business with pleasure to the benefit of a married woman.

The Atlantis hotel was modeled after the lost city of Atlantis, an island in the Atlantic Ocean said to have sunken beneath the sea during an earthquake. The designers of the resort went way out to re-create, what the city must have looked like. They had me believing, and I was still standing outside. The enormous coral and teal building seemed to be cut straight from my dreams. I stared up at the structure as Ian unloaded my bags. I loved the mythical theme already. There were sculptures of sea horses, larger than life seashells, horses with wings, sea serpents, and swordfish carved into pillars on the outside.

Once inside, I was even more stunned. The marbled floor in the lobby was breathtaking. There were even more sculptures, and large murals based around the history of the lost city. To make it to the counter, Ian and I traveled past a pool-sized fountain with mythical creatures spitting crystal clear water. The surroundings were so elegant that I felt a bit out of place, knowing that my checking account would scream bloody murder if this trip hadn't already been paid for.

I approached the check-in counter and offered a smile back at the lady behind it. After I gave my name, she quickly did her job, telling me a little about the hotel, then sliding an envelope bearing two keys over the countertop to me. I felt like a princess when I learned that my regal suite was in Royal Towers. I was ushered up to my seventh floor room by a bellman who provided me with a five-minute presentation on the hotel. He made me aware of where things could be found, from the ice machine to the water slides located by the Beach Tower.

The suite was the largest I'd ever been in. The bedroom included a king-sized bed, armoire, plush armchair television, two walk-in closets and a chair and desk. The far side of the bed was filled with pillows, and the bedspread was a real spread, not like most you see at hotels. In the bathroom, I found fresh flowers, slippers, and a bathrobe waiting for me. The toilet area was enclosed and the shower and bathtub were separate. The living room area had a sleeper sofa, armchair, four-seat dinette, and a half bath. My balcony towered over a lazy river-styled pool, and just yards away was the Atlantic Ocean. I walked onto the balcony and breathed in the cool ocean breeze as it rushed past me into the room. "All of this just for me?" I asked the wind.

It was around 6:00 and I knew that if I took a nap, I'd be in for the night. Instead, I turned on the television and flipped through the Bahamian cable channels. I was expecting some Caribbean flavor to greet me but instead found MTV, VH1, BET. I felt like I was back home; I was even able to get the local Miami news. I refused to watch it. Even though I was just 150 miles from home, I wanted believe that I was light years away. I flipped through the hotel guide and was interested in a lot of the activities, but I honestly didn't have the funds to go all out or to go out every night. My partying would have to be limited to the weekend, and after that I'd take on whatever entertainment was free.

At 8:00 p.m., I jumped up from my bath and into a dangerously sexy red slip dress. I didn't know where I was going or what I was going to do, but I didn't fly all the way to the Bahamas to do nothing. I explored the hotel by foot—the many restaurants, bars, and stores—and decided to have dinner in the Café at The Great Hall of Waters. The restaurant was built on the inside of a humongous aquarium. The walls were glass and it was as though the fish, sharks and stingrays were watching the patrons as we normally watched them in a tank.

Eating dinner alone was always uncomfortable, especially when surrounded by strangers who were laughing, talking, and mingling. I purposely positioned myself facing the glass and a stingray swam close the entire time. He sensed my loneliness, and didn't leave the area until my jumbo lump crab cakes and Caribbean quesadillas were all gone.

Though the hotel had four different bars, I wanted to visit the one called The Beach Bar. The Beach Bar was where else? On the beach. With the moon shining brightly you could watch the waves crash a few feet away. I removed my heels and carried them in my hand. On my approach, I heard the steel drum band playing, and though my ears weren't familiar with the beat, my body moved as though it was. The open-air bar was crowded and noisy with conversation, music, and laughter. The air was crisp, clean, and sexy. i sat at one of the only empty stools and dropped my shoes beneath me. The bartender walked over to me. "I ain't even gon' ask you what you want." She smiled. "I gon' give you what I think you need."

"Okay." I grinned. All of the Bahamians I encountered were so friendly. I felt like I was a long lost cousin returning home. I sat patiently awaiting her return. In a few minutes, she presented me with a drink in a martini glass. "Welcome to Atlantis." She set the drink in front of me. "Enjoy your mango martini. It's on us."

"Thank you." I took a sip and my eyes shot open. It was strong, but it was good. As most of the couples danced offbeat to the steel drum music, I became envious, wishing I had someone to hold me close. Although I planned this trip as a private getaway, if Damian and I were still together, I would've called him that night and asked him to hop on a plane in the morning. The romantic ambiance had me feeling extra lonesome.

"Can I have another one?" I asked the bartender. Within an hour, I had four mango martinis, and after the last one I didn't care about not having a dance partner. I just jumped off the stool and shook my boom-boom in the midst of the couples and girlfriends dancing together. The drums were tantalizing. Every time the mallet hit the steel it struck a nerve that wouldn't allow people to stay seated. The rhythm of the waves rushing back and forth was an aphrodisiac.

I felt a hand touch my waist. "May I have this dance, darling?" I did a one eighty and saw an older black gentleman. Why not? No one else was asking. "Sure," I said.

He placed one hand on my waist, the other held my left hand, and we danced and twirled for a while before he invited me to have a drink with him at the bar. "You sure gave me a workout," he said as we sat down.

"I don't know," I teased. "You gave me a run for my money."

He grabbed a napkin and dabbed his forehead. Now that we were in better lighting, I saw that he wasn't as old as I thought—maybe fifty, but not over fifty-five. The hair on his head was curly and sprinkled with gray, but his goatee was black. He was tall and thin, but had somewhat of a stomach hanging over his pants. How much? I couldn't see his belt. "I'm Conrad." He held his hand out to me.

"Sarai," I said as I took his hand.

He looked down at me. "Nice name."

"Thank you." I smiled. "Are you from the States?"

"Yes, ma'am." He brought his barstool closer. "From the capital of California."

"Oh, Los Angeles." I was certain.

"Is that your final answer?" he asked.

"Isn't it L.A.?"

"Sacramento." He smiled.

"Oh." I was too buzzed to be embarrassed. "Now I know."

"What are you drinking?"

I thought a second. "Mango martinis."

He called the bartender over and ordered drinks. He was actually a good-looking older man. I could see that back in the day Conrad might've been a dangerous dude to look at. But his sugar was a bit too old for my tea. However, when he pushed up his sleeve to check the time on his gold Cartier Pasha watch, he was looking more and more like my kind of man. Was he really checking the time or was he putting me in check? I witnessed India pay fifteen grand for a Cartier watch, so this brother was somebody, and I was about to find out who.

"So, what brings you to the Bahamas, Conrad?"

"Well, I come here three or four times a year." He continued, "I do a little business here."

"Oh yeah." He put it out there, so I was going to inquire. "What do you do?"

He smiled big. "A little bit of everything."

"Like?" I was nosy.

"Like everything I can," he said. "And I do it well."

I laughed. I didn't push him for more information. However, when my drink came and he started asking the questions, I left no stone unturned. Something about him made my mouth hard to stop. I told him about my father, my brother, India and Damian, my job, and my websites. By the time I was done with the second drink that he bought, the only thing he didn't know was my social security number. It felt good to vent, but at the same time I felt a little naked, revealing to a stranger that I was almost down to my last dime.

"Wow," he said at the end of my made for television movie-like life. "You've had a hell of a week then, huh?"

"I'd say."

"Well, it can't get any worse," he said.

"It better not," I said, smiling.

"So, have you been pounding the pavement for another job?" he asked.

"Nope," I answered. "I figured I'd do that after my vacation is over." I didn't realize just how incredibly stupid my decision was until I heard myself say it. There was no reason I couldn't print a few copies of my resume and distribute them before leaving town. I tried to make it sound better. "I was still trying to get my mind right after everything that went on."

"I hear you," he said, "but you have bills to pay."

"Well, my severance has me caught up for two months." Lord, why was I talking my business to this man? And why was he so interested in it?

"I'm sure you know how hard it is to get into the broadcasting industry." He paused to swallow his cognac. "Are you prepared to do something else just in case you can't get back into it right away?"

"Yeah," I lied. "I'll have to do something." I paused. "Anything until I get a bite."

"Are the websites productive enough to pay some of your bills?"

"Naw." I frowned. "I need to advertise more. Until then, they barely pay the cable and light bills."

He pushed over a napkin and pulled a pen from his pocket. "What are the website addresses?" he asked. "I'll see if I can get you some clients, and I have a friend who might be able to help you with advertising." He looked at me as though he suddenly had an idea. "Actually, I have a few associates who are flying over tomorrow. I'm certain that one of them will be able to help you generate some business."

"Great." I needed all the help I could get.

At one in the morning, the bartender rang the bell and announced, "Last call."

"You want one more?" Conrad asked.

"No, I shouldn't." I shook my head.

Checking his watch again, he swallowed what was left in his glass and said, "Let's go."

I gave him a surprised look. "Where?"   *Not to my room. No, sir.*

He chuckled. "I'll walk you to your room."

"That's okay," I said. He was nice, but who could stand a fly that was buzzing too close? "I'll be fine."

He looked me up and down. "No, you're not going to *be* fine. You already are." I bet that used to kill the ladies in the 1970s.

"Thanks." I pretended to blush. "But I'll make it to my room."

"Can't a man be a gentleman anymore? It'll be my pleasure."

I gave in. "Okay."

80

"Which part are you staying in?"

"The Royal Towers," I said proudly, like I didn't just confess to him that I was dead broke. "I'm in one of the regal suites."

"Oh, okay," he said as we began crossing the wooden bridge back to the hotel. "I'm in that part too."

"What floor?" I asked.

"Nineteenth," he said.

"Oh." Reading the hotel information earlier, I knew that the seventeenth through twenty-fourth floors were for the Royal Tower's Imperial Club members, a.k.a. big ballas. If I was paying twenty-five hundred for the week, I could only imagine what he had to pay for his room. I couldn't hold out any longer. "Conrad, what do you do for a living?"

"Let's just say . . . " He thought for a few seconds. "I'm a person in a management position."

I laughed. "What do you manage?"

"People," he answered quickly.

"That doesn't tell me much, but I guess that's all you're going to say."

He opened a door for me. "That's all that really matters."

We talked and laughed all the way to the elevator. He was carrying my shoes and joked about how they looked like they could only be worn for five minutes before the corns started to cry. He walked me to my door and didn't invite himself in, try to kiss me, or even hug me before he said goodnight. I was flattered. He handed me my red heels and I sauntered into my room alone, locking the door behind me. Those mango martinis had me feeling like the world was mine. I went out on the balcony and just stood there with the wind in my tightly sewn-in weave. I took a deep breath and realized that in spite of all the things that had gone wrong, I was still alive. "Thank you." I looked up at the sky.

Ringggggg!
Ringggggg!
"What?" I asked myself as I fought to open my eyes the next morning.
Ringggggg!
"Hello?" I grabbed the phone and pulled the covers from my head.

"Were you still asleep?"

"Yes. Who is this?" I asked.

"This is Conrad," he said. "I was wondering if you were having lunch alone."

I rubbed my eyes. "What time is it?"

"Eleven thirty," he said. "I'm sorry about waking you up."

"I didn't realize that it was so late." I sat up in bed and stretched as I looked around the room.

"Go back to bed then."

I thought of the free lunch offer. "No, no," I said. "I need to get up."

"All right. I'll meet you at the Lagoon Bar and Grill in an hour."

"Where is that?" I asked.

"It's that dome-shaped thing, sort of like a merry-go-round."

I knew exactly what he was talking about. "Oh, okay."

"So, I'll see you in an hour." Then he added, "By the way, the guy I was talking to you about came in this morning. Actually, it's a few of them that came in. They'll be joining us. I hope you don't mind."

I got nervous. "Well, maybe I should let you spend time with your friends. We can hook up later."

"They're not friends. This is all about business," he said. "It'll put your foot in the door as well," he reminded me. "Remember those websites? You might be able to get some help."

"You mean advertising, right?" I didn't want a partner.

"Yeah." He added, "Or even some financial backing."

My eyes lit up. "I'll see you in an hour."

I wasn't sure what to wear. After my shower I went through at least six outfits before I decided on an orange and yellow sundress. The thing I liked about it most was the low cut front; it dipped into my cleavage, stopping right where my nipples would start. I buttered my skin with a shimmering lotion and curled my hair at the ends, swooping my bangs to the side and watched my stunning creation unfold when I applied my makeup. Later, I slid on my orange sandals and was out the door.

It was a magnificent day. The sun seemed closer to the Bahamas than it was in Miami, but it wasn't a complaint, it was a blessing. The heat made me feel younger, sexier, and more carefree. Instead of walking through the other buildings, I walked alongside the lagoon until I made it to the other side. As I stepped into the open-air restaurant and bar, I saw Conrad with not one or two men but a group of four men. I stopped in my tracks and hoped that he wouldn't notice me turning to walk away. "Sarai." As he yelled my name, I let out a painful sigh. "Sarai, we're over here, honey." Did he just call me honey?

I spun around with a fake smile and began walking toward the group. When I approached, they all stood as he introduced me to them one by one. There was Richard from Atlanta, Julian out of Boston, and Thomas and Martin were both from Salt Lake City. As I looked at the brothas, I wished I had a camera. They were all worthy of some type of praise. I introduced myself to them, stating that I was on the radio, but currently between stations. Before too many questions were asked, I transitioned into talking about youplanmytrip.com. Julian asked a lot of questions about it, but he didn't seem overly interested.

After ordering and finishing our lunch to nonstop football talk, instead of steering the conversation more along the lines of business, preferably my business, Conrad continuously ordered drinks for me and the guys. When the calypso band showed up, he kicked into party mode. "Sarai, show Julian those moves you put on me last night."

"Excuse me?"

"On the dance floor, baby." He laughed. "Show him those moves."

I thought I would sink into the sand. "I'm not in the dancing mood right now."

Julian looked at me. "Are you turning me down?"

I glared over at him. He was cute. No, the man was fine. He had the Jason Taylor thing going on. Tall, pecan tan, bald head, and lips that looked like someone had been sucking on them. When he reached over the table for my hand and exposed his wedding band, I nearly spit into my martini. "So, are you gonna show me?"

I was disappointed but I stood up. "I guess I can."

"He's the right one." Conrad winked at me and whispered. Was this his way of helping me with my website? I thought I was coming to talk business to the guy, not bump and grind with him.

Going Broke

As Julian and I moved together, I watched Conrad at the table. Three girls, younger than me, strolled in and walked straight toward him like they knew him. They greeted him with hugs and kisses. Before long they had Richard, Thomas, and Martin on the floor. Conrad moved to the bar and just watched us. While moving his glass in a circle to stir his cognac, he smiled and gave me a thumbs-up.

"So how old are you?" Julian asked.

"Twenty-seven." I asked, "You?"

"Thirty." He moved closer to my ear. "So, what are we doing tonight?" He was smiling like I was really supposed to have something planned.

"I wasn't aware that   we were doing anything," I joked. "I'm on vacation. What about you?"

"Well, I'm only here until tomorrow morning."

"Why are you leaving so soon?"

"I was actually supposed to be in Fort Lauderdale at a convention. Today is the last day, and the only thing planned was a luncheon and a workshop that I attended earlier this year." He pointed at Conrad. "When I learned that Con was here, I hopped on the plane he sent for us."

"So, what do you guys do?"

"I do marketing for Jump Records." He pointed at the others. "I just met those guys today."

I was confused. "But you all know Conrad?"

"Yeah, he's the common denominator," Julian said as we continued to move to the beat.

We did more talking than we did dancing. In a strong Bostonian, accent he said that he was married, and had been for six years. He also had two boys, Julian Jr., who was three, and Kurt, who just seven months. Normally I couldn't stand to hear anyone with a Massachusetts accent even yawn, but he had me curious.

We left the dance floor and made our way out to the beach. It wasn't an intimate setting, but we sat side by side in the sand with the waves stopping just three or four feet away. Julian talked like he had been living on a deserted island for months without conversation. I listened to him, offered my advice and answered whenever he paused long enough. He was making money at Jump, but two restaurants that he opened had failed, and his wife had two miscarriages before getting pregnant with J.J. His mother was suffering from the same illness as my father, and he found himself in the middle of deciding if he should disconnect his sister from the life support machine keeping her alive. A month before, a car accident killed her husband and left her hanging on in a coma.

After hours of talking, Julian put his problems on hold and stood up, tossing rocks and shells at the water. They skimmed the surface a few times before falling to the bottom. I thought that after revealing all he did to me, the least I could do was make him smile. "I bet I can make mine skip more than yours." I picked up a rock and tried. It didn't make it far from the shoreline.

"What a waste of energy." He laughed and threw out another stone. "This is how it's done."

For about fifteen minutes, he coached me. Before I knew it, I beat my record of no skips at all and finished out at three. The last one I threw so hard that I fell to my side on the sand. He didn't bother picking me up. Instead, he sat in front of me. "So, how about dinner tonight?"

I was speechless. The only thing I could do was blush. "Umm." Didn't he just say that he was married with children? "Are you serious?"

He looked taken aback. "Yes." He asked, "Are you playing hard to get?"

I thought it over. What else was I going to do tonight? Of course I was going to have dinner. At least tonight it wouldn't be with a stingray, and most importantly I wouldn't have to pay for it. I was lucking out; my drinks the night before, my lunch today, and I was about to hit the dinner jackpot. "I'm not playing. I am hard to get," I flirted.

"Well, I'm up for the challenge," he said. "Dinner?"

"Sure." I smiled. "What time?"

"I'm on your watch."

I looked down at my Timex. It was almost five in the evening. "How about eight?"

"Eight is great." He stood up and helped me to my feet. "Where would you like to go?"

"I'm on your appetite," I joked as I dusted the sand from my dress.

"How about we leave the resort and see what's out there?"

"I'm down if you are."

"I'll meet you in the lobby at eight then." He smiled.

"Sounds like a plan." I gathered my things from the beach and started off in the direction of the Royal Towers then heard him say, "I'll let Conrad know."

"Okay," I said just to appease him. Why did he have to know? I certainly didn't want him joining us. I never even got a chance to mention to Julian that Conrad was a stranger to me, and I never asked him what help or advice he could offer me for my sites. Oh well, I'd have all night to find that out.

"We can get over being poor, but it takes longer to get over being ignorant."
 —Jane Sequichie Hifler

Bank Statement # 6

Account Balance: $1,068.53

Just as I promised, I was in the lobby at eight. I checked myself out several times before leaving the room. I tooted my own horn, "Damn, you look good." My Hershey's kiss-colored skin, tight physique, and my form-fitting black strapless dress accentuated my long, black hair.

I couldn't help taking a deep breath when Julian came around the corner wearing black slacks and a jacket over a pale yellow oxford shirt. I'm sure people thought we were a couple as we walked through the hotel. Standing outside, I assumed we were waiting on a cab, but a black Lincoln Town Car pulled up instead. Apparently, Julian had made plans. He told the driver the name of the restaurant and we were on our way.

He looked over at me. "You look very nice."

His staring made me timid. I was trying to sit as close to the door as I could. "Thank you." I blushed. "You're looking very dapper yourself."

"I try," he said. Lord knows he didn't have to try very hard. "Has anyone ever told you that you resemble that girl?" He couldn't remember her real name. He gave up and continued, "The one that played Bird on the movie Soul Food."

I had heard that comment countless times before. "Yes. Nia Long." I rolled my eyes, not because it wasn't a compliment but because the last person to make reference to it was Damian. He thought it was cute to call me Birdie. "I'm taller, though."

He was still looking at me. "I don't bite, ya know."

"What do you mean?" I asked.

"I mean you look like you're about to jump out of the car." He lifted my hand from the seat. "Come over here." I slid across the seat and tried not to tense up as my shoulder touched his chest. Being so close, I had to fight to create conversation until we arrived at our destination, a restaurant called Conchman's Den. The restaurant was the size of a small three-bedroom home; it actually looked like it used to be a house. "Conrad told me about this place," he said. "He said that it was great."

"Really?" I looked at it and wondered if we had the right spot. The blue paint was chipping away from the building and the door looked as though it would fall from the hinges the next time a car passed too closely.

"Shall we?" He gestured at the door.

"I guess." I was afraid to touch the doorknob.

He had the same look on his face. "I guess."

He opened the door, and when I entered it did nothing more to impress me. Though the tables were covered with white plastic, I could tell that they weren't sturdy. My purse alone might send it crashing to the floor. Being the only patrons, we expected service right away, but it didn't seem like anyone was working. There was no hostess, and no waiter rushing to seat us. The noise of pots, pans, plates, and glasses touching each other came from a room I assumed was the kitchen. We stood talking for at least three minutes before someone came out. "Oh, I sorry. I didn't hear nobody come in," A pudgy, dark-skinned woman said as she emerged. "How y'all doing?"

"Just fine, thank you," Julian answered.

"Falla me please," the woman said as she dried her hands on her apron. In passing, she hit a button on an old stereo, filling the room with the same type of Caribbean music Julian and I were shaking to earlier. He pulled out my chair and sat across from me at the table. "Here is da menu." She placed paper menus with grease stains plastered over them before us. I let mine fall to the table; I didn't want it to make contact with my fingers. "My name is Sybil. Just holla fa me when y'all ready."

When she walked away, Julian and I looked at each other and laughed. "What in the hell did I get myself into?" he asked.

"What did you get   *us* into?" I studied the menu. "Conchman's Den," I read from the sheet.

"Sybil." Julian called for her before she even made it to where she was going. She turned around with a smile and returned to the table. "What do you have to drink here?"

"What do you want?"

"I'm in the mood for a man's drink." He smiled.

She winked at me. "What about the lady?"

"She wants a man's drink too," he said with a laugh.

Sybil thought for a moment. "What about a Bahamian Rum Punch?"

"Will it put hair on my chest?" he asked.

She reached over and rubbed his bald head. "It'll even put hair on your head."

"Bring it on then. Make one for her too." Then he added, "A friend of mine told me to try your conch salad, so let us have two bowls of that to start with."

As she walked away again, I was curious. "You ever had conch?"

"No," he said. "What is it?"

I pointed at the beautiful shell housing the salt and pepper shakers. "It's the big snail-like creature that used to live in this shell."

"Are you serious?"

"Yes, sir." The Bahamas was close enough to Miami for me to be a little familiar with seafood. I had conch salad a few times, but never prepared at the hands of a native Bahamian.

After two glasses of rum punch and a bowl of the best conch salad I've ever had, our main courses and third glass of punch were before us. We both ordered stuffed lobster, crab and rice, macaroni and cheese, and potato salad. The food was so good that there was almost no talking while we ate. I was too busy studying the ingredients in everything so that I could have this experience again.

"Let's make a toast." Julian spoke with a slight slur as he raised his almost empty glass.

I did the same. "A toast to what?"

"To you, Sarai." His alcohol was talking. "Thanks for listening to me go on and on earlier."

"You don't have to thank me for that." As good-looking as he was, he could find any woman to sit in his face for three hours, and every word out of his lips would become the gospel according to St. Julian. "I enjoyed our afternoon." Then I added, "It was therapy for me." I needed to feel that men were still attracted to me, were still interested in me, still willing to spend money on me, and still wanted to know what made me tick. "I needed that."

He grabbed my hand and kissed it from across the table. "No, I needed this." I couldn't argue with his soft, moist lips. Sybil approached the table and he asked for the check. For putting her foot into the pot, Sybil got a twenty-five dollar tip from Julian. When we returned to the car, he asked the driver to take us to a club called Wet Dreams. We had warmed up to each other considerably over the past two hours, but I was astonished when he began moving his hand up and down my leg, taunting my bare flesh. "You are so sexy," he said as he kissed the side of my neck. "Sexy, sexy Sarai."

Though I was enjoying his touch, I was a little taken aback by his affection. He looked me in the face. "I'm glad you made time for me tonight."

"Made time for you?" I asked. "I didn't have anything else planned."

"I guess Conrad had it all wrong then. He said that you might have been busy."

"Conrad?" I couldn't believe that he said that. "Conrad doesn't have the slightest idea who—" His cellular phone started ringing.

He looked at it and his eyes widened. "Damn." He looked at me and I could tell that he wondered for a second if I was one of those ghetto chicks that would purposely blow up his spot. "I need to get this."

"Then get it." I smiled.

"Hello?" he said. "Hi, honey. I was just about to call you." He stayed on the phone for about ten minutes. I wasn't about to get mad. How could I? He was almost a total stranger. I honestly didn't care, and couldn't be bothered by it. I just made myself comfy next to him.

It was his wife, and his entire conversation was one big lie. It made me think about the many times Damian said the same things to me. First he said that the meeting and luncheon ran longer than expected, then told her that he was in a cab heading from Miami back to his Fort Lauderdale hotel, and lastly he said that he thought of skipping the luncheon and returning to Boston a day early, but his boss wasn't hearing it. The real joke would've been if she were at the hotel waiting on him. Oops, he checked out of the hotel early this morning. I would've loved to see him scramble to the airport trying to get back into the country on the first thing smoking.

Keeping close company with a married man really wasn't my style. I felt a little guilty hearing him tell his wife all those things. He wasn't even in America, and she'd never know. Why are some men so evil? If I wasn't almost penniless, bored, and across international waters, I probably would've turned his fine ass down. I believe in karma; what you do to others will be served right back to you. So, I wasn't doing anything that night that I couldn't stand eating a big plateful of myself, I think. "All right, baby. I love you too." Ironically, his hand was still rubbing my leg, but he stopped when he said those three little words. Did he think that pausing would validate his claim? He looked at me. "Now back to you."

"Welcome to Wet Dreams," the driver said as he pulled up and stopped in front of the building.

"We're here already?" Julian asked.

"I actually took the long route," the driver explained, "since I was supposed to be driving you from Miami to Fort Lauderdale." Even the driver didn't mind being a partner in Julian's evil game of betrayal.

"Good looking out, man." Julian was all smiles.

Wet Dreams was very wet indeed. The bar counter was an oversized rectangular fish tank, and so was the wall behind the bar. The dance floor was elevated. In fact, the steps led to the deck of a pirate ship, so it appeared that there was a party on the boat. With its sail high, the S.S. Wet Dreams had treasure chests sprinkled around it, and bogus rubies and diamonds embedded in the floor. The bow pointed to the entrance and the stern was toward the back of the establishment. Way atop the ship, where the lookout person would stand, was a machine blowing down fog. The club walls were covered with beige old-style maps, and along the walls were half-circle booths with glass-encased helms as tables. The lights in the club were shades of the ocean, and when the dizzy illuminations danced on the walls, they created the illusion of sparkling water.

Julian pointed at a vacant booth. "Are you going to be my first mate tonight?"

I blushed. "No, soy el   capitán." I loved saying the word captain in Spanish. I just haven't figured out why yet.

"Bien, si usted es el   capitán entonces yo   es el barco. Tómeme para un paseo," he said.

I gave him the ghetto stare. "What did you just say?"

"I said   well, if you're the captain, then I'm the boat. Take me for a ride."

"Where did you learn Spanish?"

"My wife."

"Where did she learn it?" I asked.

"Well, she's from Ecuador."

His worth was depreciating. "No sista   hs in Boston?" I mocked his accent.

"Plenty of black women in Boston, but I met and married her." He seemed offended.

"I think I need a drink," I said sarcastically. "Quick." I was the type of black woman he didn't want to have a conversation with on interracial relationships. Yes, I got angry when I saw it at the mall, at the movies, and on television. Yes, I allowed it to ruin my day. Yes, I wished I could snatch the brotha and scream "Why?" And now that I was single again and would be looking for a good brotha soon, it angered me even more. I said, "Let's have more rum punch." But what I felt like saying was, "Give me more rum before I punch you." He made his way to the bar and I used the opportunity to take deep breaths. One part of my brain was telling me to get over it because love was love. The other side was jealous that he hadn't chosen to share his life with a black woman.

All of the racial tension melted when   Beyonce started singing about how crazy in love she was with Jay-Z. By the time Julian returned with the drinks, I was standing, trying to shake my moneymaker like Beyonce did in the video. "Oh oh, oh oh, oh oh, oh oh," I sung. "Looking so crazy, ya love's got me looking, got me looking so crazy, ya love." I guess it was Beyonce's night because right after that song, the DJ blasted "Baby Boy." This was one of Damian's favorite songs. He loved Sean Paul.

I continued to jerk my body as Julian sat down behind me. Seconds later, he pulled my body towards him. My butt had to be in his face. I grabbed my drink and didn't miss a beat. "Baby boy you stay on my mind. Baby boy, you are so damn fine. Baby boy, won't you be mine?" Whenever I heard Sean Paul, Damian's face seemed inches away. I missed him dearly, I wanted him, and when I turned to face Julian, all I saw was my ex. I continued to dance provocatively in front of him until the temptation smoldered. His hands moved over the back of my body like they knew their way around, and in a moment I straddled him and our lips found comfort in each other.

We never made it to the dance floor. In our booth, we created our own spectacle. People on the dance floor were watching us. Still facing him on his lap, I was moving like an angry snake, and he was licking, biting, and squeezing me in places that should only be behind closed doors. Julian was fine, but when I closed my eyes, he was Damian to me. I was using Julian's body to show Damian how much he was missed. I allowed him access to places strangers shouldn't be. After two hours of drinking, dancing, and passionate fondling, he grabbed my hand. "Let's get out of here."

"Where are we going?" I asked.

He looked at me like I should know. "To the hotel." He kissed my hand and worked his way up to my shoulder, then my neck, and then his tongue was back inside of my mouth. "Let's go." Julian pulled me hurriedly out of the booth and through the club. Outside, the black Lincoln pulled up and before the driver could close the door, Julian had me sitting on his lap facing him. His fingers were like tiny snakes, slithering all over my body. They knew no bounds and I knew no manners, so I welcomed it. As he kissed my chest, I felt him growing solid beneath me. Right then I knew I either needed to put an end to our fervent play or I'd have to give up my chocolate-covered goody. My decision? I began grinding myself into his lump. My imagination ran wild. I wondered what it looked, tasted, and felt like.

This wasn't the cautious, respectable, think things out logically Sarai Emery who got on the plane. My mind, my body, and my mouth were in three different time zones. I was like R. Kelly. *My mind's telling me no, but my body, my body's telling me yeah.* Then out of my mouth was the confirmation of my stupidity. "Will you walk me to my room?" R. Kelly again. *I don't see nothing wrong with a little bump and grind.*

"I wouldn't be a gentleman if I didn't." He smiled.

We were so worked up during the ride that back at the Atlantis we trotted so fast we might as well have run to the room. We burst through the door to my suite like honeymooners. His hands were pulling clothing from my body before the hinges pulled the door shut. I wanted him badly, but suddenly I couldn't look into his face. I wanted to believe that he was Damian, or better yet Dwayne. As we bumped into the walls in our mad scuffle to get sweaty, I hit the light switch and watched the room fall into darkness. "Tell me what you want me to do, Sarai."

"I want Dwayne." I didn't care if he didn't know what it meant. I just had to say it. "Be Dwayne for me."

"Dwayne?" he asked and stopped.

I pulled his hands back to my breasts. "Just play with me." I kissed him. "Be rough and tough with me."

"Is that how Dwayne was?" he asked.

"Yeah." I was breathing heavy already.

He went along with me. "Then I'll be Dwayne."

I said with his lips still pressing against mine, "Just do me like Dwayne does."

"Are you gonna let me fuck you?" He didn't have to ask. I was already almost naked. "Answer me." I loved his aggression.

"Yes." I repeated the answer in case he missed it. "Yes."

He spun me around. "I'll fuck you like Dwayne does." He laughed as he removed my panties and rubbed in between my lower lips. "I'll fuck you like Dwayne, Rerun, and Rag." We both laughed at his reference to the

98

show *What's Happening.* "I'll even fuck you like Big Shirley."

I made it over to the sofa and pulled him along. He was out of his pants and jacket. I removed his briefs and asked him to unbutton his shirt but not to remove it. "Is this what Dwayne does when he wants that ass?"

"Yes." Many times I had pounced on Damian when he walked in from the office. I didn't give him time to get fully undressed. A few times we did it with him still in his suit. I just unzipped his slacks and said hello to my little friend. "Do you have a condom?" I asked.

"Yeah," he said, "but I thought you'd be prepared." He walked back over to his pants pocket and returned, pulling the latex over his magic wand. "Bend over," he said as he approached me kneeling in front of the sofa. "Can I have this pussy, Sarai?"

"You know you can." I was talking to Dwayne.

"Tell me." He smacked my butt. He was really reminding me of my man.

"You can have this pussy," I said in a very lustful tone. "It's all yours."

"I'm fucking Dwayne's pussy, huh?" He rubbed the tip of his sword on my open wound and made my entire body tremble. He slipped in but quickly pulled it out, teasing me. "Sorry, Dwayne. This pussy is all mines tonight." He plunged deep into me and I let out a squeal. Over the next hour, we moved from kneeling in front of the sofa to being on it. We went to the floor and then the bed. Julian was a downright freak. He was also in great shape and worked me out for all the times I was too lazy to go to the gym. After we were done, we lay side by side. He cradled me as I fell asleep knowing that my body was aching from my acceptance of him. As the sun began to rise, he kissed me on my back and woke me to have a little more. Afterwards, I drifted back into my sex-induced coma as he took a shower.

"Sarai." I felt his fingers running through my hair. "Wake up."

"What happened?" I opened my eyes and saw that Julian was fully dressed. "You're leaving?"

"Yeah." He proceeded to the desk, sitting with his back toward me. "My flight is out of here at ten. Then I'm on a flight from Miami to Boston at two this afternoon."

"Wow." Sexual acts from the night before played back in my mind and I was ashamed. I'd probably never see or hear from him again. "Have a safe trip."

"Sarai, what is the spelling of your name and what is your last name?" His back was toward me; he was leaning over the desk.

I was cheesing big. "S-A-R-A-I, and my last name is Emery, E-M-E-R-Y." Wow. Was he creating space for me in his cell phone? Maybe this wasn't a one-night stand.

"Actually, I think it'll be better to use the name of your website. What is it?"

"Y-O-U-P-L-A-N-M-Y-T-R-I-P dot com." I guessed having my web address in his cellular would be easier to explain. Not that I expected a relationship with him, but the least he could do was call me if he was ever in Florida.

Julian stood up and walked toward the bed with a piece of paper that was way too long to be a business card. "Here you go."

My mouth dropped open as I looked at the check written out to youplanmytrip.com for one thousand fifty dollars. "What's this?" I asked.

"It's for last night." He smiled. "Thanks again."

Going Broke

I didn't know if I should thank him or be offended. "What?" I was more confused than anything.

"Thanks," he said. "You made me feel as though it was a real night out."

"What do you mean?"

"I mean," he sighed, "the last time I did this it just felt like I was paying for it." He smiled. "But you were so real. At least until we got back here. Then the beast came out." He laughed.

"What do you mean the last time?" I sat up. "And why are you paying me?"

"Am I supposed to give it to Conrad?" he asked. "I wrote him a separate check. I always do."

My heart fluttered. "Conrad?" My eyes sprung open. "Wait a minute!" I took a deep breath. "What in the hell is going on?" I looked at the check again. "What does Conrad have to do with anything?"

"Look." He glanced at his watch. "I need to be on my way to the airport. Conrad and I agreed on the rate of fifteen hundred. He gets his thirty percent, which is four-fifty," he said. "You get one thousand fifty. If you normally get more than that, then you need to take that up with him. But that is what I normally pay."

I fell back against the pillow. "I'm not a fuckin' prostitute."

"I know." He kissed me on my forehead. "The politically correct term is escort. You're an escort, and a damn good one."

I pushed his face away from mine. "I'm not a goddamn whore." I jumped up from the bed naked and ran into the bathroom for my robe. "I'm not a whore."

"I never called you one."

"You're implying that I might be one. You just wrote me a check for sex."

"What?" He seemed confused. "Would you rather cash?"

"No," I cried out. "I didn't know that any of this was going on." I hoped he believed me. "Conrad told me that you might be able to help me with my website."

"Well, it looks like I just did." He pointed at the check on the bed. "Sarai, I had a wonderful time. I need to get going." He gathered his things. "I'll get in contact with Conrad when I'll be in the area again. Maybe we can hook up. I'll be sure to bring Dwayne with me." He walked over to me and couldn't smell the hurt, embarrassment, and shame excreting from my pores. He kissed me on the cheek. "Stay sweet, Sarai," he said as he walked away. He was out the door before I could say another word.

Going Broke

"When wealth is lost, nothing is lost;
When health is lost, something is lost;
When character is lost, all is lost."
–German proverb

Bank Statement # 7

Account Balance: $2,568.53

I took a shower and threw on a pair of jeans and a tank top. I was too upset to iron, afraid that I'd purposely burn myself as chastisement for being so ignorant. I called the front desk but didn't know the last name of this Conrad character, so they weren't able to tell me what room he could be found in. Maybe it was for my own good because my plan was to rip him a new asshole.

At 10:00 a.m., I was in the lobby, sitting patiently by the elevators with the check folded in my back pocket. Conrad would have to come down or be trying to get up to his room some time during the day. I couldn't believe that he was selling me without even telling me. Did he think that I was desperate? I waited a little over two hours and heard the elevators cry "ding" many times before the doors slid open and I saw the face I wanted to see. He was dressed in a navy suit garlanded with light blue accessories.

I stood up as he walked toward me with a smile. "Good morning, Miss Emery."

I couldn't say what I wanted to; the long waiting period had calmed me. I just took the check out of my pocket and placed it in his hand. "I can't believe you did that to me." I turned and walked away.

"What are you doing?" He latched onto my arm and spun me around. "What are you doing?"

"I'm not being a whore, that's what I'm doing." My words came out louder than I wanted them to. He looked around to see if anyone was paying me any attention. "Let's talk," he said.

"I have nothing to say to you." I pulled away from him.

"Let me explain," he said.

"There isn't anything that you have to explain to me." I gestured to the check in his hand. "Just take your fuckin' money and get the hell out of my face." I rushed to the elevators and he was right behind me.

"So, you're going to just let me keep your money?" He tried to whisper because there were other guests waiting for the elevators. "That's stupid. You worked for this."

I just stared at him until the elevator came. We got on with a group of people and exited on the seventh floor. "Why are you following me?" I shouted as I walked to my room. He was still a step behind me. Before inserting my electronic key, I turned around. "What do you want?"

He extended to me the check with my name on it and $450 in cash. "I'll give you my share along with yours if you'll just hear what I have to say."

I stared at the money and the check. I was caught between a rock and a hard place. Here I was trying to pretend like I was so proud when he already knew how badly I needed money. I snatched the check and the cash from his fingertips and opened the door. "You have fifteen minutes."

"All I really need is ten." He smiled as he straightened his tie and walked through the door.

"Start talking." I sat on the couch and looked at my watch.

"How many times have you been to bed with a

man and walked away with nothing?" he asked.

"That's none of your business." I looked at my watch again. "Time is running out."

He removed his jacket. "Instead of sleeping with a man and getting nothing but hurt, used, or abused, I give women the opportunity to turn the tables." He smiled. "Stop giving up the goods for free and get paid."

"Money isn't that serious to me." As the words passed my lips, I realized that it was a lie.

"It is that serious, Sarai," he said. "What in the hell are you going to do when you can't find a job in the allotted two months you've given yourself?"

I snapped, "I'll do something."

He laughed. "You'll do what?" He didn't pause long enough for me to answer. "Are you willing to flip burgers? Want to make up beds at a hotel? You want to work as a cashier? The economy is a piece of shit right now. Are you going to take your whorish man back just so he can pay the bills?"

"I'll do what I have to do." I had no clue what I'd do. "I have a college degree."

"You live in Miami and you don't speak Spanish, so that degree won't get you far." He grinned. "It means nothing and you know it."

I had to think fast. "I'll start at the bottom at a station if I have to."

He was laughing hard like I told a good joke. "You think other stations will hire you after all the drama you created at WBIG? You think other stations don't already know?"

"If it's not on radio, then so be it," I said. "I'll do what I have to do to get my bills paid."

"Great," he said with a smile. "That's the attitude to have."

"What in the fuck are you talking about?" I was getting back to the level of anger I was at before.

"You're going to have sex anyways, and you'll always have bills to pay. So, why not incorporate the two?" I didn't even bother answering. "You're not a prostitute. You're a businesswoman. You are a walking, talking billboard. You are your own television commercial, and you're a very hot commodity."

He sat next to me on the sofa. "You're a very driven person, smart, very funny, and extremely sexy." He touched my hand. "Why would you let Julian come up here, fuck you, and go back to his wife without a care in the world? Why let him skip out of here to be a loving father and husband?" He stood up. "Hell no. Tax that bastard."

"What he does isn't any of my business."

"That's where you're wrong," he said. "It's your time, it's your body, and it's your business. Let him leave you with something. He couldn't go into a store and walk out with something without leaving some bills with the cashier, could he?"

"No," I answered.

"So then why shouldn't he pay you?" Conrad asked.

"Look, I just wish I would've known that I was being used," I said.

"You weren't being used, darling." Conrad explained, "You were given an opportunity."

"But why me?"

"If not you, I would've gotten his regular."

Julian's fine physique and face came to mind. "Why in the hell is he paying for sex?"

"He pays because he knows that my girls are clean, discreet, lots of fun, and he won't hear it on the streets tomorrow. Better yet, his wife won't hear it on the streets today."

I laughed. "How do you know that I'm clean?"

"I know everything," he assured me. "Including your middle name."

"What is it?" I dared him.

"It's the word that brought your parents together."

He couldn't know. "What word?"

"Jazz." He spoke with certainty; he was right.

I stood up. "Who are you?"

He laughed. "I'm Conrad."

"No." I was nervous. "Tell me who you really are."

"I'm Conrad Johnson." He extended his hand as though we were meeting for the first time. I shook his hand then he graced me with a brief history of who he really was.

Conrad Johnson, a 50-year-old man earned a living at what he called "profit sharing." The way he saw it was he provided the clients, who provided an income for the women, who in turn "shared the profit" with him. He enticed young women with his charm and wealth to turn them into employees. Their job was to sexually entertain men. He ran a very classy, reputable, and extremely profitable organization called the Elite Establishment.

He selected what he believed to be the best merchandise: women between the ages of twenty-one and thirty. They traveled to major cities during important events such as conventions, reunions, parties, and business meetings. Among the women, there was a high code of discretion, which was why Conrad's Elite Establishment was so popular. Names never leaked, prices were discussed privately, and his girls were never tacky enough to walk the street.

Conrad gained a thirty-percent profit from every "transaction." Only under special circumstances would the money touch the hands of the woman. The men normally paid by credit card, check, cash, or money order to the establishment, then it deposited seventy percent into the woman's account. This was to avoid things appearing criminal. If one of Conrad's girls was working without his knowledge or without the man paying him first, it would result in a two-month suspension for the woman.

With girls working at all times all over the United States, Conrad never had to break a sweat. From a fully functional office in his home, his secretary took calls from members phoning to inform the Elite of their company's various events. They picked up a portion of the air, train, or rental car expenses in order to transport the girls to that city.

Conrad saw that the Elite girls stayed sexy and irresistible, but above all he stressed the importance of conducting themselves as ladies. His customers were mostly very wealthy African-American married men looking for excitement while they were away from home. The girls were considered "escorts," but they did a lot more than frequent fine restaurants and clubs with their dates. They were encouraged to earn thousands in just one night by doing "whatever" was asked.

"The men that deal with me know that I don't half-step. They pay high prices for quality and discretion. They realize that in their professional positions, marriages or relationships, getting free sex could cost a lot more, like sexually transmitted diseases, unwanted pregnancies, divorce, and blackmail." He paused. "These are men. Just like all men, they want to have sex with women that they find attractive, women that are wild, and women that are not like what they have at home."

"They're all dogs," I said, adding my two cents.

"So, you've never cheated?" he asked.

Oops, he got me. "What does that have to do with the price of cheese?"

"Everything," he said. "Most men or women under the age of forty-five can't stand the thought of sleeping with one person for the rest of their lives. It doesn't mean that they don't love their husband or wife. They just have needs away from the relationship or marriage. It doesn't mean that they love the person they're doing it with. It's just the excitement of a different body, and releasing the sexual tension they've been suppressing."

I hated to admit that he was sort of right. "Okay, I see where you're coming from."

"Thank you," he said with smile. "These men have no time to deal with jealous lovers or another relationship, having rumors sparked all over town. The grand he leaves on your pillow costs a hell of a lot less than a divorce where his wife walks away with half of everything he's worked for. These men pay high prices for beautiful women, but most of all because they know that I don't kiss and tell, they're paying for confidentiality.

"This is not the love connection. You're not in it to think that you got yourself a man. You'll be in it to keep up your appearance, which will generate more business for yourself. But most importantly, you'll be able to stay in your apartment in downtown Miami, you can keep your truck, and your father's medical care will continue."

"Are you trying to sell me on the Elite Establishment?" I joked.

"That's exactly what I'm doing." He looked at the money in my hands. "Baby, you got enough money for another month's rent in just a few hours." He stood up and looked down on me. "Now that I see what you can do for me, let me see what I can do for you. Be a part of my establishment."

I clapped my hands. "What a great speech." I stood up and walked toward the door. "Thanks, but no thanks." I opened the door.

"All right." He grabbed his coat. "I can't force you. But at least keep the money."

"One last question, though," I said.

"Shoot," he said as he walked through the door.

I asked, "How did you know my middle name?"

"Wouldn't you like to know?" He smiled. "If you change your mind, I'll have the answer to your question in the Cigar Bar tonight."

I held my hand out and offered him a handshake to signify the end of our dealings. "It was nice meeting you, Conrad." I closed the door behind him then stared at the money, wishing that there were something I could do to undo the last two weeks of my life. I should've stayed in Orlando that night because what I didn't know about Damian wouldn't have had the opportunity to hurt me. I'd still have a job and this vacation would've been a lot better.

Instead of playing the pity game with myself, I changed into a royal blue bikini, tied my black wrap skirt around my waist, and journeyed downstairs in search of the nearest pool. I needed to plunge into something therapeutic. Once at the pool, I kicked off my sandals, undid my wrap, and dove into the far end of the pool, away from people. I swam back and forth like a shark was chasing me. When I got tired, I just floated about. The sun was shining down on me and I loved it. When I bumped up to the pool's edge, I checked out the scenery. There were kids everywhere, and they all had one thing in common. Whether they were throwing beach balls, sliding down the waterslides, running through the sand, or swimming, they were all screaming.

I dipped my head below the water and was a little more thankful just to be alive. So what if I didn't have money? There were a lot of people that didn't, and they got along just fine. Actually, they were some of the happiest people I knew. I'd just have to learn how to get off my high horse; my whole life was a financial facade, a front that Damian footed the bill for.

I got out of the pool after an hour, laid out in one of the poolside chaises, and ordered a glass of red wine from the waiter circulating the area. I closed my eyes and awaited his return. "Here is your glass of wine, ma'am."

"Thank you." I twisted to face him. "I might want another one soon. Today is chalking up to be a—" I was thrown off; I was staring up at Doctor William Baker, my gynecologist. I jumped up and almost dropped my glass. "Doctor Baker?"

He laughed. "There I was, sitting at the bar. When I looked over here, I thought that I saw someone that looked like you. I told the waiter that I'd deliver it."

I sprung to my feet while tying my wrap to cover me below. "Wow." I gave him a quick hug. "What are you doing here?"

"You should know how hard I work. I need a break too." He smiled.

William Baker was a fifty-something-year-old African-American gynecologist, the only one in my area. He wasn't Denzel Washington. Hell, he wasn't even Forrest Whitaker, but he was a good man. Doctor Baker was my height but almost doubled my weight, somewhere in the area of 250 pounds. He wasn't sloppy fat, but fat and unattractive enough to be my doctor. I didn't want a stud talking to me about a yeast infection. I definitely couldn't ask Doctor Fine-ass to give me a pregnancy test, because then he'd know that I had a man. Doctor Baker was doing a great job. He was very professional and extremely nice to me during each visit. "I can't believe that you're here." I looked around. "Where is Mrs. Baker?"

"She's at home. To be honest with you, I'm not on much of a break. I do pro bono work here one Saturday a month," he said. "I normally get out of here on Sunday morning, but I decided to stay an extra day ... to treat myself."

"You deserve it." I looked over at the bar. "Come on. I'll join you at the bar."

I hadn't seen him in over a month, so we sat and talked for a while. We chatted about everything from Damian and India to my father's health. When I told him about my job, how I wasn't working and no longer had health insurance, he told me not to worry, promising that if I needed his services he'd chalk it up to pro bono work. Doctor Baker was always privy to my personal, non-medical life. I always asked his advice about my relationships, work, and finances. He also made me a part of his life. Over the past five, years I was invited to every Christmas party at his home, birthday gathering for his wife and kids, and various seminars where he was the speaker. He was more than a doctor. He was more like an uncle.

After three glasses of wine, Doctor Baker was still a sore sight for good eyes. We said our goodbyes minutes before six o'clock because he had a massage appointment. He inquired about my plans for the evening and I lied, telling him that I was meeting someone for dinner. We hugged and I promised him that I'd be seeing him in two months for my pap smear.

I walked into my suite and a joyful feeling overtook me. I looked over at the check and cash still lying there. Though I wasn't happy about how it was earned, it was still money and would allow me to stay in my apartment another month. I lounged around watching TV a while until a hunger pain hit, then the hotel phone rang. "Hello?"

"Hi, Sarai."

"Savion?" I asked.

"Yeah."

"What's wrong? Are you okay?"

"Yeah, I'm fine." He paused. "It's Daddy—"

My heart was already racing. I sat back down. "What happened?"

He knew that I was about to flip. "Well, calm down first," he said. "Dad is doing okay, but there was a little situation a couple days ago."

"A couple days ago? What happened?" I was wondering why he was talking so slow. "And why are you just calling me?"

"Everything is fine, Sarai. He had another asthma attack. He had to be hospitalized on Friday night."

I yelled, "Why didn't you call me, Savvy?"

"Calm down, Sarai. I have everything under control. I'm in Dover as we speak. I got here yesterday morning." He continued, "He was released about an hour ago. He's back at Concord."

"I mean, so what happened? Are you positive that he's okay?"

"Yeah, he's okay," he said.

I sighed. "How bad was the attack?"

"It was about the same as the one last year," he said.

114

"Okay." I was trying to process what he was saying.

"I made a joke to myself, saying that it knocked some sense into him because he recognized me."

"What?" I smiled.

"Yeah," Savion said. "He even asked about you."

"Are you serious?" I was elated. "What did he say?"

"Well, he asked how you were doing and if you were still pretty. But it didn't last very long. He went back into being five hundred miles away a few minutes later."

"Well, that's okay." I was trying to keep myself from crying. "In my dreams, we have long talks."

He continued sadly. "Sarai, I plan on helping you with the hospital bill."

"Shit." I hadn't even thought about that. I was afraid to ask the next question. "How much is it?"

I heard paper rustling close to the phone. "Four thousand three hundred and sixteen dollars."

"What the fuck?" I yelled. "Did he fuckin' die and come back?"

"Sarai, it's the two-night stay, his medication, and all of those tests," Savion tried to explain.

I put my head in my hands. "That's easy for you to say. You're not the one paying his bills." I didn't mean to say it quite like that.

"I'll try to help," he said. "I'm flying back to Atlanta on Tuesday. I'm still not working, but I can't expect you to do this all alone."

I felt like screaming. I still didn't know why he left Houston to move to Atlanta to be a hermit. "Savion, I normally wouldn't ask this of you, but I really am going to need your help on this. I'm going broke." Then I thought about it. "No, let me rephrase that. I am broke. I have just enough money to pay my rent for a couple of months and that's it."

"I just said that I'd help you." He sounded like he thought I was picking on him.

"I'm sorry." I tried to use a more soothing tone. "All I mean is that if we don't start paying this bill, it'll result in the hospital refusing to treat him if something like this happens again."

"I'm going to find a way to help you, Sarai. I promise." He sounded so sad. "I just wanted to call and let you know. Please don't let this dampen your vacation." He added, "Daddy is doing fine now."

"All right. I'll give him a call later tonight."

"I love you, sexy," he said.

I smiled. "No, I love *you*, sexy."

I looked out the glass door and wanted to scream. Who decided who would get rich and who would stay poor? Why was I chosen governor of the poor? Why are some people selected to be broke, never to have anything and live in misery? I curled up in the bed and cried, sobbing over the fact that I couldn't find anything in my life to be happy about. What happened in my life that led me to being who I was today? Where did I go wrong? Sometimes I believed that maybe Esther's curse was really plaguing my life. It was funny that I didn't think of any of this when I thought my life was on track. Reality was a bitch. This trip was turning out to do more harm than good. It had me realizing things I wasn't quite ready to take on.

I picked up the phone and received the hotel's instructions for international dialing. At three dollars per minute to dial, I called my father and gave him fifteen dollars worth of conversation. Though he thought I was some girl he went to high school with, he was very nice to me. He told me about the hospital stay and how the staff treated him like royalty. I ended our conversation by telling him that he was royalty. He was and would always be my king.

The only thing stopping me from taking a concrete dive from the balcony was the fact that without me, no one would provide for my father. I couldn't sit in the room another minute. I put on a brown-pant suit and made the journey once again to the lobby. I ate dinner at the Café at The Great Hall of Waters. Afterward I walked slowly, trying hard to find a reason not to go back to my room so quickly. I paced the halls leisurely, looking in the windows of closed stores and imagining what it would be like to walk in and purchase things on my Visa check card without saying a prayer while the clerk ran it. I noticed a red gown; it was six hundred dollars. "Do you want that dress?" I heard Doctor Baker's voice and spun around in shock.

"Hey." I was startled. "Doctor Baker."

"You like that dress, huh?"

"Yeah." I scooted back so that I wasn't so close to him. "But I wouldn't have anywhere to wear it."

"You could wear it for your next appointment," he joked and changed the subject. "How was your dinner date?"

I frowned. "He didn't show up." I wasn't lying. The stingray was a no show for our Sunday supper.

"What a jerk." He grabbed my hand. "Come and have a drink with my friend and me."

I didn't want to give off the wrong vibe. "I don't want to intrude on your friend's time." Plus, if he was with a woman, I sure didn't want to know. I wouldn't be able to look in Mrs. Baker's face again if I saw him with someone else.

"I insist." He gently guided me to the bar across the hall. "Come on."

We walked into the bar. "Where is your friend?"

"Weak bladder, I guess." He looked around. "Let me get a cigar. I'll be right back."

"What can I get for you?" The bartender approached.

"Kendall Jackson Merlot." I smiled.

"Nice choice." I heard a voice behind me. "No mango martinis tonight?"

I turned around and saw Conrad. I thought I would faint. The last thing I wanted was for Conrad to say anything in front of Doctor Baker. "I'm with company." I tried to get him to go away.

"Well, I'm your company too." He took a seat on the stool next to me. "The least you can do is be nice to me."

I tried to play it cool. "Hi. How are you?" I faked a smile.

"Oh, I'm just fine."

"That's great," I said nervously. "Can we talk later? I'm having drinks with a friend."

"I know." He chuckled. "Doctor Baker is a friend of mine as well."

"How do you know him?" My words trailed off as I looked at Doctor Baker, who was about twenty feet away selecting a cigar.

"He was the person that told me about you. One of the reasons why I came here."

"Doctor Baker?" I blew him off. "Whatever! He would never—"

Conrad interrupted me. "Your blood type is A-negative. Your last HIV test was taken last month on the nineteenth; it came back negative. Need I go on?" I was super-stunned and Conrad went on without my consent. "He has wanted to know what being in bed with you would be like for two years," he said. "He's a member of the Elite Establishment, and he knew that the only way for him to get a piece of you was to try bringing you into the fold." He smiled. "So, what do you say, Sarai?"

"I say hell no, Conrad."

"Look at his fat ass," Conrad laughed. "He has to pay for pussy."

He was right, but I wasn't going to play his game. "Please leave me alone."

Conrad didn't go away. When Doctor Baker drifted back to the bar, I asked, "Do you know him?" I pointed at Conrad.

"Oh yeah, Conrad and I go way back."

This was the most uncomfortable situation I had ever been in. At first it was like being caught between heaven and hell, but things slowly heated up then melted into being pure hell. Doctor Baker has been in the Elite for the past seven years. He told Conrad of my medical history and me, stating that I was "clean." Whatever happened to doctor-patient confidentiality?

He and Conrad spent almost hour promoting the Elite Establishment. The shock of the evening came when Doctor Baker slid three thousand dollars in hundreds across the countertop to Conrad, who extracted nine hundred and placed the remaining two thousand one hundred dollars in front of me. "Can I spend the night with you, Sarai?" Doctor Baker asked.

As much as I wanted to believe that I wasn't too good for some jobs, you'd never catch me flipping burgers, bagging groceries, telemarketing, cashiering, or selling anything in anybody's store other than my own. The two websites needed the right type of advertising and the advertising, I needed wasn't cheap. Plus I wanted to hire a web developing company to enhance the appearance.

"So, will you do it?" Doctor Baker asked me.

My financial need was great, and they both knew it. However, there were certain things I just couldn't do, and sleeping with a man for cash was one of them. Julian was a mistake. I had no clue what a twisted game was being played on me. Daddy used to tell me, "When you know better, do better." I wasn't going to knowingly be a part of something so disgusting. I stared at Doctor Baker. "How can you ask me that?" It was like talking to a stranger. "I know your wife," I paused, "and your kids."

"They have nothing to do with this." He lit his cigar. "This is between you and me."

"This is a money-making industry, Sarai," Conrad chimed in.

I turned sharply to Conrad. "Shut the fuck up. Both of you are sick." I jumped down off the stool. "Good night gentlemen."

I stormed out of the bar, and neither one of them bothered to follow me with an apology. I pinched myself all the way to my room, hoping that this was a bad dream. Each pinch brought pain, and brought me to the conclusion that this was all too real.

Going Broke

"Money is sharper than a sword."
–Ashanti proverb

Bank Statement # 8
Account Balance: $1,109.89

After the episode in the bar on Sunday night, I felt bad enough to stay in my hotel room for the remainder of my vacation, but instead I vowed not to let this trip pass me by. Holding true to my words, I shopped on Bay Street, Cable Beach, and the Straw Market, hopped on a tour bus, dashed into taxicabs, and did a lot of walking. I was truly enjoying the tranquil island lifestyle. I even went back to Conchman's Den and devoured another bowl of conch salad. The only thing I regretted was my decision to walk through the hotel's casino. I thought that playing blackjack on my computer deemed me an expert. Error! I was also cocky enough to play four hands at two hundred dollars apiece. So I donated eight hundred dollars to the Save the Atlantis Casino fund.

Needless to say, after such a loss I couldn't afford to do anything else. I was lonely, bored, and couldn't wait to get back home. I roamed the hotel like a homeless woman. I sat on the beach, window-shopped, did a little dancing and drinking at night, and ordered from the appetizer section of various menus. I met a lot of nice men, but none worthy of more than a handshake. The best part of the rest of my stay was not seeing Conrad again.

When the aircraft kissed the tarmac of the airport in Miami, I wanted to shout hallelujah. As I made my way through the airport, I hoped that Natalya wouldn't be fuming about the plane being two hours behind schedule. I entered the area where non-passengers were allowed to stand, and saw a huge, neon green sign reading: STELLA, DID YOU GET YOUR GROOVE ON? I nearly fainted. We joked about her doing that, but never in my wildest dreams did I believe her. I'm sure everyone wanted a glimpse of this crazy woman's friend.

As I approached the sign, it seemed like a billboard. "I am going to kill you."

"Stella!" she shouted and dropped the sign. Her welcoming arms made their way around me instantaneously. "I've missed you."

I had missed her too. "You are insane, Nat," I joked. "I'm gonna roll that sign up and beat your ass." Shoulder to shoulder, we walked to the baggage claim area with me telling her about the Bahamas. Nat was always worried about me in some way or the other, so I left the Conrad, Julian, and Doctor Baker story out of the mix, at least for now. I also didn't want her knowing exactly how tight my money was. I couldn't ask her for help knowing that teachers didn't make anywhere near what they deserved. I went on and on about the hotel, food, friendly folks, sunshine, water, and the breathtakingly beautiful scenery. She was in awe of the hotel, so most of her questions were in regards to it, and I was thankful. She and Nick had plans, so she dropped me off at my apartment complex.

I spent the next day, Saturday, getting my business affairs in order. I had three picnic baskets to create and nine trips to get information about. Picnictogo.com personalized picnic baskets with special items and colors to suit customers' requirements. Youplanmytrip.com was a site for lazy people with travel

123

needs. It was designed for people who didn't have the time or just didn't want to visit twenty websites in search of the best travel deals. Using the Internet, I basically found the best airfare, hotel, and rental car rates. I even went beyond that by making dinner reservations, finding out theme park fees, and even researching the entertainment in town during the the their allotted travel time.

I also arranged to have extravagant floral arrangements waiting for wives and girlfriends at the hotel's front desk upon check-in. I made phone calls to airport shuttles or limousine companies to transport clients from the airport to the hotel or vice versa. The fee for me to research all this information was fifteen dollars, but if I went the next step and planned the trip, I earned ten percent of the price of the entire trip. The site was a gold mine; I just needed the right advertisement. But at the same time, I was afraid that if I advertised, I wouldn't be able to handle the workload alone.

My Sunday was spent updating my resumé. I inserted them into professional portfolios and hit the South Florida streets early the next morning. It actually took me four days to drop my resumé off at every television and radio station from Key Largo to West Palm Beach. I didn't discriminate. I'd do country again. I was even willing to do classical or gospel. But I was hoping to get something at 99 Jamz or 103.5 The Beat. Even Y-100 would have been all right.

Two weeks went by without a single phone call regarding a job, so I decided to be assertive. I phoned the stations to ask about the various positions and reminded them that they had my resumé. My spirits were up until one receptionist decided to keep it real with me. She told me that the recording of me cursing and carrying on at

Going Broke

WBIG had been passed around from station to station via e-mail attachment over the past month. I was the laughing stock of the industry and didn't even know it. They had associated my face with the voice and looked at me without cracking a smile. I wasn't going to find a job anytime soon, and worst of all, I didn't have a plan B.

By the end of August, I was a nervous wreck. I had been out of work for a total of two months, and with both websites combined, they offered a profit of a little over $700. I used the money to keep my truck a little longer, since it could very well turn into my residence since I didn't have enough money in the bank to pay my rent. No one really knew how bad it was for me, and with a constant smile on my face, no one had to know. I was surviving on chicken-flavored Maruchan Ramen Noodles and Wal-Mart brand cola. My cable was off. Whenever my phone rang, I was surprised that it was still on, and flirting with the customer service representative who accepted my electric bill payment helped out a lot.

The first day of Dade County public school rolled around, and I kept up with the old tradition of having flowers delivered to Nat in her classroom. This year I couldn't afford the normal $75 bouquet so I opted for a dozen roses at $30. Instead of the additional $10 for delivery, I drove them there myself. Traffic at 9:00 a.m. was the pits. School buses, parents, and people driving to work were everywhere. The parking lot was full. I didn't want to park across the street, so I pulled into a handicapped spot. I was only going to be a few minutes.

When I saw the crowd in the main office, I figured it'd take a while, so I sneaked past. I didn't want to wait thirty minutes for Nat to come down or for someone to become available to deliver the flowers to her classroom. I walked through the empty halls hoping that she was in the same room as the year before.

As I trotted up the stairs and entered the math section of the middle school, a voice startled me. "Can I help you?"

"No, I'm just dropping these off to a teacher," I said quickly, not wanting to be kicked out by security.

"What room are you looking for?"

"Miss Blake's room," I said, not even bothering to look over at the voice speaking to me.

"They changed her room," he said. "She's in five-zero-six."

"Thank you," I said and looked up at the numbers, noticing that I was walking in the wrong direction.

"Hey," he said. "Don't I know you?"

I looked over and saw him looking back. "Oh, hi." I tried to remember his name and couldn't, so I just settled on, "How are you?"

"I'm fine," he said. "Do you remember me?"

I knew that he was the guy in the phantom mask from Nat's party, but for the life of me his name was a mystery. All I could recall was that he was a janitor. "Yes, I remember you." I paused. "But your name I honestly can't put my finger on." That was over two months ago. Give me a break.

"Mel." He extended his hand. "Tremel."

"Nice seeing you again, Tremel." I shook his hand. "Sarai."

Although he held a can of cleaning spray in one hand and a rag draped over his shoulder, he was still handsome. He had a fresh haircut, his goatee was neatly trimmed, and his lips still looked as though they would say "kiss me" at any given time. "I can show you where the classroom is if you want."

Going Broke

"Sure." I smiled. "Thank you." He was one step ahead of me, so I checked him out. I'm sure the middle school girls got a kick out of him being around, but even they wouldn't want to date a custodian, or even the custodian's son. His body looked even more toned than it did at the party. He had on navy pants and a light blue shirt. All custodians got stuck with such awful colors, like their jobs aren't punishment enough.

Nat's classroom was right around the corner. He pointed at the number. "Five-zero-six."

"Thank you."

"No problem. Have a nice day." He turned and walked away.

I said, "You too." I thought sure he'd try his hand at getting my number like he had at the party.

When I opened the classroom door, thirty-three pairs of little eyes turned to me. When Nat looked over at what took their attention, she grinned from ear to ear. "Happy first day of school," I said.

She walked toward me. "Class, this is my best friend, Miss Sarai Emery." I smiled at them and waved my hand. She took the flowers. "Thank you."

"Have a great first day, girl." I kissed her cheek. "I won't hold you up. Go get your math on."

She looked at the roses then looked back at me. "Thank you." A tear fell from her eye, and to me that was worth more than a field of roses. "Don't cry," I whispered.

"I cry every year. You're just not around to see it." She smiled.

"You're such a cornball." I continued on like I was one of her students. "I love you, Miss Blake."

"I love you too." For the next five minutes, I watched Nat talk about first day of school stuff with the kids, then I tiptoed out. I walked out of her classroom feeling like I had just won the best friend of the year award. I rushed down the stairs and ran into the old familiar smell of school lunch. The odor was revolting. It smelled like fish sautéed in Pepto Bismol. No wonder kids are so damn bad nowadays. I held my breath and tried hard to walk and not run out of the lobby. When I was finally close to the door, I heard a voice. "Excuse me." I turned around and saw Tremel approaching me. "I don't mean to hold you up. I'm sure that your time is precious," he said with a smile, "but you dropped these on the staircase." He held up my keys.

"Thank you." I didn't even realize that they were missing. "I guess I wasn't going anywhere, huh?"

He placed them in my hand. "Not until you went back up those stairs to get 'em."

I was grateful. "Thanks a lot. That was very kind of you."

He quickly took me back to the night we met and the comment I made to him. "All of this done by a man that has no business cards." He surely did remember me. "Have a nice day," he said.

"Wait." I was utterly embarrassed. "Would you still like my number?"

"What? I suddenly meet your standards?" he asked without a smile. "Thanks, but no thanks."

His demeanor threw me off. "I never said that you didn't meet my standards."

"You didn't have to. Everything else you said that night did." He smirked. "Or don't you remember?"

I played dumb. "No, I don't."

"Oh, I see." He smiled and started walking away backwards. "Well, if you don't remember, then I don't either."

I flirted. "Well, if we both don't remember it, then

ussell

n the best frien
e stairs and ran
nch. The odor wa
in Pepto Bismo
wodays. I held m

sta Russell

st won the best
wn the stairs an
ol lunch. The od
utéd in Pepto P
d nowadays. I h

why talk about it?"

"We won't." He quickly turned and walked away.

I couldn't believe that he had just left me standing there. "You broke motherfucker," I said under my breath then realized that I could've been talking about myself as well. I stormed out of the main entrance like a bad student. I was so upset that it was hard to find my truck. Then I remembered that I had parked in the handicap spot, and when I did find it I was praying that it was just one that looked like mine. I saw the beige ticket a mile away. "You've got to be fuckin' kidding." I snatched the ticket from the windshield. "Ninety-five dollars." This nightmare kept getting worse by the minute.

As I made it back into the apartment, the phone was ringing. The caller ID read: UNKNOWN CALLER. Over the past month I had learned enough to know that it was the student loan folks, Chase, Discover, or Sears. I looked at the phone. "Thanks for the handout, y'all. 'Preciate it." I tried to smile, but I was really flipping out inside. The phone stopped ringing, and before I could get the sound out of my head it started again. I was trying to balance my checkbook, but twenty minutes of constant on and off ringing, and the painful realization that I now only had three hundred and fifteen dollars in the bank, left me in tears. "Hello?" I said into the receiver.

"Ms. Emery?"

I asked sharply, "Who is this?"

"Well, hello to you too."

"Who is this?" I didn't feel like playing games.

"This is Mr. Johnson." He paused, "Conrad Johnson."

"How in the hell did you get this number?"

"Whoa," he said. "That's no way to greet a friend."

I was still crying. "What do you want?"

"Are you okay?" He continued, "Is everything okay with your dad?"

"What the fuck do you care?"

"Time out, Sarai. I'm actually calling to see how you're doing," he said. "I was wondering how things were with you. Did you find a job?"

"No, I still haven't found a job," I vented. "I can't find shit. I don't speak Spanish, remember? No one wants to hire me. Everybody's too busy laughing at me just like you said they would. Are you calling to laugh too?"

"You know I'm not happy about that," he said. "So, how have you been making it?"

"I'm doing just fine." I tried to sound upbeat.

"We both know that that's a fuckin' lie," he said.

"I'll be okay." I sniffled.

"How much money do you have in the bank now?" he taunted.

"That's none of your business."

"It is my business." He continued, "Because I can have two thousand dollars in your pocket by tomorrow night."

"No." I sniffled into the phone. "No."

He said, "Get a pen." I didn't have to; I already had one in my hand. "Write this number down." He called out a number and my hand moved accordingly. "Doctor Baker is still waiting on you, but at this point any pussy will do the trick," he said. "This will be my first and last time calling you. You can sit over there hungry and get evicted if you want to, or you can allow me to welcome you into this establishment. You have one hour to think about it. If I don't hear from you, then it was nice knowing you. I've never begged anyone to let me help them, and I'm not starting with you." He hung up.

I stared hard at the phone and began thinking about Daddy, his monthly expenditures, and the hospital bill. My rent was due, and life without cable was a bitch. I saw the life that I was accustomed to slipping away. I could no longer afford the things I was used to, and that was the catch—I was used to them. With Damian footing the bills, I didn't realize that I had been living beyond my means. I wanted to continue to have nice things and go to nice places.

I looked at Conrad's number and couldn't believe that I was dialing it. Fifteen minutes hadn't even passed, so he'd know just how desperate I was, but I was at a point where it didn't even matter. I was going broke.

"Hello?"

"When will I get the money?" I asked in an unsure whisper.

"He'll give it to you tomorrow night. I already have my share. We worked that out." He added, "But be sure to call the office and check in with my secretary when the deal is complete. She'll need some information from you." I could hear him smile. "Welcome to the Elite Establishment. You've made a wise decision."

For the next ten minutes, Conrad brainwashed me into thinking that there was absolutely nothing wrong with what I was about to do. He kept mentioning all of my money problems, making them seem greater than they were. He informed me that Doctor Baker would be checking into the Hilton downtown under the name Will Brown around 7:00 and wanted me there no later than 7:30. "No playing around, he has to be somewhere else at ten o'clock." Before we hung up he said, "Please know that my clients are used to the best. Be sure to take care of yourself. Go get your hair, nails and toes done and keep them done at all times. You never know when there is money to be made," he said. "Oh, and if you don't want to get on my bad side, don't try to get paid and leave me out. Trust me." He paused, "I will find out." He added, "We have a conference in Detroit next weekend. I might need you there. But the most important thing is to have fun tomorrow night."

"I'll try," I said.

"Have a nice day."

"Goodbye." I felt terrible about what I had just agreed to. But what else was I going to do? As I hung up the phone it was ringing again. I was hoping that it was Conrad. I couldn't do this and I was going to tell him that I changed my mind. "Hello?"

"Thank you again," Nat shrieked.

"Thank you for being a friend," I sang. "Traveled down the road and back again. Your heart is true; you're a pal and a confidant." I loved the *Golden Girls* theme song.

She sang the next verse, which was the way we always did it. "And if you threw a party, inviting everyone you knew, you would see the biggest gift would be from me."

We chimed in together. "And the card attached would say, thank you for being a friend."

I giggled. "What's up, girl?"

"Nothing. I wanted to say thanks again for the flowers, and I wanted to invite you to this thing they're giving free tickets out to tomorrow."

"What thing?" I asked.

"Does it matter?" she joked. "It's free."

"It could be a mass hanging. That's free," I said.

She was cracking up. When she finally composed herself, she said, "It's an invitation to Vocalize. That's that poetry reading jazz club on South Beach."

"I've passed by that place before." I added, "That sounds good." Then I remembered my engagement with Doctor Baker. "Oh, wait a minute. I have something to do tomorrow night."

"What?"

I hated lying to her. "Doctor Baker is lecturing at the community college downtown. I promised him that I'd be there."

"Aw, man. What time?" She sounded disappointed.

"Seven."

"Oh, then that's cool. This thing doesn't start until ten-thirty." She said, "If you want, we can go to the college together."

"No, no." I had to kill that thought. "I'll go. You go to the club and get us a good table. I'll meet you there. Those places get crowded fast."

"Okay," she confirmed. "Are you sure that you're coming? I'm asking because I need to put your name on the list."

"Yes, Miss Blake," I said. "I'm positive."

"All right," she said. "See ya tomorrow."

"Bye."

For the first time ever, I didn't want to see the next day; but it came anyway. I went down to Bob & Weave and they tightened my weave job. Bob blew breath into my hair, bringing it back to life. Though he had to replace a few tracks, he didn't charge me for them. He mentioned that he knew times were hard for me, and charged me only for a wash and set. I knew it wouldn't take long before the gossip king learned my story.

At Nail Wok, they took care of my nails and toes. Once home I knew that the black dress I wore with

Julian would do the trick for both Doctor Baker and Vocalize. I packed what I quickly named my slut box: condoms, extra panties, soap, a small towel, feminine and regular deodorant, lotion, perfume, and makeup.

I set out to the hotel at 7:00 and arrived at twenty after. I walked through the lobby like a zombie. I learned that "Bill Brown" was checked into room 529, and as I made my way to the elevator, I was tempted to run out. I kept my eyes on the entrance and vowed that if the elevator doors didn't open in ten seconds, I would leave. I counted down in my head. *Six, seven, eight, nine.*

"I'm glad that you came." Doctor Baker walked up next to me and pretended to be a stranger. He never looked my way. To others we appeared as two unrelated hotel guests waiting on the elevator. His presence made me feel even more like running out of the hotel, but the elevator opened up before us and he gestured with a smile. "Ladies first," he said politely.

As the doors closed, he looked at me. "Can I examine you?" Before I could answer, he pushed me against the wall and slid his tongue so far into my mouth that it felt like he was tickling my tonsil. His hands traveled up my stomach and groped my breasts. "Isn't it time for your mammogram?" He moved his hands around in a circular motion and was pinching my nipples as we came to a stop. This was the wrong night for me to be sober.

When we got to the room, I remembered Conrad saying that Doctor Baker needed to be somewhere at 10:00, so at least this wasn't going to be an all night thing. As we sat on the bed, I tried talking dirty to him, but it felt like something out of a cheap porn movie. I allowed him to kiss me and even stuck my tongue into his mouth again, but nothing was working for me. He told me about how he often fantasized about me when I was in his office and even more when I left. He admitted to having an erection during most of my exams, and said that he came on himself once during my pap smear.

After thirty minutes of me putting off the inevitable, he asked me to strip naked in front of him. He asked me to lie down on the bed with my legs opened up as though I was on his examining table. This idiot actually walked out of the room then in again with a clipboard. "Hello, Sarai." He gave me a look, egging me to go on with it.

I was extremely uncomfortable. "Hi, Doctor Baker."

"How are you?" he asked as he pulled the desk chair to the front of the bed.

"I'm doing just fine," I said.

"You are a little late for your appointment."

"Yeah." I was anticipating his touch. It would mean that this was almost over. "Traffic was heavy. I'm sorry."

"It's too late to apologize," he said. "I have a little punishment for you."

I got nervous and sat up a little. "What are you talking about?"

"Just relax." He pushed my body back. "You took so long getting here that Nurse Brooks had to leave, so it's just you and me."

I felt stupid, but quickly focused on the money I would be leaving the room with. "I thought you weren't allowed to examine patients without her in the room."

Suddenly I felt his fingers touch me below. He began rubbing me gently. "I'm not supposed to, but you made this appointment so long ago, I couldn't let you down."

"Are you sure that this is okay?" I asked.

His words trembled. "Yes, it's okay."

"What instrument are you using?"

He giggled a little. "Well, someone broke into the office last night and stole just about everything, so I'm down to the basics." He started sliding his finger in and out of me. "I'm using my finger." After a few minutes of heavy breathing he asked, "Would you mind if I used two?"

"That's fine, Doctor Baker. You do whatever you need to do."

"Really?" He doubled up his fingers just when I thought it was impossible, I began saturating his fingers with the oil from my spring. "I see that you like that," he said.

I groaned a little and I wasn't faking it. "I do."

While moving his fingers in and out of me, he used his other hand to stimulate my button. Before long, I found myself grinding into his hands and squeezed my eyes shut. I was uncomfortable, but at the same time his hands were no different than any others that had pleasured me. Plus the fact that I was getting paid made me want to do the job right. "Oh yes, Doctor Baker, yes."

Ten minutes later, he was kneeling in front of me, teasing me with his tongue. He started by pecking at me like a bird, and then he hardened his tongue and wiped it deep into me. I jumped and cried, "Oh shit! Yeah, yeah, oh yes."

"See how much fun we can have when Nurse Brooks isn't around?" He continued on below.

I was truly enjoying the feel of his tongue, so I grabbed his head and begged for more. He must've been so excited that while lashing me, he managed to undress and strap on a condom. Within minutes, he was on top of me, making faces like the world was coming to an end. I didn't see his equipment and I didn't need to, because I couldn't even feel it. Within five minutes, his sweat was draining down all over me, his eyes rolled back and he let out a loud groan as he bit into his bottom lip. I thought he was having a seizure until he yelled, "Oh fuck, that was good." All I could do was roll to the right before the big ball of brown fat collapsed on top of me.

He was out cold, snoring and all. It was over. "That wasn't bad at all," I whispered to myself as I left him on the bed, grabbed my slut box and took a warm shower. Afterwards, I did my makeup again, being sure that I wouldn't look like I had just reduced my worth when Nat saw me.

I opened the bathroom door and saw that Doctor Baker hadn't moved an inch. His feet were still dangling off the edge of the bed and he was snoring even louder. His hands at his sides helped to hide the rolls of fat littering him. The only way to determine where his back ended was where the crack began. He had no butt, just a holding area for shit. "Doctor Baker." I shook his body. "Doctor Baker."

He was startled, "Yeah?" He looked around the room.

"I'm leaving. Conrad said that you'd have the money."

He looked confused. "I do, but we're not done yet." He sat up. "Take off that dress. I want some more of that juicy pussy." He asked me to lie in bed and masturbate while he watched and stroked himself. I did so until he walked over to me. "Suck it, please." At least he was polite. He used his hand to navigate himself into my mouth. "Spit on it and suck it."

I wet him with my saliva so that I could easily gobble down all three inches of him. When he seemed like he was about to come, he quickly pulled out and asked me to stand. He stroked his piece and applied the condom as he lay belly up on the bed and ushered me on top of him.

I hated every moment of it. He kissed me harshly and continually squeezed my nipples. I thought it would be over quickly like the first time, but Doctor Baker got his money's worth. He poked me for close to thirty minutes. When he climaxed, he pulled himself out of me, snatched off the latex, and insisted on coming on my breasts. Not only did he want me to spread it over my chest, but my stomach too. Then he begged me to lick my fingers, and I did.

When I was out of the shower, dressed and made up again, I had two thousand one hundred dollars in my hand. I didn't want to see Doctor Baker ever again, but I probably would, because I had just proven to myself that for the love of money I would do anything.

"The lack of money is the root of all evil."
–George Bernard Shaw

Bank Statement # 9
Account Balance: $2,415.20

It was 10:47 when I parked outside of Vocalize and dialed Nat's number. "Where are you?"

"At the club," she shouted. The noise in the background was deafening. "Are you still coming?"

"I'm outside," I said three times before she understood. I gave the man at the door my name. "Where are you, meaning where are you sitting?"

"Up front by the stage," she yelled.

"Okay." I opened the door and heard the jazz saxophonist wailing. Vocalize wasn't that big. The maximum capacity had to be 100 people, and it looked like ninety-eight were already present. The bar was next to the door, so as I pushed my way through the crowd of about ten people, I was in front of it. I ordered two Chocolatinis.

The wall murals of famous jazz musicians brought a smile to my soul. They made me remember my mother. The building was fashioned on a downward slope, like a theatre, so the stage was down below. There were five sections each one was a step lower than the next. There were three sofas in every section with stylish coffee tables in front of them. With the drinks, I carefully stepped down toward the front of the club when the lights went down, leaving only the exit signs and the flicking candles on each table to light the way. "Damn," I whispered.

"Sarai." I heard Nat's voice to my right, and made her out in the darkness. I rested the glasses on the table then took a seat. "I got you a drink." We were sharing a

140

couch with three other ladies.

She pointed at two other Chocolatinis already waiting there. "I got *you* a drink."

We both laughed. "Well, two apiece ain't ever killed anybody," I said.

The saxophone player stopped and the spotlight danced around the club. A tall, light-skinned guy graced the stage wearing an orange dashiki and matching hat. He introduced himself as Twalik Abdul, the host. He knew good and well that his momma didn't name him anything like that. Twalik, just as I thought he would, opened the show with a pro-black poem, with the usual message of reciprocity. He introduced the next poet, an overweight black woman named Wanda Kendall. She had it all together, and before she was halfway through, most of the crowd was on their feet. I'll probably always remember this line: "Between my legs you'll find nothing but treasure. Rub it the right way and watch it spit diamonds beyond measure."

Twalik's presence, in a new dashiki, between every act was an absolute show killer. I had finished both of my drinks and wanted to grab him from the stage and beat him until he admitted that his real name was Leroy.

"Can you all take what's up next?" Twalik asked the crowd.

"Bring it on." The crowd roared the same answer they belted all night when he asked those types of stupid questions before each act.

"I don't think you can handle this brotha," he said.

Once again the crowd roared, "Bring it on."

"Our next poet is no stranger to the Vocalize family. He graces us with his talent once a week in either song or poetry." He paused. "But a song is just a poem set to music, isn't that right?" He smiled. "Ladies and gentlemen, sistahs and brothas, queens and kings, I present to some and introduce to others, Mister Tremel Colten." The crowd went wild more than they had for everyone else, but this time even Nat could barely contain herself. "Mel, do your thing, baby," she yelled as he walked onto the stage wearing a beige shirt, black jeans, and boots.

"What's up Vocalize? How y'all doing?" He smiled. "It's good to be back. I'd like to thank you all for coming back." He cleared his throat. "Tonight I've decided to do a poem." There were sighs around the room. "Come on, now. I have to rest my vocal chords. Maybe next Thursday I'll have a song ready." Applause filled the room.

I fought rolling my eyes. "I didn't know he was gonna be here," I said to Nat.

"He's the one that gave me the free tickets," she said.

I tried to look comfortable on the couch. He was just ten feet away. "He's probably no good."

Nat smacked my leg. "Stop it."

Tremel looked over the audience as he spoke. "I wrote this poem yesterday," he said. "I ran into a situation that bothered me, and the only way out were these words." He spotted Nat and gave her a little smile. If he saw me, he didn't make it known. It was like I was just another part of the chair. "The title of this piece is *Business Card.*"

My eyes widened. I felt like sinking beneath the floor. He rested the microphone back into the cradle and paused for a few seconds. When he started to speak, it was with such thunder that I jumped.

What makes me less of a man than one with a business

card?
What makes you think that I don't work my ass off just as hard?
Turning me away, not giving me the time of day,
just because I can't buy you diamonds every payday.

But then again . . . who the hell are you anyway?
You busted your ass in college,
but what are you really doing with that knowledge?
Too busy being superficial to even acknowledge
the fact that because I don't walk around in Armani suits
doesn't make me less of a man in jeans and Timberland boots.
It also doesn't mean that I'm in cahoots
with thugged-out fellas or selling illegal grassroots.
I work hard for things that I do not yet possess.
I work too hard to think about stopping to impress.
Not stressing myself to finesse the shallow valleys of your mind,
because even in a perfect world, your third eye is blind.
Princess, why are you so unkind?
I see that my uniform gives you the blues.
Stop! And live life by your own views.
Stop being so . . . materialistic,
antagonistic, unrealistic, pessimistic.
Enough of that bullshit.
Because for as long as I dwell
there's a story to tell.
And for as long as there is a heaven, there will be a hell.
And for that long I will always be M-E-L.
I'm not mad because of who I am.
You're mad because of who I am.
You're mad because of who I'm not.
But I guarantee you that it's the best I've got.
Goddess, if I wined you and dined you tonight,

tomorrow you still wouldn't allow it to be right.
It wouldn't matter that for you I opened up doors.
All that'll matter is the fact that I'm still sweeping floors
and still can't afford to take you to expensive stores.
You won't take me seriously; you barely even know my
name.
Once you learned about me, you didn't even look at me the
same.
I never claimed to be anything other than a man,
so it's all right if you don't want to be a fan.
Girl, you have issues,
so cry me a river with a box of tissues.
Don't blame me because someone left you scarred.
It's not my fault that the remainder of your heart is
charred.
The words that I put here you'll continue to disregard,
and all this because I still don't have a damn business
card.

Everyone was on their feet clapping, screaming, ranting and raving. Everyone except me, of course. I was almost in tears embarrassed as though he had shined the spotlight on me during his torture. I couldn't believe that he used this forum to get back at me. As if walking away while I was talking yesterday wasn't bad enough. He had to be the person that told Nat about the tickets and knew that if he convinced her to come, chances are I'd be there. He was on stage holding up his hands like he had just won a boxing match. He looked down at me with what I perceived to be the most evil stare in the world, then he walked behind the curtains with the audience still singing his praises.

When Nat sat down, she looked at me. "Wasn't Mel awesome?"

"Fuck Mel," I said.

"Wow," she exclaimed. "What in hell is wrong with you?"

"What's wrong with *me*?" I snapped. "What's wrong with him?"

"What?" she asked.

"That poem was about me."

"What?" She looked confused. "How?"

"He asked me for my number at your party," I said as I tried to keep my voice down. "I told him that I would take his number if he had a business card. And then yesterday when I was at the school, we exchanged words. If I knew that he had invited you here, there was no way I would've come."

"Loosen up." She shook me. "Smile."

"Smile nothing." I felt like running backstage and punching him.

"You must admit, though," she said, "that was a tight poem."

"Shut up." I managed to smile. "It wouldn't be so tight if it was about you."

There were two more acts after Mel , then a jazz band took the stage. The evening would've been delightful if Tremel had never been born. About an hour into the band's set, the house lights came on and everyone clapped and stood to leave. Since we were parked on opposite ends of the street, Nat and I said goodbye in the front of the club.

As I approached my truck and saw yet another ticket on my windshield, I wanted to scream. There was no handicap sign, parking meter, or a no parking sign anywhere. "What in the hell did I do this time?" I grabbed the paper and opened it. *I'd like to call a truce. Please meet me back inside to negotiate the terms. Tremel.* The word "please" was underlined. "Ha!" I smiled and looked at the note. "Now you wanna be friends?" I crumpled the note, threw it over my shoulder, deactivated my alarm and opened the door. When I sat behind the wheel and slid my key in the ignition, I couldn't help but wonder what he wanted to say to me.

It was one in the morning, I wasn't sleepy, and I had nothing to do the next day, but for the life of me I wasn't giving in to Tremel after what he had just done to me. I turned the key and put the gearshift into drive. As I pulled onto the street, the club door swung open and Tremel stepped out and ran into the street. I slammed on the brakes to avoid hitting him. He walked over to my window and leaned in. "So, I take it that we're not signing the peace treaty tonight, huh?"

"I think that there was enough peace in your poem to set the world in motion." I looked out of the front window. "Don't you?"

"No I don't" He laughed. "Would you please come inside?"

"Why?" I asked. "You have another poem?"

"No, but I have another side." He paused. "There is more to me than what you think."

"Is there really?" I chuckled sarcastically. "You could've fooled me."

"You know what . . . " He pushed away from the vehicle. "I've never had to prove myself to anyone, and the fact that I have to do so to you says a lot about you." He stepped away. "Have a good night." He walked back into the club while I sat in my truck, watching him with my mouth open.

I was livid. "No, he didn't just walk away from a conversation with me again." I drove up the street and into a parking spot. Without caring about turning on my alarm, I slammed the door and marched like a madwoman back to Vocalize, grabbing the doorknob so hard I thought I'd crush it. I looked to the left, then to the right and didn't see him. He wasn't in the lobby or at the bar. I stomped down towards the stage, but the area was empty.

I spotted the side door the performers trekked in and out of all night. If I had to go backstage to let him have it, I would. As I made my way to the door, I was stopped by a grip on my arm. "Why do I have to push your buttons to get you to act right?" Tremel asked. All the words I had for him disappeared when he gestured for me to have a seat on the very same couch where Nat and I were seated moments before.

"Why did you do that to me?" I asked, still standing.

"Do what?" he asked. "What did I really do?"

My forehead wrinkled. "You humiliated me in front of all of those people."

"Did I really?"

"Yes."

"You and I were the only people who knew what that poem was about." He continued. "That was your pride getting in the way, which is the same reason you wouldn't even talk to me— pride."

"Whatever!" I wasn't about to confirm or deny his accusations. "You didn't have to do it like that."

"Yes, I did," he said. "It was important to me that you hear what I had to say."

"Why?"

He chuckled. "Because you were so damn mean to me."

"I was not," I disagreed.

"You were."

"How?" I asked.

"I saw you asking Miss Blake about me, and I guess when she told you more about me, you just lost interest. You just started treating a brotha like a straight-up scrub," he said.

"Well, I'm sorry." I was ashamed.

"No need to apologize," he said with a smile. "We're even now. I just needed for you to know that men come in all shapes, sizes," he pointed a finger, "and occupations."

"I know." I felt like I was being chastised.

"So, will you have a seat?" he asked. I didn't answer. I just lowered my body onto the couch. He smiled. "I don't know exactly what your man does, but one thing is for sure, he has quite a woman."

I blushed. "Thank you." It took me a few seconds to realize that he was talking about Damian. "He doesn't know that, though."

"How do you know?"

"Well," I tried to get comfortable on the couch again, "if he knew that, then we'd still be together."

He smiled. "I'm not even gonna lie and say that I'm sorry to hear that. But I consider this an even better opportunity now." He stood to his feet in front of me. "Let's start over." He extended his hand to me for the third time since I had first seen him. "Hello, my name is Tremel. My friends call me Mel, I'm twenty-seven years old, no kids, no girl, but I do have a job." He continued. "I may not be the president of my own company, but what I do is legal."

With my hand still in his, I looked up at him. "I'm Sarai. I have no nicknames, and I like it that way. I'm also twenty-seven years old with no children, no husband, and also no job." I looked away and realized how stupid I was to still be judging him because of what he did for a living when no one would even hire me.

"It's nice to meet you, Sarai." He motioned for me to sit down. "May I buy you a drink?"

I said, "A Coke would be fine." A few minutes later, he made his way back to me with two sodas, two straws, and two hours worth of conversation.

Born and raised in Cleveland, Ohio, Tremel moved to Miami two years earlier when he encountered Cashes Jackson, an up and coming music producer who promised to showcase Tremel's sexy yet melodic singing voice. Cashes guaranteed the moon and the stars above and told Tremel that he had a deal just waiting to happen. Once here, Tremel learned that the recording studio Cashes bragged about was just a closet with an old microphone in the basement of his house and the only connections he had were to an underground radio station that people could only pick up while it was raining.

In Cleveland, he left behind family, friends, and a stable job at his father's construction company to chase a dream that he still couldn't build up the courage to believe had failed. Not wanting to return to Ohio to announce his bad news, he took the first job he could, as a janitor at Northern Miami Middle School. He also maintained the lawn, painted, and did handiwork in the home of an elderly woman he met at church, in exchange for free lodging in a spare room at her house. He hoped to save enough money to buy time at a good quality recording studio and create an unbelievable demo to help turn his life around.

He sang twice a month at Vocalize, but he was showcasing himself. There was no money associated with his performances. His voice had been compared to

Jahiem. His sexy appeal was like Ginuwine, but his lyrics were more the style of Brian McKnight. Though he was not ashamed about what he did for a living, it was not something that he wanted to do long term. Until something else arose though, he'd do it happily.

It was a little after three in the morning when Tremel walked me to my truck. "So, after learning more about me," he paused, "if I asked you for your number, what would you say?"

I grinned as we continued to walk. "I'd say that I don't have a business card, but I could write it down on a piece of paper for you."

"Hold up." He stood still and pretended to be a girl. "You don't have a business card? Oh hell naw." He walked away, then ran back over to me laughing. "May I have your number?" We reached the truck and he handed me a pen and a receipt to write my number on. "When can I see you again?"

"I don't know." I didn't know what to say.

"Well, how about this Saturday?"

"Well, it is after midnight, so it's Friday," I said. "You mean tomorrow?"

"Yeah," he said. "I guess that is tomorrow."

"Sounds good to me." I smiled. "Where are we going?" I was almost afraid to ask.

He thought a while. "To a restaurant you'll never forget." He ushered me into the truck. "I'll call you to get directions. I'll pick you up around seven. Don't wear anything fancy." He closed my car door. "Drive safely." He watched me until I got to the second light and made a left turn to head home.

My phone started ringing when I pulled into parking garage of my apartment. It was after three in the

150

morning. "Who in the world . . . " I looked at the caller ID and didn't recognize the number. "Hello?"

"Sarai?" A female's voice came over the phone.

"Yes." Then I thought. "Who is this?"

"I'm Stefani." She paused. "Conrad's secretary."

"Oh, hi." I had forgotten to call her. "I'm sorry. I totally forgot to call."

"That's all right. I was calling to find out how things went." Then she added, "I know that the first time is always a little awkward."

"Awkward isn't the word," I said. "But it wasn't as bad as I thought it would be."

"Good," she said. "And you collected two and one right?"

It took me a minute to realize that she was talking about the money. "Yes, yes I did."

"All right," she said. "Now that that's out of the way, do you have any plans this coming week?"

"Why, what's going on?" I felt a million miles away from being one of Conrad's girls while I was out with Nat, and while Tremel and I were talking, I didn't even remember Doctor Baker. Not until right now.

"Well, the Black Pastors' Association is meeting in Richmond Virginia. They want six girls there on Monday to stay until Thursday."

"Black pastors?" I couldn't have heard her right.

"Yes ma'am." She laughed. "Believe me we get calls from people you'd never expect." She asked, "Do you want to go?"

I thought about the session with Doctor Baker and couldn't imagine anything being worse. "Yeah, I'll go."

"All right. Let me go over some things with you," Stefani said. "When we affiliate with churches or church groups, we operate with extra precautions. I'm faxing pictures and profiles of everyone that's going."

"You need a picture of me?" I asked.

"I have one of you." She giggled. "By the pool in the Bahamas, taken by Mr. Johnson."

"When did he do that?" I asked.

"Honey, he gets what he wants." She continued, "Anyway, they'll be calling to let me know who wants to see who. So, before they visit you in your room, I'll have already secured the transaction via credit card. We charge the pastors two. Before he's even there, you'll get a call from me. If your phone doesn't ring, then you don't open your door," she said. "If the transaction goes through okay, I'll call and you just have a good time. For every one, you'll get fourteen deposited into your checking within two days."

"All right." I was overloaded with information.

"By the way, since our clients at times use other names to protect their privacy, you can do the same. Though they have your picture, you're listed as a number not a name, so you can give them whatever name you want to."

"Okay." I thought about the extra money. "So, how am I getting there?"

"You're flying out on Monday. I'll call you tomorrow with the details." She giggled. "In the meantime, just get packing. There is a lot of money to be made up there."

"Pastors, though?" I asked again.

"Yes, pastors," she said. "One more thing. We don't need you out of your room at all. We don't want the good guys knowing anything or raising questions. Also, some of the men traveling are traveling with their wives, so this has to be on the down low." Stefani finished with, "Get your rest. I'll call you back tomorrow."

"All right." I couldn't believe the conversation. "Bye."

The next day, Nat couldn't believe that I had gone from wanting to strangle Tremel to agreeing to have dinner with him. I couldn't believe it either. He wanted to be more than a janitor, was actively striving to be more, and that made him even sexier to me. When I told Nat that I'd be leaving town on Monday, I knew that she'd ask why. I had a lie waiting. "I sent a resume to a station in Richmond and they want me to fly up for an interview." She believed me, wished me luck, and begged me to call her on Saturday after my date with Mel.

On Saturday, I was ready at 6:30. At first, I didn't know what to wear. Tremel had called two hours prior for directions and said not to dress fancy, so I was hoping my black jeans and blue button down shirt weren't still too dressy. I was nervous. I didn't know what I was getting into, and because I wasn't in charge of planning the evening, I wasn't sure if I'd even allow myself to enjoy it. When the security guard called to inform me that I had a visitor, I entertained the shallow idea of asking what type of car Tremel was driving, but I frowned on being so tacky.

I walked to the front of the building and was delightfully surprised to see Tremel leaning up against a newer model silver Ford F-150. He met me with a smile.

"You look very nice."

"Thank you," I said. He too was wearing jeans and a white polo shirt.

He rounded the truck and opened the door for me. In the seat sat a vibrant bouquet of plum and purple flowers: daisies, mini carnations, Monte casinos, and more. I was in awe. "Thank you, Tremel." I picked them up and turned to him, remembering that I told him my favorite color was purple. "Should I go up and put them in water?"

"Naw, we'll need them where we're going," he said as he helped me step into the truck.

When he got in and started to back up, I was still wearing a purple people eater smile. "So, where are we going?"

He pulled onto the street. "Well, it's a place I've never been." He made a right, and after a while he said, "It's a place I hope you don't mind going to." He stayed in the right lane and made another right. I started to wonder if he knew his way around the area. "I do know that the chef is off the hook," he said then threw in a curve ball as he made yet another right turn. "I also heard that he's kinda cute."

I looked at him. "Where are we going?"

We pulled back into my apartment complex. "A place called Café de Mel." He laughed. "Which happens to be in your apartment."

He couldn't be serious. "Are you serious?"

"May I cook for you?" He pointed to the back of his truck; I saw three grocery bags.

Thank God I had spent the day cleaning in anticipation of our date. "In my kitchen?" I asked.

"If I lived alone, I would've done it at my place." He looked a little worried. "Is that okay?"

Mrs. White, the lady he lived with, was a grumpy old soul from what he told me. He never brought home company because he was too afraid of what she'd say that the Lord would say about it. When he moved in, she told him that fornication was a thing that had never gone on under her roof, and it wasn't about to start.

"Yeah, it's fine." It was better than having dinner for three: Mrs. White, Mel, and me.

I held onto my flowers and helped him carry one of the grocery bags. We walked into my place and his mouth flew open. "Wow." He rested the bags on the counter and walked over to the picture window. "This is nice. You must be paying a grip."

"Don't remind me," I said. As I reached the countertop, my brown grocery bag slammed into the ones he had placed there and it tipped over. Before I could catch it, I saw five or six orange-red things fall out. I thought they were oranges. "Oops." I bent down to grab one and saw legs and eyes protruding. "What the—" It started moving. "Oh my God!" I screamed. "Crabs, crabs, crabs!" I wasn't touching them. I actually ran to the door. Tremel ran over, laughing. He scrambled back and forth until he had them all back in the bag. "You should've saw the look on your face."

I was trying to get my heart to beat regularly again. "Did you get them all?" I walked cautiously around my apartment. When I got back to the kitchen, he was still chuckling. I smacked him on the shoulder. "I can't believe you're laughing at me."

"I needed a good laugh," he said. "Now I need the biggest pot you've got."

I made my way around the kitchen, first finding a vase for my flowers, then getting him a pot. For the next hour, Chef Mel did his thing in my kitchen. I'm sure my stove was wondering what the hell was happening, because the microwave was my friend. Mel didn't need my help. He seasoned the boiling pot and tossed a dozen and a half crabs into it. He added some smoked sausages, potatoes, red and green peppers, and a host of other ingredients. The boy could burn, and in an hour we had the dinner table full of things that weren't supposed to be together: blue crabs, garlic rolls, salad, and red wine.

I poured the wine. "Thank you, Chef Mel."

He joked, "That's *Head* Chef Mel to you, ma'am."

"If you're the only chef in the place, how could you be the *head*?"

He lit the two candles that he also brought. "You're right. That'll make me the master chef." He looked at me. "Lights, please." I was impressed by all that Tremel had done. He placed the candles on the side of the floral arrangement I had placed on the table. He spent a few minutes teaching me how to open the crabs and showed me where the most meat was often hiding.

Over dinner we talked a lot. He asked me questions I wasn't ready to answer, but I did. The questions were about Damian and me, my relationship with my father, and how I lost my job. He had me swallowing my wine like it was Sunkist.

Seeing how tense I was, Tremel decided to tell me more about him to even the score. Two months before he left Cleveland, he learned that the eight-month-old boy he thought was his son by his girlfriend of three years, wasn't. Sondra, his then girlfriend, confessed to sleeping with her ex-husband a few times while they were having problems. He described the feeling as being eaten alive by an alligator. "I wanted him to be mine. I wanted him to belong to me so bad." After the paternity test proved that Justin wasn't his son, he tried to stay in the relationship, but every day was an uphill battle. The little boy he had grown to love was now too painful to look at, so he walked away. The hardest thing he ever had to do was not see Justin again.

In an effort to lift our spirits, he reached for a new

bottle of wine and filled our glasses. "The rest of the night we'll spend toasting to reasons why you shouldn't eat crabs on a first date," he said with a chuckle.

After he poured my glass, I held it up. "The reason why you shouldn't eat crabs on the first date is because your date might accuse you of being a little crabby." I laughed.

"I'll drink to that." He did and then continued. "You shouldn't eat crabs on the first date because you might get snapped at." We were cracking up at our own corny little statements. I'm sure the wine was a helper. We carried on toasting even after all the wine was gone. I told him to rest on the stool on the other side of the counter while I did the dishes. Tremel was good-looking, funny, smart, a great cook, and a good man. Damn!

After the dishes were done, we had more conversation on the couch. When we were both yawning, Tremel looked at his watch and decided that he should get going. "But it's only two in the morning," I joked.

He stood up and pulled me to my feet. "If I stay any longer, then I'm not leaving."

"Oh my. Look at the time, you better get going." I smiled.

"When can I see you again?" he asked.

"Well, I'm leaving town on Monday," I informed him. "I won't be back until Thursday or Friday."

"Where are you going?"

"Virginia." I wasn't lying.

"Have fun."

"Fun?" I smirked. "Yeah, right."

"Why not?" He looked confused.

I couldn't look him in the face. "Job interview, and since I'll be not too far away, I'm planning on visiting my father." I guided him to the door.

"Well, take my number and give me a call when you're back," he said.

I grabbed a pen and something to write on and I took his number. He was in the process of getting his own phone line installed, but until then he instructed me to never call that number after 10:00 at night because Mrs. White would have a cow and a pig. I gave him my word as I strolled back over to him standing by the door. "I had a wonderful time tonight," I said. As I stared up into his handsome caramel face, his hands slid around my waist and I trembled.

"I did too," he said, then added, "The number one reason you shouldn't eat crabs on the first date is because that pretty much secures the fact that your date wouldn't dream about kissing you."

"That's not true." I stood on tiptoes and planted my lips on his. His grip on me tightened, as our tongues were gentle with each other. It didn't last long, but it was enough to imagine what it would've been like had it lasted longer, and I tasted no crab. "Drive safely," I said.

"I will." My forehead touched his goatee as we hugged. "Have a good night, Sarai."

"You too, Mel."

When I closed the door, I did the Hollywood movie thing and pressed my back against the door and smiled. I sat on the sofa awhile and watched the last forty-five minutes of *My Big Fat Greek Wedding* on HBO. When I retired to my bedroom and turned on the light, I saw a crab move sideways under my bed. "Oh, hell no." There went my heart again. "Please tell me I didn't just see that." I stood frozen for a full minute trying to think about what to do. "I'm not touching that thing." I thought about closing the door and sleeping on the couch, but the problem would still belong to me in the morning.

Going Broke

"What am I going to do?" I closed the bedroom door, ran to the kitchen and grabbed the can of Raid without thinking. "This isn't going to work." I scurried back to the kitchen and grabbed the pot we used earlier. I thought maybe it would come out and I could throw the pot over it, so by the time I got back in town it would be dead. As I walked past the countertop, I saw the paper with Mel's number on it and disregarded his words. This was an emergency.

"Who dis?" The elderly voice sounded stunned. "Hello?"

I bit my top lip. "Hello, may I please speak to Tremel?"

"Young lady, I'm in my bed." She paused. "Ain't no decent girl be calling no man at this hour. You need to—" Mel's voice interrupted. "Hello?"

"Mel, it's me."

"Tremel, you know I don't play this foolishness."

"I'm sorry, Mrs. White. She's in another time zone," he lied.

"Well, she better set her watch to this one." She slammed down the phone.

"Sarai." He sounded concerned. "What's wrong?"

"There is a crab under my bed," I said.

He laughed. "Then you need to see your gynecologist, girl." I had already seen Doctor Baker and I had enough.

"I'm serious. Please come and catch this thing." I wasn't asking.

"Are you serious?"

"Yes. I know that it's late." I begged. "Please."

"All right," he said. "But if I come, I'm not leaving."

I thought a few seconds. "I'm not sleeping with that crab underneath my bed."

Trista Russell

"I'm on my way."

"He that is of the opinion money will do
everything may well be suspected of doing everything
for money."
–Benjamin Franklin

Bank Statement # 10

Account Balance: $8,015.20
Check Pending (rent/2 mos.): $2,800
Check Pending (Daddy/4 mos.): $2,800
Check Pending (car): $550
Checks Pending 12 (misc.): $725.90
Available Balance: $1,139.30

When security called for my permission to let Tremel up, I felt the way I think people feel when they catch the Holy Ghost. I jumped up and down with the biggest smile. I couldn't tell if my reaction was because of Tremel coming back to search for the crab or him coming back period. Whatever it was, I was thankful— so thankful that I wrapped my bathrobe around me and met him at the elevator.

When the doors slid open, he was leaning against the side with a grin, wearing gray jogging pants and a T-shirt. "I can't believe I'm out of my bed at four in the morning to catch a crab."

"I'm sorry," I said with a slight smile.

As he walked into the apartment, he yelled,

"Almighty crab, show yourself." He disappeared into my bedroom, but I stayed a few feet from the door. He screamed and made a bunch of crazy noises to scare me, then ran out laughing with the crab kicking between his fingers. I hightailed to the living room. "This is the first time a woman can ever say that I gave her crabs," he joked. "What do you want me to do with it?"

"Anything. I don't care." I curled myself into a ball in the corner of the loveseat, trying to stay away from him and the sea monster. He grabbed a paper bag, dropped the crab in it, and placed it in the freezer. "Oh, that's so cruel," I whined. "It's gonna freeze to death."

"You didn't think it was cruel when I dropped them in the pot. And you sure didn't think it was cruel when you were eating them." He smiled and reached for the handle. "Would you like it back on your bed?"

"No, no thank you," I said quickly. "Sorry, mister crab."

He stared at me from the kitchen then walked over and pulled me up from the chair. "Good night." His hands enveloped me.

"I thought you were gonna stay." I hoped I didn't sound desperate.

"I'd love to." He continued in a voice mocking Mrs. White. "But what kind of a decent man would be sleeping at a woman's place?"

I giggled as I whacked him gently on the shoulder. "I know you'll be a gentleman and stay on the couch."

"I'll be even more of a gentleman if I went back home." He looked down at me.

"All right." I couldn't argue with that. "Thank you so much." We both went silent, waiting on the other to bend. "Call me when you get in so I know you didn't fall asleep on the road." I wanted to kiss him again, but I made the move the first time.

"I will." He brought my hand to his lips.

"Thanks again, Mel." I blushed.

"I'll send you the bill." He yawned, removed his hands from my back and was out the door sooner than I wanted him to be

Still too traumatized to go into my room, I grabbed a blanket and made myself comfortable on the sofa. Thirty minutes later, my phone was ringing. "I'm alive," he informed me, "and I'm not even sleepy anymore."

"See, you should've stayed." I wished he hadn't left. "I'm on the couch." I turned the television off so that I could concentrate on him.

"Why aren't you in bed?" he asked.

"My heart hasn't gotten the news yet." I giggled. "I need time to calm my nerves before I go in there."

"Wait a minute. You had me to come all the way over there to clear a room that you're still not going to sleep in?" he asked.

"Yeah," I answered matter-of-factly. "You got a problem with that?"

He laughed. "I think you just wanted me over there."

"I think you just wanted to come back over here," I teased.

He said, "I wish I would've stayed now."

I was blushing. "How come?"

"Because you have leftover crabs and a   brotha is starving." He got serious. "Naw, I really enjoyed your company." We talked and laughed until eight in the morning when the sun was high up in the sky and traffic was on the streets below.

Asleep for only an hour, I was awakened by another telephone call. "Hello?"

163

"Did I wake you?" a woman asked.

"Who is this?"

"This is Stefani."

My eyes widened. "Hi," I said.

"I have your flight information," she said.

"Okay." I reached for a pen and paper.

"You and Cherry are flying together on Delta. She's a very nice girl, so at least you'll have company. When you two arrive, there will be a driver waiting with a sign that says Elite. Give him Conrad's name. That'll be your ride to the hotel. Don't go to the front desk. Go straight to room nine-eighteen and get your room key from Judy."

"Okay." I was tired and ready to hang up. "What time is the flight?"

"Tomorrow at three, and you're coming back—"

I interrupted her. "Is it possible that I can fly back on Saturday?"

"Why?" she asked.

"My dad lives in the area and he's sick," I said. "I'd like to go and see him."

I heard her typing something. "I guess I can handle that, but the hotel on Thursday and Friday nights are on you."

I wanted to yell, "Have a damn heart," but I held my tongue. "That's all right." I had planned to rent a car and drive to Dover.

She continued. "Just make sure you have your ID when you arrive at Delta. Everything else is taken care of." She added, "I'll get you a flight out on Saturday afternoon. Judy will let you know."

"Thanks."

She said, "No problem," then she was gone.

I slept until 3:00 in the afternoon and woke up

feeling like I had been comatose for weeks. I didn't want to move or think, and I definitely didn't want to do laundry then pack. I watched TV on the sofa for two hours before I talked myself into getting up. While the washing machine washed and the dryer dried, I thought about the night before and stared at the phone, willing it to ring. I wanted Tremel to come over or call and ask to do something or go somewhere with me.

When he didn't call, I vacuumed, mopped, packed, and waited some more. After a night like the one we had, not getting a phone call the next day was a slap in the face. Maybe I read too much into what happened. The phone wasn't ringing, so I began to dissect the entire evening. Did I push him away?

When Tremel informed me that his last date was two weeks prior, I didn't want to be outdone, So I said that I was dating too. God knew that wasn't the truth but I didn't want Tremel to know that I sat in my apartment and checked my e-mail all day. The next lie I told him was that I didn't think I wanted to have kids because I wasn't good with children. I read in a magazine that if a woman mentioned that she wanted a family too soon after meeting a guy, he'd automatically throw up maybe not a stop sign, but definitely a yield. The last thing I said was people who got married before thirty-five were making the biggest mistake. That was my own stupid logic; I fooled myself into believing that because I felt too old to not have at least been engaged once.

I took the cordless phone everywhere with me. At midnight, I was angry when I hopped out of the shower and looked at the caller ID. "Well, fuck you too." I chalked it all up to another free meal, checked my room for crabs, and crawled under my sheets with images of Tremel gallivanting around town or toting a bushel of

crabs to another girl's place haunting me. "Bastard," I
whispered to myself, then my eyes closed and I waited for
the next day.

An hour before leaving for the airport, I picked up
the phone to call Daddy. i wanted him to know that I'd be
there to see him on Friday. "What the—" I didn't have a
dial tone. "Shit." What a time for BellSouth to act like I
was the only customer coming up short. I mailed out the
check on Friday, which meat they'd get it today, Monday.
Suddenly my fury cooled into a smile. The phone was
probably disconnected the day before, which would
explain why I hadn't heard from Tremel. I had only given
him my home number. In retrospect, if I wasn't so proud
and had picked up the phone to call *him* I would've
known. He may have even tried to come over, but with
the hell I raised about Damian never being able to enter
the building, security wasn't letting anyone up before
talking to me. "What an idiot," I said to myself. I looked
at the clock and wondered if I had time to quickly stop by
the school and say hi, but once I pulled onto the crowded
highway, I knew that I couldn't make it there without
missing my flight.

Walking through the Fort Lauderdale airport, I
didn't give much thought to what was ahead of me. It hit
me when I sat down in my coach seat. This venture
wasn't a regular business trip. I wasn't traveling for
WBIG and attending a concert or doing an interview. I
was about to have sex with men for money— not just any
men, pastors. After this I'd probably never see a church
again, not until they rolled me in on the big day. This
deed was sure to send me straight to hell, no lines, no
waiting.

"Sarai?" A woman walked up to the row where I

was sitting.

When I looked up, I was lost for words. "Cherry?" She was drop-dead gorgeous, light-skinned and not very tall, but thin, with long curly hair and succulent lips that even a woman would fantasize about. "Hi. How are you?" I extended my hand.

"I'm fine." She leaned over and touched my weave. "I love your hair." Running her fingers through my layered look, she winked at me, "Very chic."

I couldn't stop looking at her lips. "Thank you." If all of the other Elite girls looked like Cherry, I'd probably only end up with enough money to buy myself a Vanilla Coke and a smile. She was wearing a professional navy blue skirt suit. I quickly compared it to my beige slacks and plain white dress shirt and felt as though we weren't going to the same meeting.

During the flight, Cherry's mouth didn't stop. She told me everything about her. Her real name was Yolanda Miller. She was a professional dancer and the choreographer for a local R&B girl group, who were about to get signed to a major label. Cherry, twenty-nine, had been working for Conrad for five years. She owned her own house, a BMW, and a Benz. She didn't offer me any excuses for why she was in the Elite, and I was glad. I didn't want to have to explain my reasons. However, she advised me about what to do, telling me never to let my two worlds collide. She said, "When you're not working, don't think of yourself as that woman, and when you're working, don't think of nothing but that woman."

By the time we landed, I was feeling like what we were about to do was natural, empowering, and something we should be praised for. Conrad had her mind all jacked up, and she had me halfway there. I felt comfortable with Cherry. We exchanged numbers and promised that we'd hang out when we were back in Miami.

We were off the plane, in and out of the car, and knocking on Judy's hotel room door by 7:00. Judy was an older woman who had too much attitude. It was probably because she was envious of us since her body was 2000 miles away from being a moneymaker. There were four other girls in the room, and none of them were as friendly or nearly as pretty as Cherry or me.

When I settled into my room, I searched for my phone like a crackhead looking for a rock. I emptied everything from my purse. I needed to place a call, and nothing but death would stop me. "Eureka," I whispered as I saw the silver fold-up phone. The next thing I heard was Mel's sexy baritone voice. "Hello?"

I couldn't believe the smile on my face. "Hello there."

"Sarai?"

"Yes. Hi." I contained myself. "How are you?"

"I'm doing all right." He sounded happy to hear from me. "I tried calling you and saw that you were having technical difficulties."

I was a bit embarrassed. "Yeah, BellSouth is no joke." I offered clarification. "I sent them a check on Friday, but I guess—"

He interrupted me. "You don't have to explain anything to me. Believe me, I know." Then he added, "Why do you think I don't have a phone?" We both laughed. "So, how did the interview go?"

For a split second, I didn't know what he meant. "Well," I didn't have a lie ready, "that's not until tomorrow."

"Well, good luck."

"Thanks." Being deceitful wasn't something I

liked. "I'll need it."

"So, you'll be moving up there if you get it, right?" he asked.

If you tell one lie, you're bound to have to tell another. "Yeah."

He went quiet. "Then maybe I shouldn't be wishing you good luck," he said.

"Maybe." I jumped when the hotel line started ringing. "I better get that."

He said, "Is this your phone number on the caller ID?"

"Yes."

"Can I use it?" he asked.

"Of course you can," I answered.

"Cool," he said. "Have a good night."

"Thank you." He had no clue what type of night I was going to have, and neither did I. "Bye."

It was Stefani on the phone. She informed me that I had two hours to get myself together because at 11:00 I'd have a visitor. The ultimate rule was that the man had five hours or one door slam, meaning that once in my room, he had five hours with me. However, if he spent thirty minutes with me then needed to leave, when the door slammed, his time was up. The guy who was coming up wanted to be called Henry. He was in his late fifties and was originally from Charlotte, North Carolina.

I took a shower and ordered a bottle of wine in an effort to prepare myself. This Henry person was freaking me out and I hadn't even seen him. I did my makeup, oiled myself down in some smelly good stuff, then couldn't decide what to put on, or if I needed to put anything on. I drank the entire bottle of wine and decided that it really didn't matter. There was no need to waste an outfit. He knew why he was coming here, so I jumped

169

into some black spiked heels and skimpy, see-through lingerie.

Henry wasn't a bad looking guy, but I could tell that he was old. He was tall, slender, was well kept, had graying hair, and was very polite. After he introduced himself, I told him that my name was Sassy. The first twenty minutes were awkward. He sat on the bed and I at the table. I lied about everything; this was business, not pleasure. We could only dilly-dally around the real reason he was there for so long. I took control. I licked my lips and winked. "So, what do you want to do tonight?" I was ready to get it over with.

"Come over here and find out." He stood up and started unbuckling his pants. "Get on your knees, Sassy," he instructed, and as I made my way down to the floor, I helped him with his pants and boxers. When I saw what the old man was working with, it made me want to testify. Brotha pastor had it going on. "Very nice," I said as I stroked him. "Very nice."

"Show me how nice it is," he said. I wet my lips and gave him a few wet kisses before fully taking him in. Henry was as quiet as a church mouse, but his body language spoke volumes. With his hands on my head, he thrust into my mouth and I felt him grow even harder atop my tongue. When the time was right, I reached for a condom and started riding him like I grew up on a Texas ranch. Henry left my room after four in the morning. He must've been popping super-strength Viagra because he never showed signs of exhaustion, and he crawled back on top of me every twenty minutes.

During my entire stay in Richmond, I slept with four men. I was glad that things happened quickly because had I stopped to think, I would've lost out on something I had my mind set on doing; paying Daddy's

Going Broke

nursing home for another four months. I made $5,600 in just four days. My checking account could finally breathe a comfortable breath of relief. Cherry was right. This was an empowering position. In less than a week, I had just made a quarter of what many people make in a year.

On Friday it took me several hours to get to Dover from Richmond. Seeing the Welcome to Delaware sign reminded me of the best thing about the state, no sales tax. Once I hit the dull, old and dreary town, I headed straight to Concord Nursing Home where I found my father sleeping. I was glad he wasn't conscious, not awake to be an unfamiliar person. I stared at him for a while and pretended that he was still the man he used to be. I talked to him, rubbed his head and his bony body. He used to seem so much taller in his younger years. Lying in the bed, he looked like he went from being a buck twenty-five to just ninety-five cents.

I wanted to take him to Miami with me, not leave him in the home. But instead, I walked to the administration desk and took care of his stay for another four months. As I forked over the check, I knew that my father would die if he knew what I was doing just to keep him in a decent place. When I got back to the room, his eyes were open. I was shocked. I didn't know what to do or say. When he smiled at me, I smiled back and walked over. "You came back," he said.

"Yes, I told you I would."

"What did you do with all of that candy I gave you?" he asked.

I had no clue what he was talking about, but I went on with it. "I gave it to some children that were playing outside." I was close enough to touch him, and when I did, he held my hand. We talked about nothing for hours, laughed at television, and ate. When it got late,

171

I was asked to leave, but I promised him I'd be back the next day. I kept my word, although I knew it meant another painful goodbye. I kissed him and told him that I loved him. I repeated my name a million times, hoping that somehow he'd remember me the next time I called. "I love you more than life, Daddy."

"I love you too, Sarai," he said as my fingers slipped from his hands.

I cried all the way to the Richmond airport. I wasn't surprised that my eyes were red and puffy. I felt terrible about not being at least in the same state with my father. However, I was happy that I didn't have to watch him deteriorate on a daily basis. During my plane ride, I tried to be optimistic, thinking of the positive things that Daddy and I did together: tic-tac-toe, telling a few jokes, and we even sang a song that he still knew the words to.

I was walking through the Fort Lauderdale airport dazed, not remembering where the baggage claim area was and not seeing anyone from my flight that I could follow. In the distance, I spotted someone I thought I recognized. As I got closer, I was smiling. "What are you doing here?" I asked Tremel. I had called him in tears the night before when I left Daddy at Concord and checked into a local hotel room.

"I know you don't need a ride, but I figured you might need a hug," he said as he walked toward me with his arms open.

"Thank you." I buried my head into his chest. "Thank you so much."

"No problem." He grabbed my hands. "Now, please tell me you didn't get the job."

I smiled. "The interview sucked."

"Now, that's what I'm   talkin' 'bout." He embraced me tightly. His touch didn't feel new. It felt as though we had been doing this every day for years. I hated letting him go, but us walking hand in hand to the baggage claim area was remedy enough. After we found my black suitcase in the sea of two thousand others, Tremel asked me to follow him to Dave and Busters. We had a ball. We played tons of games, won a few prizes, and ate some of the best chicken fried outside of Nat's kitchen.

Later that night we agreed to make it a Blockbuster night. When we left the store, Tremel needed to stop and get gas, and I continued on to my apartment to get the popcorn popping. I told security that I was expecting someone and just to let him up. I was in my room starting to unpack when along with that beautiful buttery smell was Damian waltzing into my room. "What are you doing?" I walked toward him and passed him to get back out into the living room, a safe area. "What are you doing here?"

"Hi, Sarai. It's nice to see you too."

"Hi." I kept moving, not wanting him to know how afraid I was. "Did I forget to pack something of yours?" I asked.

"Naw. I just thought I'd stop by and check you out."

I grew balls. "Or are you here to check up on me?"

"Maybe." He looked me up and down. "You look real nice."

"Thanks." I was nervous. "But I need you to leave."

He asked, "Why? You told them to let me up. You even left the door open for me."

"No, I didn't." I walked over to the door. "Please leave."

"Don't you think it's about time we sat down and

talked this shit out?" He walked toward me. "We can work this out."

"No, we can't." I looked away from him my voice shaking. "Damian, you just can't show up to my place like this."

He got angry. "Why, you got company?" He began walking through the apartment. "Who's in here?" he asked as he went from room to room.

"Damian," I yelled as I unlocked the front door and turned the knob, leaving it open a quarter of an inch like I had before for Tremel. "You can't stay. I'll call the police."

"Fuck the police. You're not calling nobody." He walked into the living room and pulled me against him. "Don't you want some of Dwayne tonight?" He had a grip on me that I couldn't get out of. He tried kissing me as I squirmed and squealed.

"Stop it, Damian. You're hurting me."

"Didn't you like me to be rough with you?" He pushed me against the wall by the door. As I screamed, "Stop," the door flew open and Tremel walked in. "Whoa! What in the hell is going on?"

Damian looked like he saw a ghost. "Who are you?"

"Are you all right?" Tremel looked at me and handed me the items in his hand like he was ready to crack some skulls. I just stared at him. "Are you okay?"

"Yes." I was shaken up. "Tremel, this is my ex, Damian. Damian this is Tremel."

Tremel asked Damian. "Why are you here?" He looked him up and down.

"Sarai didn't tell you that she had a man?" Damian asked.

"Damian, get the hell out of here," I yelled. "Just

174

leave me alone." Although Tremel was there, I was still scared. Damian had been calling me, telling me what he'd do to me if he found out that I was seeing someone. "Please just leave me alone." I was crying.

Tremel opened the door. "I think she just did."

"So, who the fuck you supposed to be, Tremel?" Damian was in his face.

I saw every muscle in Mel's face tighten as he clinched his fists. "We're friends." He spoke like he wanted to say or do a lot more. "You have a problem with that?"

Damian ignored Mel's question and looked over at me. "When you're sick of having a fuckin' *friend* and you want a *man* in your life again, holla." When he walked out the door, Tremel closed and locked all of the latches.

"Are you all right?" His hands ran down my back.

"Yeah." I wiped my eyes. "I'm okay."

"What did he do to you?"

"Nothing," I said. "You came in at the right time."

Tremel was upset for a while. I laid my head on his chest and I could feel his heart pounding away. "How in hell did he get in here?"

"I told security that I was expecting someone and just to let him up. I left the door unlocked because I knew you'd only be a few minutes behind me." I paused. "I was in the room unpacking and he walked in."

He pulled me even closer. "I'm not leaving you here by yourself tonight."

"I'll be okay," I said.

He looked down into my face and spoke slowly. "I'm not leaving you." With my hands around his neck, his stare intensified and he lowered his lips to mine. My eyes were closed. He unlocked the gates, my lips parted and our lips touched for the first time since our first kiss.

I took his tongue and made it a part of me. I caressed it in between my lips and gave him mine again and again.

Tremel and I stayed up until 4:00 watching movies. Sitting on the couch eating popcorn, I nestled myself in his arms, but as I grew tired, my head fell to his lap and I covered myself with a blanket. We fell asleep just as we were.

Over the next five weeks, Tremel and I couldn't stay away from each other. I delivered lunch to both him and Nat at the school at least three times a week. He was at my apartment every other night and slept over every Saturday night. But as bad as I wanted him in my bed, Tremel insisted on sleeping on the couch. He stayed in my bed long enough to watch me fall asleep, but nothing more. However, our kisses were getting more and more passionate. Like a volcano waiting to erupt my lava was boiling.

Mrs. White didn't like Tremel staying out late, saying that her front door shouldn't be opened after 9:00. To appease her, we obeyed her commandment. So, for two weeks Tremel was in Mrs. White's house before 9:00. Though we laughed about it, I was dating a man who had a curfew. I felt like we were 15 years old. We followed her guidelines not only out of the respect he had for her and her household, but also because he was living rent-free. It also made sense for him to be there on weeknights because the school was only a block away, versus him getting up at 5:30 in the morning to battle his way north in traffic from my place. Mrs. White's rules added to our friendship. When we weren't together, Tremel and I were laughing over the phone. If we happened to be online at the same time, we'd chat on Yahoo Messenger. It made things fun.

It was now early October. "So, what are you going to be for Halloween?" Tremel asked me as I sat on his lap on the couch.

"I'm going to be you," I joked. "I'm going to put on some Timberland boots, cut my hair low, and lick my lips a lot."

"I don't do that," he said shyly and rubbed my legs.

"Yes, you do." I wasn't lying. It was probably the reason I couldn't wait for us to get our freak on. "You do it all the time." I mocked him over and over, running my tongue over my lips and biting the bottom one a bit.

"You're crazy." He smiled.

"So are you." I kissed his nose.

Suddenly he got serious. "I need to talk to you about something."

"What?" I was already preparing myself for the worst. "What is it?"

"Patience, please," he said as he scooped me up from his lap and placed me on the sofa. "I've been trying to figure out the right way to..." He stood up. "Remember when we first met and I said that I was dating someone?"

"Yes, that was about a month and a half ago." I felt like hyperventilating. "Why?"

"I told you that our last time seeing each other was two weeks before we first went out, right?"

Where was he going with this? "Yes," I answered.

I was afraid of what he was about to say. "Well, I haven't seen her since," he said. "As a matter of fact, I haven't been seeing anyone since I met you." He looked at me. "And I like it that way."

I couldn't stop blushing. "Really?"

"Really." He reached for my hands and pulled me to my feet. "Are you still seeing other men?" I was speechless. I just shook my head from side to side. "Can

177

we do this then?" he asked.

"Do what?" I knew what he meant, but you know what they say about assuming.

"Can we take our friendship to the next level?" He paused, "Let's be a couple."

I smiled. "A couple of what?"

"A couple of fools." He said with a smile. "A couple, two people in a relationship. Can we do that?"

"Yes." The way I jumped up and wrapped my legs around his waist, you'd think that we had just gotten engaged. "Yes, we can do that." Our lips met and our embrace grew stronger. He pulled away gently. "I know that I'm not everything that I could be, but I'm trying. I almost have enough money to buy time at the studio. Just be patient with me."

The phone started ringing. I jumped down and answered it, "Hello?"

"Sarai?"

"Yes, this is Sarai."

"Stefani has brought it to my attention that you've been turning down jobs over the past month," Conrad said. "Are you in this thing or not?"

I walked over to the picture window as I did a quick calculation of my ending statement balance, then thought of the fact that I hadn't even been looking for a job. "Yes, I'm still interested in the job," I said.

"Then you better start acting like it," he huffed. "I need you in Atlanta at the lawyer's convention on Friday evening."

"Atlanta?"

"ATL," he said sarcastically.

"This Friday?" I asked.

"What other fuckin' Friday you know 'bout?" He sounded pissed. "Sarai, I'm not playing games with you.

Going Broke

The Elite isn't an establishment where you can do shit half-assed. I run the show, not you. You should always be available for me, not you picking and fuckin' choosing when you want to work. I'm in the money making business. You are the merchandise, and when I need your ass on the shelf, you better damn fuckin' well be there."

"Okay. I'll be there." I wanted to hang up before Tremel got suspicious.

"You better be." He was breathing heavily. "Stefani will be calling you in the morning with the flight information." He hung up.

"Jesus," I said as I rested the phone down.

"What was that all about?" Tremel asked.

I pasted on a smile. "Job interview."

"Good for you," he said. "When is it and at what station?"

"Friday." I hated lying to him. "In Atlanta."

He smiled. "I hope you don't get it.

"No matter how rich you become, how famous or powerful, when you die the size of your funeral will still pretty much depend on the weather."
–Michael Pritchard

Bank Statement # 11
Account Balance: $1,139.30

As I rolled my suitcase to the closet in my hotel in Atlanta, my cellular started ringing. It was Tremel. He told me the shocking news of finding Mrs. White passed out on the kitchen floor when he got in from work. The medics said it was a massive heart attack and she had been dead for at least three hours. He was broken-hearted. She was like a grandmother to him, and I wished that I were there to comfort him. During our hour-long conversation, my hotel line rang twice. I knew that it was Stefani, but my man played a bigger role in my life than the Elite.

When she called back, I told Stefani that I had a problem and was late getting up to my room. She gave me the rules with the lawyers. We were to visit them in their rooms. They didn't trust us. But, they were willing to have sex with us. Go figure. Conrad charged them $3,000 since they had the balls to do something illegal.

I thought Stefani's call was just a formality until she laid it on me. "In an hour, I need you in room twenty-one thirty."

"In an hour?" I asked.

"Yeah, nine o'clock." She continued, "Calvin Ross. He's twenty-nine and I heard that the brotha is a piece of work."

"That helps." But what he looked like really didn't matter. What did matter was the fact that I couldn't get Tremel off my mind, and with every passing moment I was driving a knife further into his back.

Stefani said, "He's kinky as hell, though, so—"

"Whoa!" I interrupted. "Kinky, like how?"

"I don't know to what extent, but I flagged his name in the computer as being a little weird." I could hear her punching keys on the keyboard. "The last time he used us was a year ago, the last convention." She paused. "I do know that he's married to a white girl and just likes some black cherry every once in a while. But I don't think he did anything crazy."

"You shouldn't have told me that." I was nervous.

"Relax." She laughed.

"That's easy for you to say. You only have to deal with him over the phone." I was upset at her lack of sensitivity. "I have to sleep with him."

"Sarai, don't stress it. It's probably something like a foot fetish."

I tried to get my mind right. "Is the transaction complete?"

"Yep," she said. "Two and one will be in your account some time tomorrow."

The money was a comforting thought. "Sounds good to me." For the love of money, I was becoming a person I didn't like.

"All right, girl. Enjoy." Then she added, "I'll be calling you in the morning. You're a hot commodity this weekend."

"Really?" I didn't know if I should be proud or embarrassed.

"Yes, ma'am. They like your picture." She said, "Anyways, get ready. He's in room twenty-one thirty."

I passed the mirror and it hurt to look at myself. I resembled the picture of the woman whose face I had never seen, my mother. I quickly wondered if she was looking down on me and hoped that if she could, she'd stop me from becoming the woman I was in danger of being. I could only imagine her hurt, pain, and disappointment. What mother wants this for her daughter?

"This is crazy," I said as I continued to stare at my image. "I don't have to do this." I had no one to answer to. I could just walk out of this hotel and never look back. Or I could finish out the weekend to earn some extra money then call it quits. I contemplated for an hour before I came to a conclusion. I sauntered out of my room and to the elevator fighting tears. I was on my way to meet Calvin Ross.

He opened the door in a charcoal-colored suit. He was the soft brown complexion of the darkest of chocolate bars. He was not very tall, but his frame was solid. He had a flat stomach, jet-black wavy hair, and a goatee slicked to his skin. He smiled as he looked me up and down in my red dress. "Hello there." He extended his hand to me. "I'm Calvin."

"I'm Sarai." As my real name passed over my lips, I regretted it.

"That's a beautiful name." He took a step toward me with my hand still in his. "Would you like to join me in the lounge for a few cocktails?"

I smiled. "Sure, lead the way." I was shocked when he held my hand, not only to the elevator, but also through the lobby and into the lounge. As I sat down, he kissed me gently on the back of my hand. "I'll be right back. Please order me a vodka martini with two olives."

Stefani was right. The man looked like a statue of a bronze Zeus had come to life. However, because Calvin was labeled as a freak and Stefani couldn't remember why, I wasn't letting down my guard. I wasn't drinking; I wanted to have all of my faculties in order just in case I needed to beat his ass. When the cocktail waitress came over to find out what I was drinking, I gave her his order and kept my voice down as I told her what I wanted. "Put water in a martini glass with a cherry instead of an olive, but charge the bill the price of a regular vodka martini. For the rest of the night, whenever I order a martini, that's the way I want it."

She smiled. "That's pretty clever."

"I know." I winked. "Just don't mention it when my friend is at the table."

She gave me a thumbs up. "No problem." She walked away.

I looked around the lounge and saw a few familiar female faces that I had encountered while in Richmond. Conrad's girls were scattered throughout the hotel lobby and lounge. I could tell who they were; they were with the men who were trying to impress the next guy with their girls, rubbing their backs, their legs, being so aggressive that they shouldn't have left the room. Yet to a passing stranger, we all looked like couples.

Calvin came back and I started a conversation. "So, mister two olives, how were things today?"

"Long and boring." He unbuttoned his jacket and

slid closer to me in the booth. "Just glad that this convention is almost over and I can finally have myself some fun." He adjusted his tie. "What about you?"

"I'm fine." I put on my game face. "Glad that I have the opportunity to help you unwind."

"I'm glad too," he said as he started rubbing my legs. "You're going to help me do more than just unwind." He smiled.

I was getting nervous again. "So, what is it that you'd like to do later?" I was curious.

He ran his hand down the side of my face. "You'll see."

I'd see? I think not. I decided to take control of the night. I told Calvin that I could hold my vodka, and of course he, not wanting to be outdone by a woman, promised that I couldn't out drink him. Bingo! He fell into my trap. I had nine water martinis, and he was stuck on number seven. "Are you trying to kill me?" he asked. "Are you a woman or a machine?" I was trying to get him too incoherent to do whatever freakiness he had up his sleeves.

"Come on," I egged him on, "have one more and we'll call it even."

"All right," he slurred, quickly swallowed what was left of number seven then reached for an already waiting number eight. "Come on, let's go." He grabbed my hand and pulled me up out of the booth. "I want you." I created a monster. "Are you ready to fuck?" he asked.

I was taken aback at first. "Is that what you want to do?"

We walked out of the lounge. "That's what we came to do." As we got on the elevator, he grabbed my hand and placed it on his bulge. "You feel that?"

"Yeah."

"You like it?"

"Yeah."

He reached over and hit a button; the elevator came to a halt. "Then put it in your mouth."

"Calvin," I tried to smile, "let's go to the room."

"No, I want you to do it here." He unzipped his pants and poked his penis through. It was fat; the tip was the color of peanut butter, and the remainder was dark chocolate like the rest of him. "Suck it."

"Calvin, I don't think that this is the best idea," I said.

"I'm paying for what I think is the best idea." He put his hand on my shoulders and pressed me down. "Suck it."

I looked up at him. "Let's go to the room."

"No." He seemed aggravated.

"We might get caught here," I whined.

"I want you to do it now." He pulled me to my feet. "Just put it in your mouth."

I tried to convince him. "I just think that this is a little risky."

"Sometimes business is a risky thing." He pushed me to my knees. "I'm paying for head, not excuses." With his free hand, he unbuckled his pants and they fell to the ground. "You suck my dick right here and right now." I dropped to my knees and took him into my hand. "I'm paying three thousand dollars and you telling me where and when I can and can't have it? Suck my dick." He was so thick that I couldn't get my hand completely around it. He grabbed the rail on both sides of him as I spit him down. Then stroked and sucked him hard. I was taking him in almost to the shaft. He was long. An inch more and he'd be performing a tonsillectomy. In a few minutes, he pulled out of my mouth, ejaculated into his hand and licked his fingers clean. I guess that's the kinky shit that Stefani was talking about.

Once we were in his room, I threw myself on the bed. I was drained. "No sleeping tonight." He had already stripped down to his bare necessities. He climbed on top of me and he was already hard again. "I want you to fuck me."

I asked, "Right now?"

He rolled off of me. "Take off your clothes." He looked serious. "Everything." He grabbed his suitcase.

"Whoa, what are we going to do?" I was concerned. I thought him licking his own cum was what made him a freak. "What's in there?"

"Just get naked." He looked sober.

"This isn't going to be anything crazy, right?" I asked.

"It might be."

I wanted to run. "Calvin, you're scaring me."

He unzipped his bag and pulled out a leather panty harness with a black 8-inch rubber cock attached. "You don't have to be scared." He walked toward me and placed it in my hand. "I want you to put this on and fuck me in my ass."

I wanted to throw up. "Are you serious?"

"Very. I treat myself to this every once in a while." Then he looked at me cautiously. "I'm not gay." Yeah right, and neither is Elton John.

"You want me to do you?" In a way, I was relieved that that's all he wanted me to do, but at the same time I was absolutely grossed out that that's what he wanted me to do. I didn't even have to sleep with him. This was easy money. I thought about my bank account and got down to stripping. I strapped on that harness, lubed the rubber dong down with some KY gel, and as he lay on his back with his legs wrapped around my thighs, I entered him. I started gently and then got rough. He was a man that could take it. I fucked him like the dick was really mine. I manhandled that li'l punk bitch the rest of the night. Had him calling out my name. I spanked him and even made him suck on the dong after I took it out of his ass. Yuck!

The next day I received a call at noon to tell me that I was meeting a man named Norman Hall in an hour. Stefani informed me that Mr. Hall wasn't a lawyer but a businessman who happened to be in town. He was forty-two years old, from Ohio, and didn't mind using his real name. "He ain't a freak like the one I had last night, right?"

"Not to my knowledge. He used us once before. I don't have anything listed on him other than him being a big guy."

"Big like what?" I asked.

She laughed. "I don't think he's fat, just built."

"He better not be fat. After what I had to do last night, I can't take any more." I was serious.

When Norman answered the door, I was living in a world of intimidation. He was NFL defensive lineman big and reminded me of Suge Knight. He was tall, built, and sexy. "Hi, I'm...my name is Michelle." I struggled with my name.

"Hi, Michelle." His handshake pulled me into the room then he pointed at the bed. "Have a seat."

There was a high-tech camera mounted on a tripod right in front of the bed. He walked over to the closet then came back with an envelope and handed it to me.

There were five $100 bills in it. "What is this for?"

He smiled as he stepped behind the camera. "I want to take some pictures of you."

"Pictures of me?" I asked. "I don't know if we do that."

"Yes." He put his finger over his lips. "This is our little secret."

"I don't know if I can do this."

The flash went off and I jumped. "You do now."

"I don't think I should do this."

His huge frame moved over to mine like an elephant to an ant. He took my purse and placed it on the dresser. "Take off your clothes." He was wasting no time. "Take off your clothes and let me see your ass."

"Who's going to see these pictures?" I asked as he helped me undress.

"Just me. I jack off a lot," he said and pulled off my shirt. "Nice tits." He took my breast into his mouth and sucked hard. "Get on the bed and do something sexy." For the next thirty minutes, I posed at his command. "Smile." "Pinch your nipples." "Open your legs." "Spread your pussy lips." "Finger it." I figured as long as I was in the pictures alone they couldn't do any harm. Maybe he'd be nice enough to send me some copies.

He continued, "Look mean." "Look horny." "Finger it some more, yeah girl." He got naked as he was taking snapshots and detached the camera from the stand. He walked over to the bed and asked me to sit up. He held his erect penis out. "Here," he angled the camera down at it. "Suck it."

I smiled. "Put the camera down first."

"Come on," he begged playfully.

"Put the camera down and we can play," I said. "I don't want you to take pictures of me doing that."

He moved his hand and ran it over my head aggressively. "Suck the fuckin' thing."

"No." I tried to stand up, but he pushed me down and grabbed my neck. "Bitch, suck my dick or I'll hurt you." His hands were big and strong, and I was afraid that I wouldn't leave the room alive if I didn't comply.

"Okay, okay." I managed to get the word past his tight grip. I put him in my mouth and closed my eyes Trembled each time I heard the flash go off. "Take it all the way in," he instructed over and over again, picture after picture.

"See, that wasn't so bad now, was it?" he asked as he rested the camera on the dresser and got a rubber from the drawer. He slid it on as he walked toward the bed. "I'm a rough guy, Michelle. Just do whatever I tell you to do and everything will be all right."

Though I felt like crying, I was glad that the picture session was over.

"Come here." He wanted me to lie belly up on the edge of the bed. He pushed himself inside of me. The weight of his body told me that I wasn't going anywhere until he wanted me to. "Why are you so damn stiff?" he asked, upset with my lack of participation. "Move your ass."

"You're too heavy," I said.

"Fuck you." He slapped me so hard that I almost didn't think it happened. I just felt the sting. "Move that ass."

"What the fuck?" I cried. "You don't have to hit me."

"I will beat your ass if you don't fuck me right." The way he was looking at me told me that this wasn't just a fetish; he was a violent guy.

I grinded into his body wildly. There was no

passion, I was just scared out of my mind. "Please don't hit me again." I closed my eyes I don't think I prayed as much in my whole life as I did while Norman was on top of me. If this was the lesson I was supposed to learn, then I had. A few minutes into forcing my body to enjoy him, I heard the sound of snapping and the flash of the camera. I opened my eyes and saw a naked man walking around the room taking pictures. "Oh my God," I said.

"That's right, baby. Two for the price of one," Norman said as he pulled out. "Get on your knees." I did, and he tore into me like there was no tomorrow.

The other man was also tall, but he was thin. He was taking pictures of everything that Norman and I did. I stared at him. I couldn't see his face behind the camera, but I kept mouthing the word *please,* hoping that he'd pull his friend away from me. Instead, he put down the camera and positioned himself on the bed in front of me and started touching himself.

"Suck him." When I hesitated, Norman grabbed me by the back of my neck and forced my head down on the man. I was crying and the man could see it. As I sucked him, he wiped my tears away. I was trembling. He pitied me and pulled his tool away from my mouth.

I continued to move my head up and down so that Norman, watching from behind, would still think I was doing it. "That's right. Suck that dick, you nasty whore," Norman commanded. The man made faces and groaned so that Norman would believe even more.

Just when I couldn't take it anymore I heard a faint digital cry. "Shit," Norman said.

The man said, "You better get that. I told her you were gonna to call her back. She's gonna to think something."

"You wanna fuck her, Tee?" Norman asked the

man.

The man lied, "Naw, she's doing a good job right here." I continued to pretend to have him between my lips.

"Okay." Norman pulled himself from me and spanked my behind twice. "Keep sucking. I'll be back." He picked up his cell phone from the top of the television. "Love of my life." He chuckled. "I know, Shelia, I was out taking some pictures of the landscape earlier . . . " His voice trailed into the bathroom and I heard the door close.

I jumped up and looked at the man. "Please let me go."

"He won't be long," he said.

"Will you let me go?" I cried and begged. "Please."

He thought about it. "Hurry up."

I jumped out of the bed and grabbed my jeans, shirt, shoes, and purse. I left the envelope with the money next to the lamp but grabbed the camera and the three rolls of film sitting next to it. I looked at the man. "Get out," he whispered.

"Thanks," I mouthed, then ran to the door and out. I was naked but who cared. There was no one in the hallway, but even if there were, they'd have to deal with it. I ran my narrow brown behind to the stairwell and continued running all the way from the thirteenth floor to the eighth floor before I stopped to put on my clothing. Even then I rushed, putting my shirt on backwards and my jeans on the wrong side. I finally made my way down to the third floor and burst into my room like I was a burglar.

I packed up everything I brought with me and called the front desk to get me a cab. The receptionist said that one was already waiting out front. I scurried from my room and walked through the lobby looking like someone who didn't belong. I didn't check out, I just left.

"Take me to this address, please," I said to the cab driver. I looked around and cried as we pulled off.

Thirty minutes later I was pulling my suitcase behind me to door number nine of the Red Bush apartment complex. "Who is it?" he asked.

"Sarai."

"Who?" I knew he'd be surprised.

"It's your sexy sister," I said anxiously. It had been a year and a half since I'd seen him. "Open the door, Savion."

It took him a minute to do so, and when he did, I saw why he hesitated. My brother looked like he had lost fifty pounds. He didn't call Jenny Craig; something was wrong. "Savvy, what's wrong with you?" It was the first thing I could say. He was so malnourished it seemed as though it hurt him to walk. "Are you okay?"

He threw his arms around me. "No." He held me tightly. "No, I'm not okay." I walked into his apartment and didn't make it past the sofa.

"Talk to me." I pulled him next to me. "Talk to me."

This evil grip that this day had on me was a tight one. Savion confessed to me that while he worked as a personal trainer in Houston, not only was he sleeping with female clients, but also his male customers. He had been living a double life as a bisexual man for the past five years. His choice of lifestyle wore him down fast in Texas, but the most devastating blow of all was learning that Trina, his ex-girlfriend back in Dover, was killed by a man who learned he had contracted HIV from her. Seeing how dangerous things could get, he packed up and moved to Atlanta, without informing any of his female, gay, or "straight" partners. He was afraid that

193

once they found out, his life would be in jeopardy in more ways than one. I held his frail body in my arms, and my twin soul and I cried together.

Later that evening, Conrad called. Before he had a chance to ask me what happened, I told him what Norman did to me and that I was out. He begged me not to quit, promising that he'd never put me in a dangerous position again. All of his words fell on deaf ears; I wasn't going through that again. He vowed to change the screening process for his clients, but my answer was still no.

Just like that Conrad baited the hook and sweetened the bargain. He offered me business for youplanmytrip.com, telling me that I no longer had to entertain. Stefani needed help, so I would be in charge of all the Elite's travel plans. He had me; I was still in the establishment.

I stayed in Atlanta a week longer than I was scheduled to, which meant missing Mrs. White's funeral, but Tremel understood that I wanted to help my brother deal with his illness. I went with Savion to his weekly doctor appointment and also to see his counselor. We might not beat it medically, but Savion and I had planned to beat the disease emotionally. He needed to know that someone still loved the mess out of him—me. He wasn't dying from AIDS; he was *living with* AIDS.

Going Broke

"You aren't wealthy until you have something money
can't buy."
–Garth Brooks

Bank Statement # 12

Account Balance: $5,339.30

I walked through the airport trying hard to hold back a smile. I was anticipating seeing Tremel at any moment, certain he'd surprise me again. However, I made it all the way to my truck without spotting him. As I loaded my luggage into the trunk, I looked around on edge, expecting him to startle me. I wanted to feel his presence, smell his sexy cologne, and look into his eyes. I had been unfaithful, and longed to tell him that I was sorry with my body, because he'd never forgive me if I said it with my mouth.

I pulled into my apartment complex and the security gate wouldn't open. I blew the horn until Manny wobbled from the booth with an envelope. "Bonita lady," he had the heaviest Spanish accent outside of Cuba, "someone bringa dis fa joo."

I smiled as I looked at the padded yellow envelope. Eviction notices were normally pink. right? So, it wasn't that. When the gate opened, I couldn't wait to park. It didn't matter how far I was from the elevator; I pulled into the first space I saw. In the envelope, there wasn't a note but a CD. The cover of the CD was a sexy picture of Tremel from the back, sitting on the beach without a shirt. In big, bold black letters on top it read: **TreMelody**. On the bottom, it simply said: *Forgotten*. I looked at the CD again. "Forgotten?" I said aloud. What was he trying to say?

I rushed out of the garage and all but burst into my apartment. Forget unpacking, peeing, eating, and making phone calls. I raced to the stereo, jammed the CD in, and turned the volume to the highest. The music was seductive, starting with a saxophone, then a piano joined, the drums came in slowly after, and Tremel said, "Yeah." The digital synthesizers dropped in with a sexy funky beat and I fell into the loveseat. It seemed like Tremel was right there. "Oh yeah."

It's been a while since I've been in this boat.
But the one thing I remember, lady, is how to stay afloat.
Please don't swim away,
There's something I have to say.
Baby, you don't have to respond,
Just don't stop feeling our bond.
You are something I thought only dreams would let be.
I can't remember my life prior to you and me.

I had forgotten how to live, forgotten how to give.
I forgot how to trust, and how to lust.
But through you I learned to care.
Please forgive me if this seems rare.
But before you came along, and way before I wrote this song,

I had forgotten.

Willing to do whatever it'll take.
Willing to move slowly, can't afford a mistake.
Ninety-nine just won't do;
Make one hundred percent man out of me.
Put my key in your lock; set your soul free.
If you passed me by, it would've been a great regret.
I want you to be that one person I'll never forget.
Because you took the time to walk my way
Lady, this is what I've been longing to say.

Give me reasons to forget everything I knew.
Give me reasons to remember only you,
the one that finally got through.
I don't need to know any that I've forgotten.
I'm opened to you and I'll spoil you rotten.
I'm no longer afraid; love me.
Make my heart what I know it could be,
So that forgetting will be just a memory.

I had forgotten how to live, forgotten how to give.
I forgot how to trust, and how to lust.
But through you I learned to care.
Please forgive me if this seems rare.
But before you came along, and way before I wrote this
song,
I had forgotten.

Now that I've found you,
My life seems brand new.
So you'll never be . . . forgotten.

"Forgotten" was absolutely beautiful. I sat in shock

for at least three minutes after the song was over. Tremel had sung for me prior to this, but we were always joking around. However, on the CD his range was something serious. He sounded like he had a recording deal ten years ago and was still on top of the charts. His voice, the lyrics and the music took me to another place. It made me not only wonder whom he was singing to, but whom he was singing about. "Was he singing to me?" I asked myself. "That was about me, wasn't it?" I giggled and turned the volume down only to play the song three more times. I decided that if "Forgotten" weren't about me I sure as hell would love to know who the lucky girl was. "It's about me," I said as I blushed.

I was startled by a knock on the door. "Who is it?"

"Chinese," a muffled voice said from the other side.

"Yeah right," I whispered. "Who is it?" I didn't order any Chinese food.

"The Chinese restaurant," the foreigner said.

I looked out of the peephole and sure enough, standing there was Liu from the Chinese place down the street with a carton full of food. "Hi, Liu." I pulled open the door. "I think you have the wrong apartment number. I didn't order anything."

"I did." Tremel stepped around the corner with an assortment of flowers in shades of purple. I was so happy to see him I swung the door open. Liu knew where the kitchen was.

"Tell me you didn't get the job." He smiled as he wrapped his arms around my waist. He asked me over the phone, but decided he wanted an answer in person.

"You don't have to worry. Atlanta radio stations want no part of me," I said.

"Thank God." He kissed my lips. "I want every part of you."

"I go, I go now." Liu covered his ears jokingly.
"Tank you, Mister Mel. Sarai, I see you lata." I closed and
locked the door behind Liu.

"I've missed you a lot." He placed the flowers on
the counter. Minutes later, I was kissing him like my
mouth had been slurping only holy water during the past
week. I never wanted to let him go. I was his tail for the
rest of the evening. Wherever he went, I was less than
one step behind. He was surprised with all of the
affection.

After dinner, we lit candles and I played
"Forgotten." We sat on the floor. I sat facing him with my
thighs atop his and my feet on both sides of him. The
flickering of the candles hid his face a bit. He rubbed my
back as I leaned into him. "What inspired you to write
this song?" I asked.

"This couple that I know." He pressed his forehead
against mine and continued to stroke my back gently.
"They just seemed so right, so caring, and so happy," he
said.

"Sounds like a special pair," I said.

He kissed my nose. "Sarai, I have some good and
bad news for you."

"What?" I backed away a bit so that I could see his
face better.

"Which do you want to hear first?" he asked.

I actually didn't want to hear anything. "The bad."

He didn't waste any time. "Mrs. White's son,
Jason, is putting the house up for sale. He wants me out
in a week."

I smiled. "That's not too bad."

"I wasn't finished. I'm moving to Daytona Beach to
live with Ralph, a friend of my father, who has a
plumbing business. He's promised me a job."

"In Daytona?" I couldn't have heard him right.

"Yeah."

I thought about the last time I rode that far. "So, it wouldn't have mattered if I got the job in Atlanta," I said with a pout.

"Yes, it would've. Driving to Miami beats driving to Atlanta." He smiled. "Plus, I like the weather here."

"It's five hours from Daytona to Miami and six hours to Atlanta." I rolled my eyes. "Not much difference."

"Just listen to my good news," he said.

"What?" I couldn't believe him.

"The reason I'm moving to Daytona is because I'm flat broke." He had the nerve to laugh. "While you were away, I took off from work and bought studio time. I spent all the money I had been saving to complete an eight-track demo." He pulled the CD out of his jacket pocket.

"Oh my goodness." I hugged his neck. "You did it," I squealed.

"I have a hundred copies, and twenty-three of them have already been mailed out to different labels." He smiled. "So, I hope to hear something soon."

"I'm so happy for you." I felt as though he was already signed. "I know you're going to make it. That song was incredible, baby." I was in tears.

"Don't cry."

"I can't believe that you wrote the song about me, about us." I managed to get it out. "Your dreams are coming true." I got up and turned up the CD. After every song, I was more impressed than the one before. Tremel had the talent, he owned the sexy look, and his drive was tremendous. When song number eight faded to silence, we were still holding each other. I couldn't lose him. I wanted him in my life. "Don't go to Daytona." My mouth said what my heart was feeling.

"Jason wanted me out of the house a few days ago, but I asked him to give me a week," he said.

"I know, but don't go." I pulled him closer and brought his lips to mine. "I'm just getting used to you being around."

"I'm getting used to you too." His CD started over again. We stared at each other without words for the first two songs. Our hearts had started a fire that only passion could extinguish. Our lips connected and our tongues raced to meet. He caressed my back gently. My hands fumbled from his forehead back to his neck. We kissed, our breathing was heavy, and our bodies were hot. Somehow we untangled ourselves. My back was flat against the living room floor and Tremel was on top of me.

His hand traveled from my waist to my breasts and that was all the incentive I needed. My eyes rolled back and I was ready to go into convulsions. I had to concentrate, think of something else so that I wouldn't look like I was having a seizure. I couldn't believe the excitement I was feeling from his fingertips on the outside of my shirt. We had never been this close before; he'd never touched me like he was doing now. Over the past few months, I started to think that he had something to hide, but according to the knot that was pressing up on me below, Tremel didn't have a thing to be timid about.

Through the speakers, he was singing a song called "Have My Baby." I felt him all over me as I listened to the words of his song. "Let's make love to make life, have my baby and be my wife." Tremel slowly removed my shirt as the speaker sang. *No baby mama drama between me and you, no breaking up to make up like some others do.* He littered me with kisses from my belly button back to my lips. *Lady, have my baby; let me put life inside of you tonight. Take this ring, let's do this thing, help me do it right.* He seemed shocked as I tugged on his shirt and lifted it over his head. *If the test says no, then I'll cancel my show, just to rush home and make life nice and slow.* Feeling his bare chest on mine and hearing him singing in the background was a dangerous combination.

Before long, we were both completely naked. I was suddenly afraid of what the next step would do to our friendship and new relationship. "Sarai." Tremel looked down at me. "Please believe that this isn't all I want from you." At the moment, it didn't matter, because all I wanted was him in any way I could.

"I believe you," I said.

He lifted his body a bit and when he brought himself down, he slid right into me. I took a deep breath and closed my eyes. I felt like Goldilocks; he wasn't too big or too small, he was just right. Our bodies melded together like they were cut from the same cloth, and now here we were joined together to create a royal garment. Other than our breathing, my whimpers, and his groans, the only sound in the room was *TreMelody* crooning through the speakers. When the music stopped, the sound of our bodies loving each other had an even better melody.

Out of the still of the night I uttered, "Stay with me." He plowed deeper into me again and again. "Don't move away. Stay with me." I kissed him and moved my body to match his pace a little more. "Move here, Tremel." I wrapped my legs around his thighs and grinded my pelvic area around in circles. "I have more than enough room here." Our bodies continued to gently slap against each other. "Forget Daytona." I rubbed his back. "Stay here."

He pushed himself upward with his hands palmed down on the rug on both sides of me. "Here?"

"Yes."

He asked, "Are you serious?"

"Yes."

"But I don't even have the money to give you to start out," he said. "I spent over nine thousand dollars in the studio, which was all—"

"Shh," I interrupted him then pressed my hands into his hips. "Just give me you." He started moving again, and he didn't stop until we were both speaking in tongues, sweating, and calling out each other's names. Tremel fell to my side and I rested my head on his upper arm. "So, when can I move in, landlady?"

I was excited. "Well, you just put down the deposit." I walked my fingers down his chest. "Let's see what you've got for first and last month's rent." We both laughed.

We started moving his things into the apartment the next day. Within a week, Damian's old office space was converted into Tremel's new music room. It was nice to have someone around again, and Tremel being that someone was an added plus. During my days, I not only booked flights, cars, and hotel rooms for Elite, I also called various record labels to gather information and mailed out Tremel's demo to anybody who was anybody in the music world.

Over the next month, whenever there was an envelope addressed to Tremel, with our fingers crossed we'd open it together. Rejection was a nasty game to play. The letters always sounded like this: *Thank you for allowing Blah Blah Blah Records the opportunity to experience your talent. Though your work is truly amazing and unique, at present our establishment is not in search of an artist of your genre. However, we wish you lots of luck in all of your future endeavors.* Some of them returned the CD, some didn't.

Each piece of mail we sent out included professional photographs, the CD, a lyric sheet, and a memo selling Tremel Colten. Before long, I started taking the rejection personally. I was his biggest fan. I believed in him and couldn't see why we couldn't find anyone else who did. Whenever I was discouraged, all I had to do was turn on his CD or listen to him sing while sitting behind his Casio, and I'd run to lick stamps or drive to the post office to dust myself off and try again.

It was early November when the phone rang. "Sarai, I have a guy in Miami that wants a girl tonight. I figured I'd let you work this one," Stefani said. "You have someone local that's free? It'd be dumb to fly someone there on short notice. We'd be spending more to get them there. You think you can find somebody?"

"I'm sure." I grabbed a pen. "Let me get his information and I'll make some calls."

"Cool," she said. "His name is Dwayne Cart, but he'll be checked into the Marriott on Biscayne under the name Damian Carter. I took care of the transaction already. He spoke to Conrad and they worked out a special rate because the girl he had a few months ago bailed early. Conrad will pay whoever you find directly, so this Mr. Cart character is getting a free ride."

I almost dropped the phone. She had no clue that she had just told me that my ex-boyfriend was paying money for sex when he was supposed to be in a relationship with my former friend.

"He'll be checking in at six and wants her until midnight. We need someone there no later than seven. Okay?"

"Hold a second." I clicked to my other line and listened to the dial tone while my heartbeat forced itself to become regular once more. "You are a nasty bastard," I said into the phone, wishing that somehow the lines would cross up and Damian would hear me. I went back to Stefani and held back the temptation to scream. "Yeah, I'll have someone there." I looked at the clock; it was a few minutes to four. "I'll take care of everything." And I meant just that.

I made four calls the first one to Cherry. Since I hadn't heard that R&B girl group's name on the radio, I figured she'd probably needed a few extra dollars. I assumed correctly. Cherry knew exactly where the hotel was and agreed to be there at 7:00 sharp. I instructed her to wait on my next call, and I'd tell her what room number to go to. The second call was placed to Damian around five. I called him using a calling card so that my number wouldn't show up, and I also did a little to disguise my voice. "Mr. Cart, this is Michelle from Elite."

"Hello, Michelle," he said in a flirty tone. "How are you?"

"I'm doing great," I lied. "I was calling to let you know that Cherry will be meeting you at seven. Please leave a key at the front desk and tell them that your wife will be picking it up."

"Okay. Thank you." Then he said, "Conrad and I already worked things out. Are you aware of that?"

"Yes." I wanted to curse at him. "Have a good time."

He laughed. "Why don't you come instead of sending someone?"

I bit my bottom lip. "I'll be there in spirit."

"Flesh is always better, though." He asked, "Where are you?"

"I'm not into that part of the business, Mr. Cart." I continued, "Have a good night." I hung up.

My next call was to the hotel, confirming that Mr. Carter had checked in. Sure enough, the bastard was already waiting in his room. Cherry was informed to go straight to room 1412 and not to the front desk. I placed my last call from inside my truck parked in the hotel garage. It was to a number that I thought I had forgotten, but when payback is a factor, you're liable to remember anything. "Hello?"

"Hi, India. How are you?" I asked.

"Sarai?" She sounded nervous and surprised. "What, what do you mean?"

"I mean how are you?"

"Fine," she said. "You?"

"Great." I continued. "Look, I'm not going to beat around the bush and waste time. I was calling to find out if you'd like to have a drink or something. We need to talk."

"Are you serious?" Her voice was filled with glee.

"Yes." I faked it. "Yes, I am."

"You, Nat, and me?" She was probably too scared to be alone with me.

"Just me and you. We've got some talking to do."

"Okay," she paused, "where?"

"Let's see." I pretended to think about it. "Let's go to that restaurant inside the Marriott on Biscayne. A friend of mine said that they have the best pasta."

"Cool." She fell for it. "When?"

"Well, I have to be somewhere later. Is it all right if we do it right now?"

"Now?" she asked.

"Yeah. I'm really ready for us to get back on track."

"Wow, I'm lost for words," she said. "I'm already dressed. I'll be there in thirty minutes." I had her hook, line, and sinker.

With Damian's room key safely tucked away in my purse, I sashayed into the restaurant and told the host that I'd sit at the bar until my friend arrived. From my stool, I watched Cherry in her sexy business suit enter the lobby and turn heads as she made her way to the elevator to entertain her client. India was pretty, but Cherry was prettier. I had picked the right girl for the job.

My Merlot was doing the job. I was loose and ready for anything to happen. I ordered another glass, paid for it, and finished it before the bartender had a chance to place the bottle back on the shelf. A dark, evil shadow overtook me when I spotted India walking through the lobby doors. My blood was boiling like it was when I saw her curled up, hiding in my bathtub after she had just jumped off of my man. I had to breathe and try to think good thoughts or security was going to have to call higher authority to handle me.

She was smiling just as she had many times before while sleeping with Damian behind my back. The look on her face said that she wasn't sorry. It was actually telling me she was happy that I finally came around and saw things her way. I was ready to rumble. I was Mike Tyson minus the 'what the hell' tattoo over half of my face.

As she walked toward me, her steps became shorter. It took her forever to get to me. I couldn't hold back. "You miserable bitch." I paused. "Why did you do this to me?"

"I knew this was too good to be true." She stopped a few feet from me. "I said that I was sorry, Sarai. What in the hell else do you want me to do or say?"

"Just tell me why you did this to me."

"Damian and I just connected. I didn't plan on it, I just fell in love with him." She looked me up and down. "He loves me too."

"He didn't love you, India, he was fucking you. He didn't even love me. But if he loves you so much, then why is he calling me? Why is he still trying to get me back? Did he tell you that he sends me flowers, cards, and candy?" I took a breath. "He's no good." Looking at her, I knew that she thought the words were just from a woman scorned.

She had the nerve to say, "Will you just accept the fact that we're in love?"

"How can you fall in love with a man that was supposed to me mine? You were supposed to be my friend." I was in her face.

She waved me off. "I knew that there was a fuckin' catch." When she tried to walk away, I grabbed her hand. "You want a catch?" I took the key from my purse. "Go catch your man in room fourteen twelve showing another woman how much he's in love with you." I placed the key in her hand.

She giggled. "Whatever. Damian is in Shreveport. His flight gets in at midnight."

"Midnight?" I laughed and looked at my watch. "I guess he meant midnight in Iraq, because the brotha is upstairs. I can guarantee you that you and I will have a whole lot more in common when you walk into that room and meet a woman riding your man's dick." I walked back over to the bar and ordered another glass of wine while she stared at me.

"Why in the hell are you playing with me, Sarai?"

"I'm not the one playing with you. It's Damian that thinks you're a toy." I looked away from her. "Room fourteen twelve." As she started to walk away I yelled, "And don't you ever say another fuckin' word to me for as long as you live. This does not mean that we're cool." I sipped from my new glass of wine as I watched her walk to the hotel exit. However, she paused then turned around and strolled to the elevator. My work was done.

Tremel was home; I could hear him playing his keyboard. I gathered the mail and opened the door to the music room. "Hi there."

"Hey." He gestured for me to come in. "How was your day?"

"A little crazy." I giggled. "I'll tell you about that later. We have mail to open." I sat on his lap and handed him everything with his name on it.

"I don't want to go through mail today, baby." He held me around the waist and put his head on my shoulder. "It's so draining, one after the next. It's starting to play with my mind. This can really drive a person crazy."

"I know, but good news is only considered good news when you've had a little bad news first." I tried to encourage him. "Come on, let's open the envelopes and see what we have." One by one, we opened the four responses, and sure enough we had been had again. All four were bad news. I was ready to jump off of this Ferris wheel we were riding. We just kept going in circles.

"Something has to happen. This is my dream." Those were his last words before falling asleep.

I sat around the house the next day wanting to throw out the letters that we'd received, but he insisted on keeping them, saying that in the future they'd keep him humble and appreciative for the one chance he was given. Remembering Tremel's words from the night before haunted me, and as I thumbed through the stack, I got an idea. I wasn't going to just sit back and help only to watch his dream sink.

"Jump Records, this is Julian Odom speaking."

I was clutching the phone so hard I was surprised it worked. "Hi, Julian. How are you?"

"Oh, I'm just fine." He continued, "Who do I have the pleasure of speaking with?"

I didn't know what he would to say about me contacting him at a number he never gave me. I went through the Elite Establishment's computer files to get it. "This is Sarai Emery."

I could tell that he stopped doing whatever he was doing. "Who?"

"Sarai." If he didn't remember me, I was hanging up "We met down in the Bahamas at the Atlantis. Remember?"

"Ah yes." He was concerned. "Is something wrong?"

"No." No, I'm not pregnant or calling to tell you to get tested. "Everything is fine."

"Hold a moment for me, please." I listened to music produced by Jump for about two minutes before Julian came back. "Are you there?"

"Yes, I am."

"How are you doing?" I was surprised by his friendly tone.

"I'm fine. Thank you for asking." I was nervous. "You?"

"All work and no play unless you're in my area."

"No, I'm in Florida." I felt like an idiot. "Listen, I was calling to ask your advice, or to see if you could be of any assistance to me."

"About your website?"

"No, my site is actually doing all right," I said. "I'm calling because I have a friend who just finished a dynamic demo. However, we're having a problem getting it past the receptionist's desk at many record labels. The CD hasn't been reviewed by anyone who matters. We've been getting back a bunch of form rejection letters, but I know that there is major talent there."

"Is she fine?" he asked then laughed.

"*He* is very attractive," I said.

"Can he sing, though?"

I thought he'd never ask. I pressed play on the stereo and held the phone toward it for ten seconds. "What do you think?"

"Well, he sounds good, but I'll need a copy of the demo so I can get a better listen and pass it on to the right person."

"Thank you so much, Julian," I said. "Let me get your address at Jump."

He said, "Don't send it here. A friend of mine will be down in West Palm Beach this weekend."

"Who?"

"Dwayne." He chuckled. "For old time's sake, how about a little fun in exchange for doing you this little favor?"

I knew what he was trying to say. "I'm sorry. I really don't do that anymore, Julian."

"Then I'm sorry. I really don't work for Jump anymore, Sarai," he said. "One good turn deserves another. I even guarantee you that I'll get Martin Bonnet to listen to it, and if he's deserving of it, I'll give the man props." He paused. "I know how hard it is to get into the music industry, and believe me, everybody that gets in knows somebody who knows somebody who knows somebody on the inside."

"So, I can't just send you the CD?"

"No, that's boring," he said.

"So, what do you want, Julian?" I asked.

"It's not what I want. It's what Dwayne wants, and he wants that g-spot."

"Can I just pay you?"

"No, baby. We're not talking cash, we're talking about the CD." He paused. "You bring it to my hotel room in West Palm, I get that pussy, and I'll promise you that it'll end up in the right hands."

I was desperate. "Can't I just pay you to take the CD?"

"You will be paying me, but I don't accept dollars, just sex." He cut the conversation short. "I'm due in a marketing meeting in two minutes."

I took a deep breath. "Okay."

"I'm sure that your friend will appreciate how much you're willing to do to help him," Julian said. "I'll call you on Saturday, Sarai."

"Money doesn't change men, it merely unmasks them. If a man is naturally selfish or arrogant or greedy, the money brings that out, that's all."
–Henry Ford

Bank Statement # 13

Account Balance: $8,339.30

Julian called while Tremel and I were at the mall. I asked Tremel to excuse me. Then exited the Foot Locker and sat on a bench in front of the store where I politely told Julian I couldn't take him up on his offer because I was no longer in the Elite for the purpose of entertainment. I tried to be businesslike and propose a deal with him, telling him that I'd pay any amount to get the CD heard, but Julian wasn't having it. He reminded me of all the positive things that could be produced through our reunion, mainly Tremel's CD.

After ten minutes on the phone, Julian won. I'd never get a chance to help Tremel like this again. Julian said that he had a meeting with Mr. Bonnet, CEO of Jump Records, on Monday morning, and promised that he'd hype the CD and make something happen, even if it was just a phone call. I reluctantly agreed to see him.

I told Tremel that it was a high school friend of

215

mine who was in town and wanted to meet me for dinner. When we got home, I couldn't keep Tremel off of me. The best thing was that he wasn't hungry for sex; he just wanted to be close to me. We cuddled in bed for a couple of hours and watched a movie. Being in Tremel's arms made getting up out of bed to be with Julian real hard, but each time I talked myself into not going, Tremel would bring up something dealing with the music industry, something that made me want to make his dreams reality. What he didn't know was that I was standing between him and the door he needed to be open for him. I wanted things to happen for him, so I pulled down the covers and started to walk into the shower and into his dreams.

"So, what time will you be back?" Tremel asked from under the sheets as he watched me get dressed.

I couldn't even look at him. "I really don't know." The lie had grown bigger than I wanted it to. "I was so surprised to hear from her." I even went as far as asking him if he wanted to join us, but before he could answer I gave him three reasons why he'd be bored out of his mind.

"So, when did she get here?" he asked.

I was nervous. "Yesterday, I think."

"What time are you supposed to be there?"

"Around seven-thirty or eight." The truth was I told Julian to expect me at eight and it was already after six, so I changed the subject. "What do you think I should wear, baby?"

"Sarai, I don't want to be a part of the getting dressed process." He fell back on the bed and shook his head, smiling.

"Help me," I yelled jokingly. "Please ... I need help."

He said, "Wear that blue dress you wore when we

216

went to Levels."

I laughed. "I think that's a little too dressy. We're just going to dinner."

"It looked good, though." He smiled. "Put it on for me when you get home."

"No, I'm going to put it *on* you when I get home."

"Put it on me. Put it on me, girl," Tremel joked.

A little before 7:00, I was dressed and ready to go. "I'll see you later." I walked over to the bed and kissed him on the forehead.

"Wait, I'll walk you down." He started to get out of bed.

I pushed him back. "No." I couldn't let him walk me out because I had a bag next to the couch with panties, condoms, deodorant, and other items that I couldn't let him see me leaving with. "You don't have to walk me down." I kissed him. "As a matter of fact, I want you right here in this bed when I get home." I trailed my fingers down his chest.

"Can I get up to pee, warden?" he joked.

"No, that way it'll stay hard." I laughed as I walked away. "See ya later, baby."

I sat in the parking lot of Julian's hotel for twenty minutes. I was trying hard to rationalize what I was about to do. Tremel would be thankful for the opportunity, it could really open up the doors that were being slammed in his face, but I also thought about how I had to betray him to help him. I'm sure there weren't enough words in the dictionary to make him understand why I thought this was the best thing to do.

I slipped the CD into my car stereo, and as I listened to the power in Tremel's voice, tears came to my eyes. I couldn't tell if it was love that made me want to go this far for him, or if it was lack of love leading me to go this far. "Here I go." I touched up my makeup and left the car.

In Julian's hotel room, we talked like we knew each other well. I laughed at his jokes, pretended to be interested in life, and ignored his sexual advances. After all of that, I dropped the bomb on him. I told him that the singer I wanted him to check out was really my boyfriend and I was willing to write him a check for a thousand dollars instead of doing what I came to do.

"You know I can't accept your money," he said. "I know how hard you have to work for yours."

I begged, "Julian, just take the money. I'm doing all right now as far as cash is concerned."

"Naw, I have all the money I need." He stood up and started undressing. "Let's do something where we'll both walk away from this business deal happier. You'll get the CD played and I'll get laid."

I smiled. "Yeah, but I really don't feel right about this."

"What is there to feel bad about?" he asked. "This is what the business is about. If you don't do it, he might have to do it with someone else." He kept undressing. "Which one would you rather?" He was naked. "Nothing in life is free, baby, not even good talent. You scratch my back and I'll scratch yours."

Moments later, I was doing more than scratching his back. I was kneeling in front of him with a mouthful. Julian, bent on making the night a living hell, insisted that we play Tremel's music on his laptop, claiming he really wanted to get a good feel for his talent. It was like Tremel was standing right next to me. I closed my eyes and he was all I saw. I tried to pretend that I was kneeling in front of him instead of Julian, but the physical dimensions of Julian's baton were off. By the time Forgotten started to play, I felt like I needed a straightjacket, a psychiatrist, and holy water. I was going insane. As my head bobbed up and down, tears dripped and dropped onto his pubic hair. "I can't do this." He tried to force my head back down. "Stop." I pushed his hand away and wiped my mouth. "I can't do this."

"What are you doing?" he asked.

"I can't do this." I stood to my feet and looked at him. "I'm sorry."

"Where are you going?"

"Home." I grabbed my purse.

He stood up. "So, you're just going to leave me like this?" He pointed at his private part as it pointed back at me.

"I'm sorry." It was all I could say as I sobbed and made my way to the door. "You don't have to help me. We'll make it on our own." I opened and closed the door as Julian stared at me.

I walked down the wall talking to myself. "I love him too much to do this to him." Those were words I hadn't spoken to Tremel yet. "I love him."

I got to my truck and cried like a baby. I rinsed my mouth with Listerine and spat out of the window every chance I got. I threw the bag that held my condoms onto the shoulder of the road. I was done forever with being that woman that money wanted me to be. I was an emotional wreck and when I heard my phone ring, I wanted to throw it out the window, too, but I answered instead.

"Sarai, what in the fuck did you do yesterday?" Conrad asked, making me wish I had gone with my initial instinct. "Are you trying to put me out of business?"

"What do you mean?"

"You know what in the hell I mean," he insisted. "Do you know Dwayne Cart?"

Damn! I was caught. "Yes, I do," I whispered.

"What in the hell did you think you were doing?"

"What did I do?" Playing stupid was always fun.

"What did you do?" he paused. "You gave his girlfriend a key to the damn room. You got Cherry caught up in some bullshit. The damn girl tore her weave out and all. Cherry said that the woman kept screaming your name and said that you gave her the key to the fuckin' room."

"Well, if that's what Cherry said, then that must be what I did." I had been through enough in one week; I was going to speak my mind. "Dwayne Cart is my ex-boyfriend. I caught him fuckin' one of my best damn friends, and this was my way to get back at him. Sorry for doing it on your time clock, sorry if you lost a few dollars, and I'm sorry if Cherry is bald right now."

"You're sorry all right. Your sorry ass won't work for me again."

"Fine, Conrad," I shouted. "Not like I can claim this bullshit on my taxes any damn way."

"Ya broke bitch, let's see how much business your website is gonna get now. Youplanmytrip.com— more like youplanbullshit.com. I told you not to fuck with my money. Now you got this man's woman all up in my business because of you. Security had to take them all out, and the police were called." He was angry. "I swear if my shit goes down I will be on your doorstep, and it won't be to deliver no goddamn Sunday paper either."

He had me scared, but I turned the tables and put some fear into him. "Conrad, if you threaten me again, I swear I'll call the Sacramento police station after we hang up. I know too much of your business for you to piss me off," I said. "Stay the hell out of my life. I want nothing to do with anything that has to do with you or your establishment. There was a Sarai before Elite, and they'll damn sure be one after it."

"You're pretty damn cocky today," he said with a laugh. "What, the fucking janitor got a promotion?" He hit a tender nerve.

"Fuck you." I hung up.

I was so angry that I knew I couldn't hide it from Tremel. I was still crying when I walked into apartment. I saw him on the couch watching boxing on HBO. He was so engrossed in the fight that he didn't notice I was there until I slammed the door. "Hi, baby." His eyes didn't leave the screen, but when I didn't answer, he looked my way. "Hey." His smile turned into concern when he looked over at me and quickly realized that something was up. "What's wrong?" He turned off the fight and walked over to me.

I placed my index finger over my mouth and shook my head from side to side, signaling that I couldn't talk about it. He wrapped his arms around me. "Sarai, what happened?" We moved to the couch and I didn't know what I would tell him, I just knew that I couldn't tell him what the tears were really about. Feeling his heart beating against my side made me believe that he deserved to know the truth. However, the thought of losing him or him never trusting me again outweighed my guilt. I stared into his eyes and what I said wasn't a lie. "You mean the world to me."

His eyes lit up and he smiled. "Is that why you're crying?"

"No."

"Then what's wrong?" he asked. "How was

dinner?"

"I didn't go," I said.

"Why not?" He looked confused.

"There was an accident." Another big fat lie instead of a little bit of truth passed my tongue and rushed through my lips. "An accident that happened right in front of me. A teenage girl died." Where was I getting this stuff? "It could've been me. It just made me realize that life is too short. I stayed at the scene a while and then just came back here to you." Every part of the lie was leaving an open wound. "I love you, Tremel." If I had said it one day earlier, it wouldn't have meant what it meant at that moment. "I couldn't go another day without you knowing that." I kissed him. "I love you."

He squeezed my body tighter and took a deep breath. "I love your hips, I love your thighs. I love your lips and the way you roll your eyes. I love not just what you say but the way you say what you say. I love being with you, love coming home to you every day. I love when you're strong, but I love it when you're weak. I love when you're happy, but even when you're bleak. I love the big things, but also the simple things that we do. For you I'd do anything, Sarai, because I love you too."

If I weren't already crying, I would've started then. "You're so sweet." He was full of surprises. "When did you make that up?"

"About a week ago. I was just hoping you'd give me a reason to recite it to you." He kissed me and my head fell to his shoulder. I felt as though I let him down even more by lying, but one thing was certain, I was in love with him. We didn't do any more talking. I fell asleep later and he carried my motionless body to the bedroom, placed me under the sheets, and never left my side.

Going Broke

On Monday morning I checked my website e-mail and found a query from a customer named T.C. I knew that it was Tremel. He had paid fifteen bucks a few times to submit queries before. In the past, he jokingly asked about flying to Paris, Japan, and Rome. But this time he asked me to make arrangements for him and his girlfriend to fly back to his hometown of Cleveland in three weeks for Thanksgiving. I researched the information and sent it to him as I always did. However, I was shocked when he sent me a return e-mail the following day with his credit card information and instructions to book the trip.

He stepped into the apartment after work looking as sexy as ever in his blue uniform. The way I rushed him daily, you'd think he was wearing an Armani suit. "Hi, Tremie." He hated to be called that and would normally tackle me to the ground playfully when I did.

"If I didn't have business to take care of with you, I'd hurt you." He grabbed me by the waist and kissed me.

"What business do you have with me?" I asked.

"Our trip to Cleveland."

I laughed. "You're such a jokester."

"What?" he said. "Didn't you get my e-mail?"

"About the trip?"

"Yeah," he said seriously. "Were you able to find an evening flight on that Wednesday?"

"Tremel, if I put your credit card number in, it'll really buy the ticket." I giggled.

"Okay, and?" He looked at me strangely. "That's what I want."

"Whatever."

"Sarai, I'm serious."

I looked at him. "You want me to go with you to Cleveland for Thanksgiving?"

"Yes."

"Won't your family be there?" I was nervous already.

"Yes, that's the reason we're going." He laughed. "You don't want to meet them?"

"No." I was confused. "I mean yes. It's not that I don't want to meet them, but you don't think it's too soon?" Strangely, the good thing about Damian was that he had no family. Therefore, I never had to worry about anyone judging me. Tremel knew that I wasn't a big fan of seeking approval. When I saw the area code 216 on the caller ID, I shouted for him to pick up, and if he wasn't home, the call went straight to voicemail.

"We've been together over two months now." Then he added, "I thought we were looking to be long term."

"We are, but I'm not good with parents, meeting family and all that stuff," I said. "Why don't you go and I'll just stay here? We can go together another time." I wasn't the average woman; I couldn't even cook. "What if your mom asked me to help her in the kitchen?"

"Then I'll call the fire department," he joked. "I'm just kidding. Relax. Everything will be all right."

Relax? I was about to have an anxiety attack. "Maybe we can go for Easter or something." I was making up anything, any holiday, just not the one that was three weeks away.

"I've told my mom about you," he said.

"You did?" My heat skipped about eight beats. Mothers wanted their sons with girls who loved to cook, clean, bake, and sew. The majority of things I cooked were also microwaveable. Why bake a cake when you can buy it? If something had to be sewn, that meant it went to Goodwill. I was clean, but only where it counted. I didn't lift up the rug or move a chair to look for dirt more than once a month.

"My mother will love you." He took my hand. "Let's book our flights."

It was settled. We were flying to Cleveland late Wednesday night and coming back on Sunday afternoon. To me, the stay was too long. I had no idea what I could do with strangers for four days. Tremel was pumped up about us staying in his old room, which meant even more time around his family. I wasn't thrilled. Thank God when he called his mother and learned that both of his grandparents, an uncle, and a few aunts would also be there, he elected to stay at a hotel so that his older relatives could enjoy the comfort of his parents' home.

On Thursday as I cleaned, I stumbled upon the safe in my closet and found the camera and three rolls of film I stole when I left Norman's hotel room in Atlanta. Quickly I wondered what the pictures looked like. For a moment, I wondered what Norman's real intentions were, who the other guy was, and how many times they had done what they did to other girls.

Call me foolish, but I wanted to see the pictures. I jumped in my truck and didn't stop until I was thirty minutes south, in Kendall, in front of Will's house. William Tout, a gay white photographer I met in college, was a good friend of mine. Seeing some of the pictures he took and developed in his personal darkroom, I knew that my shots would be just another walk in the park for him.

"So, what's on these rolls, missy?" he asked as I handed him the envelope.

"You'll see." I grinned. "But this stays between you and me, Will."

"Honey, I do more than gossip with these lips," he

joked. "When do you want them back?"

"When do you think you can have them ready?"

"In the morning if George doesn't come over tonight."

"And if he comes over?" I asked.

"Then next week." He laughed. "I'm kidding. I'll have them tomorrow."

"Thanks." I hugged him.

He waved his finger from left to right and left again. "I'm not charging you since I know that you're broke and shit, but you will be getting black and whites."

"No problem." I kissed him on the cheek and left. He was ready to get into my business. He couldn't help it. Before I even pulled back into my apartment complex, my phone was ringing. "You nasty bitch," Will said. "I am so jealous of you."

"Why?"

"I only have two done right now, but they look great," Will said.

"Which two?"

"Let's just say you have a mouthful."

"Oh." I sighed. "They get much worse."

"One question. Does he have a brother?"

"You are such a tramp. What about George?"

"I'm sick of Italian sausage. I think it's time for a long, fat, juicy African treat," he joked.

I was about to throw up on my steering wheel. "Can you see my face in these two pictures?"

"Yes. But honey, I know that you aren't married." He paused. "However, your friend needs to know that if he wants to be in pictures he should remove his wedding band because a broke bitch like you might try to find his wife and sell these pictures to her to use against him in court." He laughed. "I'll have them ready tomorrow. I just had to call you and tell you what a sexy slut you are."

"Thanks." A light bulb went off in my head. "I'll pick them up tomorrow," I said. "Talk to you later, sweetie."

"All right." He hung up.

Will had turned on an idea that I immediately began to work over in my mind. I sat in my truck for about fifteen minutes, figuring out exactly how I was going to make Elite work for me. I had made all the arrangements for the Elite girls to attend the ending of the Black Businessmen of America Association convention being held in Trenton, New Jersey this week. This was a big event. Thirty girls were set to arrive in Trenton the next day, which was Friday. I knew who would be with whom and at what time. I had all of the men's real names, hotel information, aliases, profiles created by Stefani, and their credit card information, which included their home billing addresses. I had everything I needed to put some money in my pocket and help some of these men's wives walk away from their men financially fat.

That's right, I was about to unleash havoc on the Elite. "In your face, Conrad." I smiled as I looked at the camera. I ran upstairs and used my site to plan my own trip. I was going to New Jersey the next afternoon to bring the pain. I did a few loads of laundry, and as soon as I started packing, Tremel walked in. "Whoa," he said. "Where are you going?"

"To see Daddy," I lied.

"Is everything all right?" He was concerned.

"Yeah, a mild asthma attack," I said. "I'm leaving tomorrow afternoon. I'm flying into New Jersey. Everything else was costing way too much."

"Is he okay?" Tremel asked.

"Yeah, he didn't have to be hospitalized." I actually did call Daddy. "But I just want to be sure that everything is okay."

"How did he sound?" Tremel asked.

"He sounded all right," I said. "But I just want to check him out, just to be certain."

He didn't sound too pleased. "And you   *have* to go tomorrow?"

"Tremel, I want to see him. I'll be with you and your family during the Thanksgiving holiday, but Daddy will be all by himself. I know it's short notice, but I really want to be sure that he's all right."

"Okay, I feel you." He sat next to my suitcase on the bed. "I guess I can't keep you to myself all the time."

"Aw, you're gonna miss me." I smiled. "I'll be back on Monday."

He picked me up around the waist and rested me on the bed. "I can't wait until Monday."

For the next two hours, I thought of nothing while Tremel put a move on my heart. When we made love, it was more than just two bodies pressed up against each other. We were connected in every way; I could feel his inner man. He was the kind of lover that made a woman think there wasn't another man on the planet like hers. Whenever Tremel and I made love one thing was always certain; at the end I was in tears, not from physical pain or emotional angst, but tears of the purest joy.

In Trenton, I checked into the hotel and rushed to my room to get set for the big weekend. All weekend I wore baggy clothing, ponytails, glasses, hats, and anything else I could find to alter my appearance. On the first night I strolled into the lounge with the camera and immediately befriended Javier, a young Latin guy. Javier had no clue that he was a part of a well-conceived plan. It was falling in line too easily. After a few drinks, I told him that I was a photographer at a fashion magazine based in Miami and asked him if he was a model. I acted completely flabbergasted when he said that he wasn't. I pretended to be intrigued by his style and told him how I knew someone that was searching for a model with his look.

I convinced Javier that I was vacationing in Trenton and didn't have my professional equipment, but would love to take photos of him with my regular camera. I told him that I'd see to it that the right people saw the pictures and he'd be receiving a call. Javier jumped at the deal. While he posed, I pretended to be focusing on him, but his surroundings were really getting all of the attention. The zoom lens was a marvel. I had close-ups of the Elite girls and their men kissing, touching, bumping and grinding on the dance floor. I knew who each girl was by the pictures on their profiles on my computer at home, and it would be a cinch to go look up the man I had scheduled her to be with.

I told Javier that I wanted some other shots of him, and he decided on the pool. It was pure genius; this guy was in my head. The poolside was Black Businessmen paradise. They were everywhere, and had no shame as they partied with girls young enough to be their daughters or in some cases, granddaughters. Javier was acting like he had hit the rollover lottery with me. He even bought me a few drinks. The poor soul didn't even know that in most shots I only got his arm, the top of his head, or his kneecap, but there was big money to be made in the things going on in the background.

Javier and I went to the eighth floor; the floor

where the girls were staying. I had him stand by an artificial tree next to the elevator. I snapped shots of men holding hands with their girls as they stepped off. The elevator doors opened up with not only girls wiping their mouths, fixing their dresses and hair, but also with men patting napkins to their mouths and zipping up their pants.

On Monday morning, I flew back to Miami with nine rolls of film. Four guys believed that they'd be hearing from a modeling agency within the next seventy-two hours. Error! I drove from the airport to Will's house. Without giving too much information, I promised him two thousand dollars to develop the pictures and not speak of word of them to anyone. I got home and researched on my computer. Jackpot! Everything was at my fingertips: phone numbers, addresses, and most importantly, names.

Tremel walked in. "Hi, honey," I said from the living room as I approached him.

"Hey." He wasn't as enthusiastic as I imagined he'd be.

"How have you been?" I grabbed his hand.

"I'm fine." I could tell that something was wrong. "How is your father?" He let go of my hand and walked to the kitchen.

"He's okay," I said.

"He's okay, huh?"

"Yeah." This was the trip where I really hadn't done anything wrong. "Why?"

"Nothing." He opened the refrigerator and poured milk into a glass.

"What?" I was nervous.

"Nothing, Sarai." He looked at me for the first time

since walking into the apartment.

"Tremel, what's wrong?" I regretted lying to him. "Why are you giving me attitude?"

"Attitude?" he asked. "I'm not giving you attitude. I just asked how your father was doing."

"But why do you keep asking me that?"

"Probably because the nursing home called here early this morning looking for you," he said calmly.

"Oh my God." My heartbeat was off the chart. "What happened? What did they say?"

"You tell me, Sarai." He raised his voice at me for the first time since I'd known him. "Where were you?"

I was speechless. "I told you where I was."

"Please don't lie to me." He lookcd at me with eyes I knew needed to know the truth. He begged me. "Please tell me the truth."

I still wasn't giving it up. "What did they say when they called?" I asked.

"It was a Nurse Gray. She said that it was an emergency. She also said that you needed to call her and oh, she said that she hadn't seen you in a while." Then he repeated, "She hasn't seen you in a while." He got closer to me. "Tell me where you were."

I dialed the number to the nursing home on the speakerphone while Tremel stared at me. "Hello, may I please speak with Nurse Gray?" She had never called me before. I just hoped that everything was okay. I was shaking by the time she picked up the phone. "Nurse Gray, this is Sarai Emery. Did you call me? Is everything okay?"

"Ah yes, Sarai," she said. "How are you?"

"I'm fine," I rushed. "Is my father all right?"

"Oh yes, he's doing great."

"Okay. Was there a reason you called?"

"Yes, it seems that every time you come to town to see him, I'm off. I haven't seen you in quite a while. The only reason I knew that you were here this weekend is because I was processing the check that you left, but you forgot to put your driver's license number on it." She continued. "I can't put the payment through without it."

"Oh okay, hold a sec. Let me get it." I grabbed my purse and fished through it. I did visit my dad on Sunday. I drove from Trenton to Dover, 160 miles roundtrip. I spent four hours with him and paid for another two months, so he was good until March. I returned to the phone and gave Nurse Gray what she needed. "Anything else?" I asked.

"No, darling," she said. "Just call me the next time you're coming so that I can plan to see you."

"I will." I pressed the speaker button off. Tremel was quiet. He had the word embarrassed written all over his handsome face. I made a move to leave the kitchen, but he reached for my hand and pulled me over to him. "Oops," he said.

"Where did you think I was?" I punched him on his arm gently.

He smiled a little. "You weren't here."

I rolled my eyes playfully and said, "You owe me fifty apologies."

As I looked at the tiled floor, he lifted my head with his hand beneath my chin. "I just missed you." He kissed me softly on the lips. "I'm sorry." He slid his mouth down to my neck. "I jumped to conclusions." Tremel lifted my shirt above my head. "I was wrong." My bra was unhooked next, and I watched it fall to the floor. "I just allowed my mind to over-think." His fingertips roamed my hills and valleys, and I allowed my body to enjoy his touch. "I was dead wrong, baby." He unbuckled my pants and pushed them toward the ground. "I apologize." He didn't remove my panties, but he picked me up, laid me on the dining room table, where he pulled my thong to the side and I became his five-course meal. He penetrated me with his tongue and I trembled. "Damn, I've missed you," he said.

We moved to the loveseat where he gave himself to me for dessert. I was facing him as I lowered my body to him and wrapped my hands around his neck. I felt him within me as I softly bounced up and down on him. "Do you accept my apology?" he asked with his hands on my waist.

"No," I said as I grinded myself into him.

"You don't?"

I shook my head from side to side. "Nope."

Tremel suddenly stood up and lifted me, putting my back against the wall. As he slid more of himself in, he looked me in the face. "So, you're never going to forgive me?" he asked.

I wrapped my legs around him and looked into his eyes. "Why should I?"

He began poking me hard and fast. "Shit." I thought I had died and gone to some sort of heaven. "Oh my God," I said as I held onto him around the neck.

"You forgiving me now, huh?" He smiled.

Lord, he felt good. "Damn." He moved a little faster, and I thrust myself to him each time.

"Tell me that you're sorry for not believing me," I said into his ear.

"I'm sorry," he said.

"Say it again."

"I'm sorry." I made him apologize about ten times, and each time he sunk himself deeper than the time before. I wasn't going to be upstaged. I started wiggling, jiggling, and whipping him with it. "Damn girl," he groaned. "Oh yeah." He kissed me. "I love it." Just when I thought I had control, he sped up and ran me out of power. "Ah, you can't take it," he said. "You can't handle me." My eyes rolled back and my body began shaking like I couldn't remember it doing before. He completely filled me. "Oh God, oh God, oh God," I yelled over and over. I didn't care if the folks in the next apartment could hear. He slowed down and looked at me. "You forgive me now?" he groaned.

"Why should I?" I asked him with a playfully intense stare.

He guided his chocolate wand deep into me again and made magic with it. He cast spells of love, lust, passion, and screams within my walls. My flesh called out to him, and before long my mouth was doing the same. He kissed and felt me everywhere, but one thing remained the same, he kept asking my forgiveness. In my heart, I had forgotten the situation, but the passion that built by saying no was incredible. He knew the game I was playing; it excited him too. He asked me over and over and continued to make mad fervent love to me. "I'm not gonna stop until you say yes." He thrust himself faster and deeper into me. He seemed hotter and thicker than ever before. "Do you accept my apology?" He was too good. I was biting my lips, digging into his back, screaming, groaning, and grinding him. I lost the battle. He was the victor, too much of a challenger for me, so I succumbed to him. "Yes, baby. Yes, I forgive you."

"Say it again." There was sweat coming from every pore.

I moaned. "I forgive you." Tremel let out a loud grunt, closed his eyes, and fastened his lips to mine. I felt his body freeze, shiver, and then collapse onto mine as we slid down the wall together. Our night was far from over, though. Tremel apologized to me four more times using, his body as the peace offering.

"A man who loses his money gains, at the least, experience, and sometimes, something better."
–Benjamin "Dizzy" Disraeli

Bank Statement # 14

Account Balance: $29,489.30

On Monday I sent overnight mail to sixteen different women. The packages all included pictures. The pictures that they received were innocent yet questionable. I was hoping that it'd make them want to see more. In the photos their husbands were talking to, touching, or having dinner with another woman. Each envelope also contained a note that read: *Shh! Be expecting my call.*

I wasn't phoning Tronquesha up the street. I had to know what I was doing to get through to these women. It was going to take more than street smarts, Ebonics, and old school girl talk. These women were probably highly educated, self-sufficient, and not easily intimidated. They had money; their husbands were partners at law firms, physicians, business owners, producers, and dentists. I was praying that they were smart enough to see past my obvious blackmail scheme and see that their black males were scheming.

Tuesday afternoon using my cellular phone, I reluctantly dialed through my calling card to the first number. My breakfast was gone, butterflies overtook my stomach, and I was shaking like a leaf. I had written out what I was supposed to say and practiced the script numerous times, however, what were these women going to say to me? "There is only one way to find out," I said as I pressed the final digit. Before I placed the phone to my ear, someone was already on the other line. "Hello?" She picked up on the first ring. "Hello?" the middle-aged female repeated.

"Yes." I tried hard not to use my regular voice. "Hello, may I please speak with Mrs. Stewart?"

"This is she." She sounded pissed. "Who are you?"

"Good day, Mrs. Stewart." I had to keep my cool. "My name is Tatiana Graham." I paused. "Did you receive a package in the mail today?"

"I sure did." Then she went off. "Who are you? Why in the hell are you trying to break up my home? How long have you known my husband?"

I tried to remain focused. "Mrs. Stewart, I can explain, but first I'll need you to calm down."

"Don't tell me what you need me to do," she screeched. "I don't know you."

"Mrs. Stewart, I am not the woman in the picture." I needed her to trust me. "I'm calling to try to help you. Like I said a moment ago, my name is Tatiana Graham. I am a private investigator out of Trenton, New Jersey." I read from my script. "While I was working a case last week. I ran into your husband and this other woman and I thought you should know about it."

"How do you know my husband?"

I did my research. "That's not important. The fact is that I knew that he was married and the woman he was with wasn't you."

She started crying. "Well, who in the hell is she?"

"Honestly, Mrs. Stewart, that is a question only

your husband can answer." I took a deep breath. "I don't know her name, but I do know that she is someone that Mr. Stewart is seeing intimately whenever he's quote-unquote out of town on business," I said. "I'm contacting you and other women like you today because I walked five miles in your shoes. I was married to a man that lied and cheated every chance he had. You, just like I did, deserve more than this."

"When was this picture taken?" she asked.

The picture she was looking at was her husband and Star, the Elite girl, sitting in a booth in the hotel lounge having drinks. Innocent photo, you think? Try again. Star was sitting on his lap dangling the cherry from her drink on the tip of his tongue. "The picture you're looking at was taken over the weekend at—"

"The Black Businessmen convention." She finished my sentence then let out a sound of pain. "That lousy fuckin' bastard." Forget being proper, emotions had this sistah catching a ride on the bus to Ghettoland. "I can't believe that this li'l dick, fat muthafucka has the nerve to be cheatin' on me." Her rage intensified. "After all these goddamn years."

"Mrs. Stewart, I'm truly sorry," I sympathized then went right for the jugular. "I went through the same thing, which is the reason I started my PI business." I took a breath. "I followed my husband on what was supposed to be a business trip, but instead I walked into his hotel room and met a woman on top of him."

"Oh my God," she exclaimed. "I would've killed him." She didn't stop there. "I would've grabbed him by his shit and bit it off."

"Well, I did the next best thing. I filed for divorce and showed the judge the pictures of him and his mistress around town that a friend of mine had taken a week before I caught them. Honey, I cleaned his ass out completely." I laughed and added, "Alimony is a lovely thing. That's how I started my own business, *and* I kept both houses." I sweetened the pot.

"You go, girl." She tried to laugh but sniffled instead. "That's what his trifling ass gets."

"That's what they all need to get," I said.

"You're absolutely right," she said weakly. "I still can't believe that this is happening to me. I am so damn good to this man. I cook, clean, take care of the children, make sure that I'm in shape, and fuck his bad body ass whenever he wants me to . . . " Her voice trailed off and I couldn't make out anything else.

"Forget being his wife for free; being his ex-wife might be more rewarding." I continued my pitch. "Mrs. Stewart, with the pictures that I have of your husband, you'll walk away with—"

"Pictures?" she interrupted me. "I only have one. You have more pictures?"

"Yes, I do," I said.

"Why didn't you send 'em all?" she asked. "Send them to me. I want to see all of 'em."

"I'll send them under one circumstance," I said firmly.

"What?"

"Don't turn the other cheek and let him do this to you again." I had to play the role.

"Oh, hell no. You don't have to worry about that. I always thought that fat fuck was up to no good," she said. "Send me the pictures. You only get one chance to make a fool out of Virginia."

I smiled. "The picture I sent you is sadly just the beginning of his evening with this young lady. I have eighteen more of Mr. Stewart during the convention but

240

they may be hard to look at." I wasn't lying. I actually had a picture of Star on her knees in front of Mr. Stewart in what they thought was a dark alley. After Will brightened it up, the picture was a sight to behold.

"I can't believe this." She was sobbing. "Please send them."

"I'm sorry, Mrs. Stewart." I really was. "Are you okay?"

"Yes, I just can't believe this." She was hyperventilating.

"Mrs. Stewart, I didn't call you today to hurt you. I just wanted you to be aware of what was going on. The truth of the matter is that I can't send you the pictures without you being a client of mine. I could lose my business taking pictures of your husband without you hiring me to do so. Mr. Stewart could actually sue me. He's a lawyer, and he knows all of that."

"Well, as of right now, I am your client. You have my consent to go to the convention and find out what he's really doing," she said. "I want those pictures. What do I have to do to get them?"

I took a deep breath. "First off, you might want to keep your findings on the down low until you make a definite decision and speak to a divorce attorney. Telling him about the pictures will give him too much time to confer with his legal team. We have to catch him off-guard." I had no idea what I was saying, but it sounded good. Watching Court TV was paying off.

"That's what I was planning on doing." She continued hurriedly. "How much do you want for the pictures?" She was making this too easy for me.

"I won't charge you as much as I normally do." I pretended to be calculating figures. "How about two hundred and seventy five dollars each?" I closed my eyes and waited for the rejection.

"I don't give a damn. It's his money anyway," she huffed. "Send me all of them."

In another forty minutes, I promised Mrs. Stewart that she'd receive all of the pictures as soon as the blank money orders, totaling $4,950, were in my hand. To guarantee her that I was looking at pictures of her man, I told her what he was wearing in some of the pictures. I also told her that if she didn't have the pictures at least four days after sending off the money orders, she could call the police. My fingerprints were all over the picture that she had in her possession, and that was the truth.

By the end of our talk, she was willing to Western Union the money to me. I declined her offer because I'd have to give her my real name in order to claim the money. I instructed her to send the money orders to a post office box that I opened while I was in Trenton. However, I asked the postal worker to forward my mail to a Miami post office box, belonging to Mrs. White. Tremel had given me the key to check his mail two months ago. I still checked it twice a week, and I had the only key.

For the next six and a half hours, I talked to fourteen other women, but only eight of them bought into my black male photo gallery. Six women were comfortable with not seeing anything more. They claimed that they knew about their men, and as long as they were was bringing home the bacon and not an STD, it didn't matter. I was cursed out several times, called everything, and told that they'd report me if I contacted them again. One brainwashed asshole of a wife had the nerve to put her "dick been everywhere" husband on the line. But still, after the chips were down, they didn't fall the way I had planned, but I was still looking at collecting $42,300 within a week.

Going Broke

In the midst of my jubilee, I suddenly thought of what those women were feeling, what I had selfishly put them through just so I could pay my rent. I tried to justify my actions, reasoning that I did what I did to free them from their doggish men, but once again, I was in it for the love of money. I had once more proven to myself that not only was I willing to hurt myself, but also others all for the love of that mean green.

The last call I made was a courtesy call. It was to the wife of the owner of the camera, Norman Hall. It turned out that he was the owner of several jewelry stores in Ohio. His wife sounded like she was going to meet her maker when she answered the phone. I expected that reaction from her because her package was different than the ones sent to other women. I sent her twelve pictures of Norman and I having sex. I didn't ask her for money; I just wanted her rapist of a husband to be exposed. I told Sheila the truth: I was the woman in the picture, and her husband paid to have sex with me but played too rough. I told her how I begged him to stop but he wouldn't. His friend snapped the pictures, and I was able to escape only when she called Norman on his cell phone.

By Friday, over half the money I was expecting was already in my bank account. I mailed out all of the pictures and was sitting pretty until I thought about the dangerous reality of what I had done. I was sure that the husbands would somehow want to know who the private investigator behind the pictures was. I was paranoid times ten, walking around like a crackhead, looking over my shoulders, swearing I heard someone calling my name, and scared to turn corners.

I was even reluctant to meet Nat at the restaurant

243

on Ocean Drive where we agreed to have drinks. Nat and I hadn't seen a lot of each other lately, so I made the sacrifice and drove the short distance. I got there at 7:00. We first wanted alone time to catch up on all of the talking we missed out on, so we asked Nick and Tremel to allow us two hours together and to meet us at 9:30 for dinner. "So, how are you treating my buddy Mel?" Nat asked from across the table.

My mind was still cloudy. "Mel is fine." I added, "You should know, you see him every day at school."

"I know, but I asked how you're treating him." She smiled.

"He's okay." I hadn't touched my drink yet. "We're okay." I looked over at a man at another table. I thought sure I heard him say my name. I was trippin'.

"Are you okay?" She looked at me strangely. "You're like on another planet."

"I'm fine," I lied. "Just thought I heard something."

"Well, hear me, damn it," she joked. "Are you still looking for a job?"

"Not really," I said.

"So, what are you doing for money these days?"

I snapped. "What are you trying to say?"

"Whoa, li'l mama." Nat threw her hands up jokingly. "Who you think you talkin' to?" She playfully put her dukes up.

"Damn." I dropped my head. "I'm sorry."

"What's wrong with you?" She pushed her drink aside. "Don't tell me that Tremel has insufficient funds in his dick account," she said with a smile.

"Naw." My eyes welled up with tears.

"Talk to me." I stared at her for a while. There was too much to say. For me to tell her about what was happening now, I'd have to start from how I got involved

244

in it all in the first place. I opened my mouth. "Nat, I got myself involved in something crazy." I was close to crying already. "It's a long story."

She looked at her watch. "We have two hours before they'll be here. It can't be that long of a story." She reached over and touched my hand. "Start talking."

"I don't even know where to start."

"At the beginning. My ears are wide open," she said.

I took a deep breath. "Well, it all started when I went to the Bahamas . . . " Over the next thirty minutes, I told Nat everything from my first meeting with Conrad all the way to me playing photographer in Trenton then making the phone calls. By the end, she had moved from across the table to sitting next to me in the booth.

"You made a few bad decisions, Sarai, but that doesn't make you a bad person." "Especially if you've learned from your mistakes."

"Honestly, I don't know if I've learned. I'm just scared about getting caught."

"Caught by whom?" she asked.

"It eats me up to think of what will happen to me and Tremel if he finds out. I've been lying to him since day one. I slept with Doctor Baker right before our first date. It's been one lie after another, over and over and over again." I wiped my eyes. "If I loved him so much, then why would I do this to him?"

Nat's voice was so soothing. "I believe that you love him, but you're also human."

"Humans know better, though."

"But they also make mistakes." She continued with her logic. "Now you have to confess them to him."

"Confess to him? He ain't a damn Catholic priest." We both laughed.

"You've got to tell him, Sarai," she said.

"Tell him?" I looked at her like she had just slapped me. "I can't tell him about any of this."

"Yes, you can," she said.

"What would I tell him, Nat?"

"Tell him the truth about what you've been doing."

I tried hard to decrease the value of what I did. "It's not like I'm still doing it."

"But in order for you to have peace of mind, you have to tell him something."

I rolled my eyes. "The only thing my mind isn't peaceful about is Conrad and these men coming after me," I said. "I'm through with everything else."

"Okay, I understand. But what if he finds out from someone else?"

"Shit." The thought made me sick to my stomach. What Nat was trying to get me to do was right, but I'd rather be wrong and still have a man. "I can't lose him."

"The way I see it if, he loves you, then you won't lose him." She smiled.

"What are you smoking? I want some." I tried to keep my voice down. "He is not gonna want anything to do with my trifling ass if I tell him."

"Trust me, Sarai, you won't be able to keep this a secret very long. Something is bound to fall out of line. Tell him something, a piece of the truth. It's better than nothing at all." She believed every word she said.

"Even a piece of the truth is too much." I was angry. "I was having sex with other men, and it doesn't just stop there. I was doing it for money. Nat, I can't think of any man who would want to stay with a woman knowing that she's been fucking other men while they've been in a relationship."

"Sarai, you're never going to have peace of mind if

246

you're always worried about Tremel finding out."

"Nat, I actually wasn't worried until I started talking to your cleanse my-soul-ass," I joked. "I was fine. The only thing I was worried about was those men looking for me, but you've got me on a brand new level."

She looked at me. "That damn boy is crazy about you."

"I know, but he'll go crazy *on* me if I tell him."

She asked, "Do you love him?"

I rushed my answer out. "Without a doubt."

"So, how do you feel about lying to him?"

"I feel terrible about it."

"Would you rather him learn about this through somebody else?" she asked.

"No. I wish I could tell him," I whined, "but I can't."

"You know what? Don't even worry about hurting his feelings, because I have something to tell you." She turned the table on me. "He's been sleeping with a math teacher for the last six months.

"What?" My anger spiked off the charts. "What?"

Nat answered nonchalantly. "I hear that they might still be messing around, but I don't know."

I thought my stomach was coming out of my mouth. "Why didn't you say this before?"

"See, that's exactly what I mean." She laughed. "Isn't it worse to hear something from someone who doesn't know the story, or someone who only knows the bad part of the story, rather than hearing it from the horse's mouth?" She added, "Compare what I just said, which was gossip, to Tremel coming to you and saying, 'I just want you to know that I used to date a teacher at the school where I work. She and I were still trying to establish something when I met you, but when you and I started getting serious, and I realized that I had feelings

247

for you, I told her that I didn't think that we should see each other like that any longer.' "

I took a deep breath. "You were about to get him a severe case of foot in his ass."

She laughed. "You can't get mad at anybody."

"Yes, I can," I said.

"Okay, now all jokes aside, didn't it sound better coming from him than from someone who is adding on or doesn't know exactly what's going on?"

"Yeah," I agreed. "I see your point, but please see mine."

"I see what you're saying, Sarai." Nat and I talked a lot more, and at the end of our conversation, I had concluded that I still wasn't confessing anything to Tremel. Knowing that our relationship was new, I didn't feel that it was strong enough to handle what I had to say. I also couldn't figure out what avenue of my life could ever lead to Tremel finding out. I was willing to take my chances. I hated lying to him, but I loved him too much to tell him the truth.

By the time Tremel and Nick arrived, I had already returned from the restroom where I washed my face, reapplied my makeup, and was looking just like I did when I arrived. Nat, Nick, Tremel, and I ate together, danced, and drank late into the night. Later, all four of us did something that people living in Florida could do on a daily basis but rarely take advantage of. We walked on the beach.

Holding hands and kicking sand reconfirmed that Tremel was the best thing that had ever happened to me. I regretted blowing the first opportunity I had to be with him when I met him at Nat's party; that would've given me extra time in his arms. However, in four months he went from being a janitor I didn't deem worthy of

248

conversation to being the light that lit the way in my life. I was in love with him. When I was with him, I smiled the way five-year-olds did when they see a McDonald's Playplace.

When my feet touched the Cleveland soil the night before Thanksgiving, I was a ball of tremors, not from the plane ride, but from pure nervousness about meeting his family. We grabbed our bags from the conveyor belt around 10:00, and I was glad that Avis Rent-a-Car had a crowd. We didn't get out of the rental office until after midnight. I welcomed his thought that it was too late to visit his parents' house, so we rode straight to the Hyatt and checked in.

Tremel had no problem getting to sleep, but all I could think about were his parents, his three sisters, and two brothers. It didn't stop there. Both sets of his grandparents were alive. He had a total of eight uncles and six aunts who would be there too, not to mention all of his cousins, too many to count.

I was from a very small family. My father had no brothers or sisters, so I didn't have uncles, aunts, or cousins, and his parents died long before my birth. My mother's family was in Utah. Savion and I saw our maternal grandparents once a year, but they both died before we were ten. Once they were gone, no one bothered to keep in contact. Thanksgiving was always just a Cornish hen, Daddy, Savion, and me. Big family gatherings were new to me.

When Tremel rolled over at six and started rubbing my arm, he thought that he had woken me, but I was up, never down. "Good morning," he said.

"Hey." I turned over slowly. "How did you sleep?"

"I was out for the count," he said. "I can't even

remember saying goodnight to you."

"You didn't. When I came out of the shower you were gone."

"I'm sorry." He apologized but he didn't have to. The previous day when he got in from work, all he had time to do was take a shower before we hit the road to the airport.

"How did you sleep?" he asked.

I wanted to pretend that things were fine, but I lied to him enough. "I haven't had a moment's rest."

"Why not?"

"I'm nervous," I said.

"Baby, I thought we were past that."

"I thought so too, until we got off the plane." I laughed.

"Get some rest baby. We have a long day ahead of us." He hummed softly and rocked me to sleep. When I woke up, it was after 11:00 and he was looking out of the window, completely dressed. As I stretched, he walked over to the bed. "How did you sleep?"

"Fine, thank you," I smiled.

"Good." He looked at his watch and joked. "Now get your ass up and let's get out of here." He lifted me out of bed. The next stop was the bathroom where he dropped me off and closed the door behind him. Damian and a few other ex-boyfriends all had Tremel beat financially, but they paled in comparison to Tremel's love for me. In just a few months, he had outdone everyone in my past. If his family was anything like him, they'd love me just as he did, but the guilt of what I did behind his back made me believe that it'd be written all over my face and they'd sniff me out.

"Stop the car. I think I'm going to be sick," I joked

right after Tremel announced that we were less than five minutes from his parents' house.

"You always have a bunch of mouth," he touched me on the cheek, "but you're nothing but a scaredy cat."

"I don't wanna go," I whined jokingly then reached for the door handle. "I'm gonna jump out."

He laughed. "Go ahead. I'll slow down." I smacked him playfully on the arm. In a few minutes, we pulled up in front of a light blue two-story house. The violets carefully planted all around the house played up the color, and so did the beautiful, freshly cut, thick green grass. As we walked up the sidewalk, I became even more curious about what was going on being behind the frosted oval glass of the white French doors.

"There is no turning back." Tremel looked at me and slid his key into the lock. "Don't be scared." He kissed me on the forehead and pushed the door open. As the air inside rushed out past me, I smelled turkey, dressing, macaroni, potato salad, pumpkin pie, cranberry sauce, and much more. He didn't have to beg me. I wanted to run inside. As I entered, I heard a lot of talking, laughing, pot and pans, but over everything was the loud voice of a sports commentator describing the last play of the current football game.

The white tiled floor sparkled as if diamonds were scattered over it. A chubby little boy about three feet tall peeked out of a door and pointed. "That's Uncle Mel." Before he could put his finger down, people flooded the hallway with hugs and smiles. I was introduced to everyone but couldn't remember a name if my life depended on it. Right after learning a name, I had a new name and a new face to smile at. I shook hands and said, "Hi, nice to meet you," or "Hello, I've heard so much about you."

Tremel's father didn't look like I imagined he would. He was very light-skinned and tall. He was also thin enough to fly away with a kite on a not so windy day. I blushed as Tremel introduced me as his girlfriend. His father talked to me a while before he yelled for his wife to come out of the kitchen. "This is Sarai, Mel's lady friend." His mother was about my height, with long, straight brown hair combed into a neat ponytail. She weighed more than her husband, but who didn't? She was peanut butter brown like Tremel and me. I felt faint for a split second as she stared at me. "Nice to meet you, honey. Welcome to Thanksgiving at the Colten's house." She wrapped her arms around me. "I told Mel that you have such a pretty name. Did he tell you?"

I looked at him. "No, ma'am, he sure didn't."

"Why didn't you tell her what I said?" She embraced her baby boy. "I missed you so much." She kissed him on the cheek and squeezed him again. We stood in the corridor talking until some other family members strolled in and we had to move out of the way. Tremel held my hand and started to show me around the house. As we were going upstairs, his mother sideswiped us. "I need some help with the greens," she said to me.

My eyes widened. "You mean collard greens?" Yes, I am an African-American woman who has no clue how to prepare those things.

"Uh-huh," she said.

Everything else happened in slow motion. "Okay," I said and looked at Tremel, who offered me a look of concern then smiled at his mother, who in turn took my hand away from his. "Don't worry. I just need you to strip the pot." He kissed me on the cheek and watched me walk away to the kitchen.

Sabrina Colten was as sweet as she could be. After

252

spending time with her, I saw that she was no one to fear. We weren't alone. Her mother and mother-in-law were both sitting at the kitchen table giving their old-time recipe instructions. Two out of her five sisters were also present, and though they were twice my age, they looked like they were clueless about cooking. However, Tremel's three aunts on his father's side were burning right alongside his mother. She really didn't need me to do anything; I think it was her way of breaking the tension. It was obvious that Tremel's father's sisters thought that they were master chefs. So by talking to me every once in a while, Mrs. Colten didn't have to pay them no mind. Along with asking me about myself, she'd throw in a "Baby pass me the salt," or "Sweetie, let me get some sugar," or "Do you see that spoon I left over there?" every time her sisters-in-law got on her nerves.

I heard the front door open and close many times, but if someone didn't come into the kitchen, I wasn't going to meet them. It was my golden rule. I found comfort in the family members I had already met. Before long, I was walking through the garden with the grandmothers. They loved me already. Mrs. Colten, Tremel's paternal grandmother, was eighty-one and Mrs. Hall, Tremel's maternal grandmother, was seventy-nine. However, they both had a lot of spunk in them. There must have been something in the Ohio River. As we strolled, they talked about Tremel being such a mischievous child. In his younger days, he was always playing tricks on people and starting up some form of trouble.

Everyone in Tremel's family was shocked that God would give such a sweet singing voice to such a little clown. No one even knew that Tremel's li'l bad butt could sing until he was ten years old and was in the Sunday school Christmas play. When he opened his mouth to sing "Silent Night" the church folks were on fire. The boy had them shouting like the pastor had just delivered the Word three times over.

Once we were back inside, it was almost time to eat. Tremel's mother issued me the task of walking through the house to count how many people were present. She instructed me to open any and every closed door so that she'd have an accurate headcount. The older people were watching football in the family room. I counted fourteen folks there. Eight teenage boys were in a bedroom flipping back and forth from the football game to BET videos. In the kitchen, there were eleven people including myself. In a bedroom down the hall, I found ten children playing and I ran into seven teenage girls upstairs.

I saw a closed door at the end of the upstairs hall and sashayed toward it. I knocked on it twice before I tried to turn the knob. It was locked, so I shrugged my shoulders and turned to leave. Less than a foot away I heard the lock click. "You need something?" I heard a man ask. I turned to say no but ended up not being able to say anything at all, the man I was staring at was Norman Hall, better known as the cameraman. I was frozen, and when his eyes focused in on who I really was, his face reddened with anger.

It took him one step to get into my face. He grabbed me by the neck and pulled me into the room. "What the fuck are you trying to do to me?" Before I could say a word, his hand squeezed even tighter around my throat. "Don't you think sending those fuckin' pictures did enough? What the fuck do you think you're doing?" he asked.

I couldn't talk; I couldn't even breathe. I was

losing oxygen and he didn't give a damn. I reached for his hand and tried pulling it away, but I couldn't. I shook my head from side to side. My eyes were pleading with his, but it didn't matter. I had never been so afraid of anyone in my entire life, and in a split second things got worse. There was a knock on the door. "Uncle Norm." I heard Tremel's voice outside the door. "Uncle Norm, you in there?" I wanted to scream for help, but I couldn't, and even if I could, I'd have a lot more explaining to do.

Norman's eyes got even wider, like they'd pop out and roll to the ground. "Gimme a minute," he yelled, then held his finger to his mouth and pushed me inside the closet. Through the vent, I watched Norman's shoes trail back to the door. "Hey, what's up Mel?" he said as he opened the door. "How you doing? When did you get here?"

I saw the bottom of Mel's jeans move closer to Norman. They hugged quickly. "Me and my girl flew up from Miami last night," Tremel said.

"All right. Good to see you again, man. Damn, you're pretty buffed. You still lifting?" Norman asked.

"Yeah, I've been doing a little something," he said.

Norman asked, "So, how are things with your music?"

"Well, I finished my demo. I've been sending it out to different labels, but getting in there is a bitch." He paused. "My girl has been helping me get in contact with the right people. Hopefully by the time we get back home, we'll have some good news." He asked, "So, what's up with you and Aunt Sheila? Mom said you're staying here for a while?"

"Yeah, for about a week. I'll be in an apartment soon. Sheila is trippin' over some stuff she heard and saw," he said. "She kicked me out. Came home and my shit was on the lawn."

Tremel laughed. "Told your ass to settle down. You better start listening to your nephew, boy." I heard them slap hands then watched Mel's jeans disappear past the door. "I'll see you downstairs. They told me to tell you that the food is almost ready."

"All right. Give me a minute, I'll be down there," he said as he closed and locked the door and made his way over to the closet. "You need to get your ass out," he whispered and pointed at the window.

"I'm Tremel's girlfriend." I spat out my words before he reached for my neck again.

"What?"

"I'm his girlfriend. We came from Miami together."

"Ah shit." He asked disappointedly, "You?"

"Yes, me." I pushed my way past him and kept my voice down. "I didn't come here to start any trouble. I had no clue that you'd be here, so don't put your damn hands on me again." I marched towards the door.

"What's your price tonight, bitch?" he laughed. "Wait until I tell him."

I abandoned the doorknob and walked back over to him. "Please don't do that."

"Fuck you," he said with an evil laugh. "My wife is staring at pictures of me fucking you, won't let me see my kids, and she's filing for a goddamn divorce because of you, and you think I'm not going to tell him?"

"Please don't say anything. I don't even work for the Elite anymore."

"That's all right. You used to, and that's all that matters."

"What can I do to make you shut up?" I asked.

He groped himself through his pants. "I'm sure something will come up."

Going Broke

My head swung from left to right. "No, I'm not doing that." I was desperate. "I'll pay you."

"How much?" he asked.

"Anything." I was willing to do anything except sleep with him again. "I'll write you a check. Just please don't mention what happened."

"You sure you don't want this dick?" He pressed himself up against me.

I pushed him away. "How much should I write the check out for?"

Looking down at me he said, "Well, your pussy was fat and good as fuck, so it's probably been selling well. I think you can afford ten grand."

"Ten thousand dollars?" I wasn't whispering anymore. "Are you out of your mind?"

"Mel!" he yelled. "Hey, Mel! Come here."

"Okay." I swiftly placed my hand over his mouth. "Okay. Okay. I'll write you out a check for ten thousand." I was nervous. "This is a deal, right?"

"Money talks." He offered me his hand as a signature to our contract.

We shook on it. "Thank you."

"Bullshit walks," he said. "Don't walk out of Cleveland with my money."

"The rich would have to eat money if the poor did not provide food."
–Russian Proverb

Bank Statement # 15

Account Balance: $50,639.87

Out of all the families in the world—in America, in Cleveland—Norman had to belong to this one. He was Tremel's mother's baby brother. I couldn't get my head right. The house quickly became a maze; getting to the stairway was nearly impossible. Though I could see it, I just couldn't get there. I was freaking out. I remembered how to walk, one foot in front of the other. Soon I was skipping down the steps like I had just seen a mouse. My stomach muscles tightened when I heard Mrs. Colten's voice. "What's the headcount, sugar?"

"I—" I couldn't remember. "I counted fifty-seven." I made up a number and prayed that I was close.

She rounded up the bunch. "All right, everybody. Let's meet in the dining room."

I followed her down the hall to the large dining room. It seemed built just to host this occasion. Draped in white linen, the long rectangular table could seat twenty people, and four round banquet-sized tables would hold eight each. The room was dressed with festive fall colors: orange, brown, yellow, and green. Artificial cornucopias adorned the round tables, but the main table had two fruit baskets on it. The sterling silver utensils and place settings were perfect, even at the kids' table.

When everyone was in their seats, Mrs. Colten, her daughters and I rolled three long carts to the room from the kitchen and arranged the Thanksgiving buffet alongside the wall. Smelling the apple, cherry, and sweet potato pies, the children dashed toward the cart. "Uh-huh, no sir. Y'all know we don't do it like that." Grandpa Colten clapped his hand. "Go sit down." They obeyed his command and took their seats. He struggled to stand, and when he did, the room fell silent.

"Everyone stand, please. Hold hands and let's say grace." I was at the main table, next to Mel. We held hands, then I bowed my head and reached for his sister, Paula's hand now standing to my right.

Grandpa Colten began his prayer. "Father God, we come before You today thanking You for the many blessings that You've given us. Lord, we thank You for yet another day. Heavenly Father, we thank You for allowing our family to be together one more Thanksgiving Day. Lord, we're thankful for the clothes on our backs, shoes on our feet, food to eat, and a roof over our heads."

He took a deep breath. "Jesus, we come before Your throne this afternoon to say thank you, thank you for dying on Calvary's tree. Oh Lord, You thought it not robbery to hang Your head and die for sinners like us, and we thank You today. Jesus, for You I live, and soon, Lord, soon for You I'll lay down my life."

He breathed deeply again. "Thank you, Lord, for life, strength, and good health today. Without You we'd be a bunch of nobodies, and we wanna thank You, Father." He paused. "Oh Lord, bless our homes, bless our family, bless the food which we are about to partake. Bless it Lord. May it do our bodies good. Bless the hands that labored so that our bellies can get fat." I heard the

Going Broke

kids giggle. "And Lord, when this life is over, give us a home in Your kingdom. In Jesus' name I pray." We all closed the prayer together. "Amen."

Grandpa Colten cleared his throat and spoke once again in his deep voice. "Look at the food. Look at the meat . . . My Lord, it smells good. C'mon kids, let's eat." The children cheered and rallied around him, and surprisingly, they let him be first in line.

My heart was still racing, but I had forgotten why until Norman walked into the dining room. He stared at me and suddenly winked. I looked away. Mrs. Colten walked over and greeted him with a hug. "I thought you were dead up there." She was just talking, but oh, how I wished that it was so.

"No, I had some calls to make." He glanced over the room. "I had some things I had to line up." He walked over to his mother, Grandma Hall, and started a conversation.

As good as the food looked and   smelled, I had no appetite. If I could have requested one thing to eat, it would have been invisible ink. As long as Norman was in the room, I didn't want to be there. Tremel was talking to me and I didn't have a clue about what he was saying. All I could think about was how unbelievable this whole thing was. Norman and I were in the same house for Thanksgiving.

"Uncle Norm," Mel shouted above the noise and gestured for Norman to come our way.

I turned to him sharply. "What are you doing?"

"I want you to meet my uncle," he said with a smile. "Don't tell me you're still scared."

"No, but I've just met so many people, I can't remember any names." I tried to sound upbeat. "You have a huge family. Give me a minute. We're here until

Sunday." It was too late. Norman was already walking toward us with a stupid grin from ear to ear. Mel stood and they slapped hands again. I pretended to be looking elsewhere while they talked about the football game. Moments later, Norman initiated the introduction.

"This must be the young lady you were telling me about?"

"Yes, this is Sarai." Tremel looked down at me and rubbed my arm. "Sarai, this is my uncle Norman."

I turned around in my seat and offered him a half smile. "Hello."

"Sarai, huh?" He reached his hand out to me.

"Yes." I wanted to slap his hand, but I took it.

"Man, you look like someone I know," he said.

"Oh really?" I couldn't read his expressions. I didn't know what he was going to say next.

"Yeah," he kissed my knuckles, "but you're a lot better looking."

Mel grabbed my hand from his uncle's. "All right, all right. Enough of that," he joked. "You're in a world of trouble as it is."

"You know how I do it." Norman laughed and walked away.

I used my time during dinner to get to know Mel's siblings. They were all very smart, laid back, friendly, and polite. I felt as though I was having dinner with Sandra, Denise, Theo, Vanessa, and Rudy. They made me feel welcomed, not like the outsider I thought I'd be. I managed to eat a full plate of food. I figured that if I didn't eat, Mrs. Colten might be offended. I kept a watchful eye on Norman because he was throwing back drinks quickly. I was concerned about him turning into a babbling idiot.

Going Broke

After dinner, the banquet tables were folded down and the stereo turned on. It was dance party time, and the children were first on the floor. And whom did they take with them? Grandpa Colten. Keith Colten, eighty-five years old, had been a church deacon and trustee for forty-seven years. Tremel talked about him so much that meeting him felt weird. It was like I had met him months ago. It seemed we all had gone bass fishing in Lake Eerie together. I imagined him reading stories from the books of the Bible, and I pictured him teaching Tremel how to ride a bike.

Grandpa Colten was stepping big on the floor with his grandchildren and great-grandchildren. It was a sight to see. All eyes were on him as the music played. We all laughed, clapped, screamed, and then panicked when we realized that after ten minutes of dancing, Grandpa wasn't showing us a new move when his eyes protruded from his skull. He grabbed his chest and fell to his knees, then forward to the ground. The house was in hysteria. Anyone that had breath in their body was screaming. I couldn't recall whom, but someone had enough sense to call 911. The paramedics were there quickly, and as they left with the patient in the ambulance, we all followed in our crowded cars. We forgot anything rational and burst through red lights, expecting traffic to adjust to our situation.

The Colten and Hall families filled the emergency area and were relocated to a private waiting room. There were about twenty chairs in the room, magazines, and a television tuned to Cartoon Network, but even the kids weren't interested. They wanted to know what happened to Granddaddy. Tremel sat next to me in a chair and buried his head in his hands while I rubbed his back. Hour after hour went by. Sometimes we laughed, but the majority of the time we just stared blankly at something, anything.

Finally the doctor walked into the room wearing a neutral face. He closed the door behind him. "Hello." He took a seat next to Mr. Colten and addressed us as a group. "I know that this is a hard time for you all since it's Thanksgiving Day, but any other day this would've been just as terrible. You have my sympathy." We all held our breath; no one was sure what type of sympathy he was offering. "I wanted to let you know exactly what took place."

The doctor continued, "His heart's arteries were blocked, and Mr. Colten suffered a massive heart attack." There were sighs and cries all through the room. "We performed heart surgery and sewed in a new piece of blood vessel to bridge over, or bypass the obstruction. We fixed the immediate problem, but there were other arteries that were leading to a blockage, so we fixed them as well. We repaired three arteries altogether, so what we performed is what is called a triple bypass." He took a deep breath. "His age plays a major part on how, or if he'll pull through this." He paused. "The next seventy-two hours are extremely critical. He is currently in ICU. In the morning, you will be able to see him two at a time, but as for tonight, let's limit it to just two members of his immediate family."

Tremel's father and Grandma Colten followed the doctor. A few minutes later, Tremel got restless and sprung from his seat and out the door. I was right behind him and so was his mother. His face was flooded with tears. He started punching the air with his fist and let out a few loud grunts. His mother gazed at me, gesturing for me to take control. I guess I had to. He wasn't her little boy anymore; he was my man.

Going Broke

I walked up behind him. "Baby, I'm sorry." I ran my hand slowly over his head and then his back. "I'm here for you." He didn't say a word, but I felt him trembling underneath my fingertips. "All we can do now is pray. That's what he'd want us to do." He looked at me as though I was right. I gave him a little smile. "Mel, let's pray for him." He slowly turned to me, grabbed both my hands and right in the middle of the hallway of Saint Michael's hospital we silently asked God to restore the same health and strength that Grandpa Colten was so thankful for just hours earlier in his prayer.

When other family members left to drive home, Tremel didn't. He refused to leave the waiting room, stating that someone should stay. It took his mother and I an hour to convince him that there was nothing he could do by sitting there. At 1:00 in the morning, we were finally on our way back to the hotel. We took a shower together, and as much as I admired his beautiful brown body, I couldn't expect him to be aware my desires. I pulled the towel from his hand and bathed him just like a servant did to her king. I lathered him from head to toe and he never said a word. All he had to do was stand still. He was my emperor, and I was willing to humble myself before him.

I moved the cloth over his chest, felt his heart beating and wondered what my life would be like had I not fallen victim to Conrad's sweet talk. I still wouldn't have a job, but I would've taken something, anything, even if I had to leave my apartment and get something meager down south. I would do anything to change the decisions I made. Two good things came out of my time in the Elite: daddy's care and the money being sent to Savion to help with his illness. However, the worst thing that could ever happen, Norman being Mel's uncle, meant the road of my life that Tremel knew nothing about was making a U-turn and headed to the truth.

I thought of many ways to avoid giving Norman money. The only way around it was to tell Mel about everything before his uncle did. If I told him about Norman, then I'd have to tell him about Julian, Doctor Baker, the pastors, and the lawyer. I was now faced with making a decision to lose or to keep the one thing that made sense to me.

I joined Tremel in bed where he didn't talk much. His mind was still at St. Michaels'. He was thinking of a man he loved and was afraid to lose. And so was I. This night there was a different kind of moaning and groaning. It was all done in our hearts. We both longed for the betterment of something we believed in and loved. His situation was out of his hands, but I had the ability to change what I was going through.

We were at the hospital early the next morning. As soon as it was visiting time, Tremel and I were standing by his grandfather's bedside. Liquid-filled tubes and wires ran back and forth from Grandpa's body to the machines nearby. Tremel was better composed, though melancholy, and not a tear was in sight.

With his eyes closed, head upright, and hose coming out of his mouth, Grandpa Colten was laying there so still it seemed like his spirit had left the building.

Mel said into his ear, "Want to hear a song?" His hand moved over Grandpa's snow-white mane. "What about your favorite hymn, Pops?" He grabbed his stiff hand. "How about a little Precious Lord?" he chuckled and then cleared his throat. "Precious Lord, take my hand. Lead me on, let me stand. I'm tired, I'm weak, I'm 'lone. Through the storm, through the night, lead me on to the light. Take my hand, precious Lord. Lead me home." Tremel sang three verses of the song and had nurses, doctors, patients, and visitors all tearing up and amazed. Though I didn't see It, Tremel said that at the very end of the song his grandfather squeezed his hand. It was the first sign of life anyone had seen since he fell ill the night before.

I left Tremel and ran toward the waiting room to tell the family that there was a sign of life. However, on the way there I ran into trouble— Norman. "I changed my mind. I don't want a check. I want cash," he said.

I scanned the area for family members. "I'm not traveling with that type of money."

"Then go to the bank," he said.

I lied. "I bank with a credit union, and I can't take out more than two hundred a day at the ATM, so you'll have to wait until I get home." I was sick of him.

"I'm not waitin' on shit," he said. "I want that money before you leave."

"Why?" I tried to keep my voice down. "You own a bunch of jewelry stores. You don't need my money." I wanted to spit on him. "Why are you doing this to me?"

"You did it to yourself, bitch," he said. "You sent those pictures to my wife and fucked up my family." He pointed at me. "Because of you, my life is hell. And you're right; I don't need your money. Ten grand ain't shit to me. But because you tried to ruin my life, you better believe that I'm damn sure gonna to try to fuck yours up too." He walked away and left me standing there like we were two passing strangers who weren't talking.

Norman was like a termite; he was eating away at me and I was about to crumble. What do people do when they have pests? They call an exterminator. A friend of Damian's, Big Ralph, was "hired help," and all I had to do was compensate him for his skills and time. I was ready to pay a price to see that Norman did not talk to Tremel or to anyone ever again. Many times I had watched the news and saw people get busted for hiring a hit man who was really a detective or some loser working for the cops, but that hadn't turned me off from the idea. The verdict? Do or die. What I wanted to do would cause someone to die.

I continued my walk to the waiting room. I moved very slowly, trying to remember what it was I was supposed to say to Tremel's family. Before I made it there, a doctor rushed past me, and by the time I got there, everyone was screaming and crying. Grandpa Colten had given up the ghost. Shortly after the announcement, a nurse ushered Mel into the room and he fell into my arms.

Because of the funeral arrangements, we ended up staying an additional week in Cleveland. During that time, I truly felt like a part of the family. You couldn't tell me that my last name wasn't Colten. Tremel and I spent day and night at his parents' house, helping to make arrangements, phone calls, and decisions. We never left the house for the hotel until after midnight each night. Though Norman was always there, he acted the way a human should. I guessed the death had humbled him. He was actually nice to me when we were alone together, and he never mentioned the money.

"There's no place like home," Tremel said as we walked into the apartment from the airport. "Seems like we haven't been here for months." He rested our luggage on the living room floor. "I can't wait to get to bed."

"Me too." It was just 5:30 on a Sunday evening.

"But we have a lot of mail to go through." I looked at the blinking light on the answering machine. "And twenty-six new messages."

"You're checking all that stuff on your own." He dragged the bags from the living room to the bedroom. "I'm about to lay down."

"No," I whined. "I'm not doing your dirty work." I ran behind him and pounced on the bed. "Get out of this bed. We have to do this stuff together. All of that mail isn't mine." He closed his eyes and faked a snoring noise pretending to be asleep. "Get up, Mel. Even Rip Van Winkle can't fall asleep that fast." I started tickling him.

"Stop." He was laughing uncontrollably. "I'm going to hurt you, girl."

"Come on. Let's go through the mail so that when we get in bed we can stay." I grabbed his hand and tried dragging him out of bed.

He hopped up. "All right, fine. But you owe me a massage."

"Deal." We walked into the living room and sorted the mail as we listened to the messages over the speakerphone. We went through almost twenty messages before hearing a young woman's voice. "This message is for Tremel Colten. My name is Alexandria Mitchell; I am an executive producer at Jump Records." My heart leaped as she continued. "We had a chance to listen to your demo a week ago, and I've been trying to contact you ever since. I decided to leave you a message this time." Tremel and I stared at one another. "We were very impressed, and are hoping for the opportunity to work with you. A proposal was priority mailed to you, but we still haven't heard from you. Please review it ASAP, and if you're still interested, please call me here at Jump. My number is . . . " I couldn't believe what I was hearing, but she continued. "If possible we'd like to get you out to Boston right away."

Tremel and I were still staring at each other. We were both in an extreme state of shock. I couldn't believe that Julian had done me the favor anyhow. I hadn't told Mel about trying to submit to Jump, and he never submitted because he didn't think he stood a chance with such a major record label. He didn't say a word. His smile said everything that he couldn't.

A full minute went by before he whispered, "Play it again." I hit the button, and this time we giggled dizzily during the entire message. At the end he said, "This can't be real." We hugged. "Is this a joke?" He repeated the question over and over again. "I can't believe this." He kissed me several times before he realized that we had business to tend to. "We have to find that proposal," he said anxiously. "I'm calling them first thing in the morning to let them know that I'm still interested." He added, "Very interested."

I was sitting in his lap by this time. I squealed, "Baby, we did it." I corrected myself. "Well, you did it."

He looked at me like I had just pinched him. "You were right the first time. *We* did it. You've been there for me, helped me get all of those demos out, made phone calls." He paused. "We did it." He kissed me softly. "I love you."

My stomach was quivering. Though we still didn't know exactly what was up, the fact that something was up had me on a high. "I love you too." I got up from his lap and began to look over the mail. We opened envelope after envelope in search of the dream. In the midst of our search, the phone rang. It was Nat. She notified me that

Going Broke

Nick had asked a teacher at school to find out her ring size. I shrieked with happiness for her. It was the beginning of December, so Nick no doubt had a big question to ask her on Christmas day. "Wow." I walked into the bedroom, leaving Tremel to sift through the mail alone. "I'm so happy for you." I sat on the bed and smiled like it was my special day.

"I can't believe this," she said. "How do I act surprised, though?"

I thought about it a bit. "Just pretend that he's asking for your size to buy you a pair of gloves," I joked. "So when he pulls out the diamond, you just fall to the floor."

"I can't believe this, Sarai," she said. "After all of these years, I finally found the one."

Did she mean the one as in one inch? I laughed to myself, "Who did he ask for your size?"

"Mrs. Cooper." I could tell how happy she was.

"He should've asked me. I wouldn't have let you know anything." In a way, I was disappointed that she already knew. "She should've kept the secret."

"Well, she never actually told me," Nat said. "See, this is how it happened. Nick met Sharisa, Mrs. Cooper, at the Thanksgiving thing at the school last week. I saw them talking a lot. I even caught a little attitude about it, but I kept cool, though. I didn't say anything, but I had major beef." She paused. "Anyways, what happened was she came into the lounge today with this jewelry magazine and sat with me. All of a sudden we're discussing jewelry, and she asked my ring size." Nat took a breath. "At first I thought I was just paranoid, but when I was in a restroom stall, she came in and I heard her on her cell. When she said 'Nick? She wears a size six,' I thought I was going to die."

"Whoa!" I smiled. "I say you just go on with business as usual. Don't let him know that you know." My heartbeat was racing for her. "So, we have a wedding to plan, huh?"

She screamed with joy. "Oh my God."

"I'm jealous," I said. "I want a big fat   diam—" My sentence was interrupted by Tremel's voice.

"Sarai."

"Oops." I had forgotten all about Tremel's good news, but I didn't want to prematurely discuss anything. Plus, it was Nat's moment. "My man is calling me. Let me get back to you." I hung up and walked into the living room.

"Did you find it?" I asked as Tremel stared at me like he had seen a ghost. "Is that it?" I asked, looking down at the oversized envelope in his hand.

"No." he pointed to the manila packet on the sofa. "That's it." He reached inside and showed me the contents. "But I found this." The saying 'what you do to others will come back to slap you in the face' slapped me smack-dab in the kisser. Even after taking a deep breath, I realized that there was nothing I could say to explain the pictures he handed me of his uncle and me doing it doggie-style. My life slipped into a coma. I knew that when I woke, up nothing would make sense and everything that I had before would be worthless.

"What the fuck is this, Sarai?" His eyes welled up with tears and seeped with anger and disbelief. He hit the photos. "What the fuck is this?" He snatched the pictures out of my hand and flipped through them quickly. "How could you do this to me?" His lips trembled with fury. "My uncle?"

"It's not what you think. I can explain, Tremel." I wanted to reach for him but was too afraid, so I took a step toward him instead. He stepped back. "That didn't happen in Cleveland. It happened a while ago."

"My uncle?" He frowned at me as though I had an odor. "My fuckin' uncle?"

"I didn't know that he was your uncle back then." I was trying to sell him on that statement.

He asked, "Back when?" and before I could answer his question he continued. "Why didn't you tell me that you knew him?" He threw the pictures and sent them scattering all over the floor. "When did this shit happen?"

My emotions caught up with me, but more devastatingly, so did my lies. I was crying, "When I went to Atlanta."

"Atlanta?" He did a quick calculation. "Weren't we together then?"

I was sobbing. "Yeah," I whispered. "Please let me explain."

"You were supposed to be there for a job interview. I can't believe this." He couldn't keep still, but he kept his cold, cheerless eyes on me. "You cheated on me."

"No. It's not what you think. I wasn't cheating on you," I said.

He yelled. "You weren't cheating?" He picked up one of the pictures and pushed it in my face. "If you weren't cheating, then what the fuck were you doing, Sarai?" He shouted, "You cheated on me. You lied to me, you . . . " He paused. "You did it with my uncle."

"It's not what you think," I said weakly.

"It doesn't matter what I think. I think that that's blatantly obvious," he shouted. "You don't give a damn about me."

"I do." I reached for him but he turned away. "Please just hear me out."

"Hear what? You don't have to say anymore. I don't

want an explanation." He pointed at himself. "I gave you no reason to cheat."

"I did it for money," I blurted out in an effort to be understood.

"Money?" he asked in utter disbelief.

"I was broke, Mel. I had no money, nothing." I tried to contain myself. "I was about to get kicked out of here, my car was about to be repossessed, and my dad's fuckin' nursing home bill had to be paid," I shouted and cried. "I slept with men for money."

"Whoa. Wait a minute. Men?" he asked in a clarifying tone. "How many men?" Before I could say a word he was back at me again. "You're a prostitute?" He chuckled out of madness. "I can't believe this shit. Here I am respecting you, wouldn't even sleep in the same bed with you until we both decided to be exclusive, and you're a fuckin' ho."

"I needed the money." I grabbed his hand and he yanked it away from me. "Just listen to me, please," I begged.

"I have nothing to listen for. And you don't have anything to say to me." He continued, "Don't say anything else to me." He disappeared into the bedroom and I followed him. "I'm getting the fuck out of here." He grabbed his already packed suitcase then pulled clean clothes out of his drawers and began stuffing them into his luggage. "Just get the hell out of here so that I can do this."

"Tremel, I love you."

He stood still and looked at me. "You don't love me. You didn't even like me in the beginning when you learned I didn't have any money. You never thought anything of me. I offered to help you with the rent and you told me that you didn't need my help. Trying to be all independent instead of—"

I stopped him. "That's because I knew that you couldn't afford it."

He yelled, "Don't tell me what I can and can't afford. I offered to help you many times, and you wouldn't allow me to. You made it seem as though you weren't hurting." He walked over to me. "I might not be Damian or them other cats, I may not be able to afford to pay rent here, but if I knew that you didn't have the money, we could've moved into something that I could afford." Tears were streaming down his cheeks.

"You refused my help and allowed other men to help you by sleeping with them. I guess you really have changed from the night of that party. I guess it really does matter that I don't have a business card, a flashy sports car, or a house of my own." He looked me up and down. "I guess I'm just your charity case, huh?" He continued, "Well, I'd rather sleep on the damn street tonight than sleep with you." He zipped up his suitcase.

His words were like grenades; he threw them, didn't care where they landed, and left me wounded and confused. "Please don't leave me," I begged. "I'll tell you the truth about everything."

"The truth don't mean shit to me now." He put his hand in my face.

"Okay, just please don't leave me." I was hyperventilating and snot was draining from my nose. "Just hear what I have to say."

He was annoyed. "What?" His eyes looked back at me and hit me like a fist. "What in the fuck do you have to say, Sarai?" He backed up into the dresser and leaned on it. "You have the floor. What in the hell more does your sorry ass have to say?"

I spent the next hour telling Tremel the truth. It all

started with Damian leaving me penniless and me losing my job. I confessed that it all started in the Bahamas as a mistake but turned into the only way it seemed my life would get better. I told him about my doctor, the men in Virginia, my Atlanta trip, and my trip to Trenton to take the photos. Without issuing the gory details, I stayed completely honest with him. However, I didn't tell him about Julian and Jump Records. I worried that he'd think he didn't deserve the chance and wouldn't take it.

When I was done, he asked me tons of questions that I could tell he couldn't stand the answers to. Though we were both in tears, he wouldn't let me get close enough to comfort him. It wouldn't have mattered if I had said sorry in every language; Tremel made it clear that he was through with me. In silence, he grabbed the handle to his suitcase, picked up a couple of pairs of shoes, and strolled out of the bedroom. When I heard the front door close, it felt like he had physically closed it on my heart. I let out a scream so loud I was sure that my neighbors were contemplating calling 911.

Though I had done many outrageous things to obtain it, now that I had it in abundance, I couldn't use my money to get what I needed most, Tremel's love.

Going Broke

"The last time I saw him he was walking down Lover's
Lane holding his own hand."
–Fred Allen

Bank Statement # 16
Account Balance: $56,639.27

A week went by, then two, then came the holidays.
I drank no eggnog, didn't put up a tree, and refused to
hang a stocking. The only thing that made it feel like a
holiday was the pain of being alone. On Christmas Eve, I
claimed I was too ill to attend Nick's Christmas party. On
Christmas, I complained that I thought I was coming
down with the 48-hour bug that had been plaguing
Miami. I was fine! I stayed home and watched T.V.
specials, cried, and waited for the phone to ring. On
Christmas Day, I sang carols all alone and opened up my
one gift. It was perfume, Weekend by Burberry London,
from Nat. I had a gift for Tremel in case he came by. It
was musical and songwriting software for his computer. I
typed up and printed out over fifty songs that he had
handwritten in a notebook. He didn't come.

On January 3, two men showed up at my
apartment with a letter from Tremel. It read: *Ms. Emery,
I've hired movers to collect my possessions. Please be kind
enough to show them what belongs to me. Thank you for
your cooperation. Mr. Colten.* In front of two strangers, I
was forced to realize that he really wasn't coming back. I
allowed the movers in, and while they moved his musical
equipment, I heard them bickering about how long it'd

278

take them to drive to Boston.

"Boston?" I whispered then wept as I folded Tremel's clothing and stacked it neatly into the three boxes the men provided for me. In two hours, the only physical remembrance of Tremel I had was the dead crab in the freezer and a bottle of his cologne that it would kill me to part with. Ever since the night he walked out, I sprayed a little on the backside of my hand so that through the night I could pretend he was close by. "Boston," I said again when I let them out.

I turned on my Billie Holiday CD, poured a glass of Kendall, and rummaged around the Internet to find out the exact distance between Miami and Boston— 1,520 miles. I sipped my wine, and after the alto saxophone cried, Billie sang, *Good morning heartache, you old gloomy sight. Good morning heartache, thought we said goodbye last night.* The song was over fifty years old, but it seemed like it was written just yesterday for me. How did Billie know?

In one of the boxes with his clothing, I put his still-wrapped Christmas gift, and along with his songs I typed out, I included one that I wrote for him, entitled "Come Back."

Didn't know how good I had it until I didn't have it anymore.
Thought you were coming right back when you walked out the door.
I can't bring myself to wash your pillowcase,
I need your smell near . . . just in case
I get lonely, I get worried, or I get scared.
My house can't be a home if you're not in my bed.

Trista Russell

Chorus:
If I said I'm sorry in every language, would you forgive
me?
You're right, what I did was wrong, and I have no good
reason.
I miss you, return to me; in you arms is where I long to be.
If love grew on trees, this would be my season.
Make an exception; I know that you don't backtrack,
but baby, just come back. Please come back.

Damn, I was stupid. How could I hurt you that way?
I remember our first date just like it happened yesterday,
I still think of the night you came over and never left.
That was the same night that I reported a blatant theft.
You walked in and stole my heart without a gun to my
head.
Look at me now. Pull the trigger, 'cause I'm better off dead.

Chorus:
If I said I'm sorry in every language, would you forgive
me?
You're right, what I did was wrong, and I have no good
reason.
I miss you, return to me; in your arms is where I long to
be.
If love grew on trees, this would be my season.
Make an exception; I know that you don't backtrack,
but baby, just come back. Please come back.

Come back, come back.
Yes, I'm down on my knees.
Come back, come back.

Going Broke

Not ashamed to beg, please.
Come back, come back.
I don't know what else to do.
Come back, come back.
I can't go on without you.
Come back to me.
Come back to me.

I didn't expect anyone to pity me or feel sorry for me, and I couldn't say that people were wrong for uttering the words "that's what she deserved" when they thought of me. Some said that I got what was coming to me; others said that I didn't get enough. But they all agreed on one thing, and that was that I rode the wave of my lies too happily and for too damn long. When I told my story to people, I changed my name to Deborah, to protect the guilty, and the general consensus was, "That's a nasty bitch. if I was Travis, I would've left her too." The more feedback I received, the harder it was to keep coming home to an empty house.

As I rolled over in bed and looked at the clock, I whimpered, "Boston." It had actually became one of the first words out of my mouth every day since I heard the movers say it, and that was two months ago. It was early March. I was giving myself until Saint Patrick's Day to get over Tremel or I'd check myself into an institution. Tremel and I were only together for four months, but it felt like four years, and I was acting like it. I was still crying over spilled milk like it had chocolate cookies in it. Women only mourned over a man this long if he was hella fine, rich, or throwing it up and slapping it back down in the bedroom. Tremel was two out of three and had me about to lose my mind. Lord, if he had money, I think I would be in a diamond-studded straightjacket right now.

When the phone rang, I was still answering like it could be him. "Hello?" I said anxiously.

Nat asked, "When are you going to get over it? I can still hear it in your voice."

"Well, good morning to you too."

"Good mornin', Ms. Emery," she joked. "What are your plans for the day?"

"Why?" I looked at the caller ID. "Where are you?"

"On the road," she said.

I scanned the calendar for a holiday. "No school?"

"I called out. I have something important that I need to get done," she said.

I asked, "What?" She never missed school unless it was a real emergency.

"Put on some clothes and pack a bag. We're going to Naples for the weekend. I'll be picking you up in twenty minutes." Before I could protest, she continued, "I'm already on my way."

I hardly ever left my apartment these days. As we spoke I was still in bed. "You should've called me and told me before right now, Nat."

"What in the hell do you have planned other than sitting and thinking about the dick that got away?" she joked. "Not a damn thing. So, get out of that bed and be ready."

"Oh my God. Are you serious?"

Nat yelled, "Yes!" Then she asked, "Do you have five hundred dollars cash on you right now?"

"Yes. Why?"

"Just bring it." She continued. "I'm not coming up there. I'll call you when I'm downstairs." With that said she hung up in my face. What a friend.

"Shit." I jumped out of bed, ran into the bathroom to turn on my hot curler, brushed my teeth, and jumped into the shower. After that was done, I raced around the room talking to myself as I threw clothes into a suitcase. "How in the hell did she just plan a trip to Naples?" I gathered a few pairs of shoes. "She could've asked me first." I curled my hair. "What is in Naples anyways?" I gathered my things. "Isn't that where all the old people move when they retire?"

Nat actually gave me an hour. It was close to noon when she phoned and told me to get downstairs. In the car, she stuffed my money into her purse then informed me that during our weekend, if I spoke Tremel's name she'd deduct ten dollars each time. If I cried, she'd take twenty-five, and if she caught me with a frown, for whatever reason, the price was fifty dollars. Those were her rules, and she didn't wait for me to agree. Those were the rules.

Pulling up in front of The Ritz Carlton in Naples was all I really needed. The lobby was a treat all by itself. I was already in a better mood. The Gulf of Mexico was right in back of the hotel, so Nat and I wasted no time changing into our bikinis and walking out to the beach. After lying out in the sand and talking for a while, we decided to get into the water. Nat was afraid of the fish; even the tiniest guppy had her screaming like the people did in *Jaws*. We were in water up to our belly buttons, which was as far as she was going. "I can't believe that you're scared of these little things." I tarried closer to the shoreline with her.

"It's the little ones that cause the problems." Nat stared into the water and jumped whenever she saw anything fishlike. "They can swim up inside of you and lay eggs." She laughed. "Soon you'll be walking around thinking you got a yeast infection, but what you really got is a two-piece fish and chips plate."

"You are foolish." I laughed like I had been wanting to for months. "You are too foolish."

She got serious. "I'm so happy that you came with me."

I playfully threw some water her way. "Thank you for inviting me."

She pointed out into the distance. "They say that the ocean is supposed to be soothing, so go out there and sooth yourself, and don't come back until you're cured." She smiled. "I'll be right here waiting for you."

I joked as I swam off. "That's if the fish don't take you away." The temperature, water, and its movement felt so good. Nat was right; it was soothing. I don't know exactly how long I was floating around and bobbing up and down, but boy, did I cry. I still hadn't forgiven myself, and I wasn't sure if I should. Since Tremel left all I had managed to do was beat myself up. It took me up to now to realize that if living meant living without him, then that's what I had to do. I was never the victim, but I fooled myself into thinking that I was, nursing invisible wounds and taking medicine for a heart that I had broken on my own.

Finally, I started thinking realistically and not selfishly. Damn, what was in this water? It was like my tribulations had solidified and were floating on the waves. Though I could still see them, they didn't seem so great anymore. Someday soon they'd crash upon a distant shore, and I prayed that they would never find me again. A white flag was waved, and the battle between my heart and mind was done. I plunged beneath the surface and returned to the top like I had just been baptized. I ran into peace of mind somehow, and was ready to throw away the bottle of cologne that I used to fool myself with at night. It was time to let go. It was also time to stop Billie Holiday's "Lover Man," "Solitude," "Them There Eyes," "Crazy He Calls Me," and "Good Morning, Heartache" from being the soundtrack of my life.

The ending of a relationship is a lot like going broke. First it hits you, but you don't believe that your funds could really be that low, so you call your bank's automated system to confirm the balance. You're more comfortable dealing with the computer, too embarrassed to talk to a live representative. Second, you hang out with your friends and pretend that all is well, but you're really counting every penny, every drink, and hoping that the gas in your car will take you where you need to go. Third, by the time you decide what to do to help your financial situation, you have a negative balance and a bunch of overdraft charges, which means that whatever you do, any deposit you make will still go toward mistakes you made in the past.

Nat and I had a very meaningful weekend. I couldn't say thanks enough. It was exactly what I needed, time away from mourning. We had facials, massages, ate at ritzy restaurants, and had our hair done in the hotel's salon by an old white lady who turned us into a black Laverne and Shirley. We went in only for a wash, but Margaret insisted that she curl us too. On the elevator, we laughed and sang, "One, two, three, four, five, six, seven, eight. Sclemeel, schlemazel, Hasenfeffer incorporated." Our dreams came true when we shook, combed, and hot curled those grandma curls out of our hair back in our room that Sunday afternoon. We reflected on our trip and agreed that it was the best time we had spent together in a very long while.

During the two-hour ride back to Miami, we discussed the wedding. Nat and Nick were planning a winter wonderland Christmas-themed wedding set for Christmas Eve, one year from their engagement date. Nat asked me to use the drive to look through a bridesmaid's catalog and tell her which of the seven I liked the best. Wine and black were her colors. I thought it was a great combination and knew that wine would work with my complexion. I turned the pages and found a dress that made me not want to turn anymore. It was a European satin, strapless, three-quarter length dress with a two-inch ribbon tied at the natural waist. It was ivory and the tie was black, but for Nat's event it would be wine with a black tie. "This is the one." I hit the page.

She kept her hands on the wheel and looked over. "Great, that's my favorite." She focused on the road again. "I think I want y'all in those shoes too."

"I don't know about that." I looked at them. "But I can see me in that dress."

"Me too." She smiled.

We both went quiet long enough to hear the radio. I didn't know what station she was listening to, but it had to go. Elton John's "Can You Feel the Love Tonight" was playing. "Oh, hell naw." I reached for the knob. "We need some soul up in here with another hour on the road, sistah."

I flipped through station after station until I got to 99 Jamz. A song had just started. It sounded familiar, and as the intro played, I told myself that it absolutely couldn't be. My heart accelerated. I stared at the radio and waited until Tremel started to sing "Forgotten."

It's been a while since I've been in this boat, but the one thing I remember, lady, is how to stay afloat.

I tapped Nat and pointed at the radio repeatedly.

Please don't swim away, there's something I have to say. Baby, you don't have to respond, just don't stop feeling our bond. You are something I thought only dreams would let be. I can't remember my life prior to you and me.

Right before the chorus I cried, "That's Tremel!"

"What?" Nat's eyes grew big.

"That's Mel," I said out of breath.

"Are you serious?" She turned it up.

"Yes." I was smiling from ear to ear. "He did it." I knew the words, but I was too excited to even sing the song. For a split second, I thought we were still together. I reached for my cell phone, but there was no number to dial. As I listened to the song, I remembered that it was written for and about me.

After the song went off, the female radio personality spoke. "Yes, ladies, we have in the studio with us the newest addition to the Jump Records family, Tremel." She paused. "How you doing today, sweetie?"

"I'm all right. Thank you guys for having me."

"The pleasure is all mine. Believe that," she flirted. "This song is tight to death. We played it for the first time three weeks ago, and now that's all they want us to play. Congratulations, boo."

He had to be blushing. "Thank you."

"Did you write *Forgotten*?" she asked.

"Yes, yes I did."

"Okay, you know you just opened up a can of worms, right?" she asked.

"Oh boy," he responded jokingly. "Naw, what's in the can?"

She asked, "Since you wrote it, we ladies want to know. Who is it that you can't forget?"

There was silence and my heart almost stopped. "Well, I actually wrote it for a friend of mine that was contemplating asking his girl to marry him."

"Did he ask her?"

He laughed. "No. Things didn't quite work out with them."

"Well, forget him," she joked. "It worked out for you."

"It did, it did. I got a hit single out of it."

"You sure did," she said, "and I can't wait to see the video."

"Is that right?" He sounded like he was flirting back.

"That's right," she said in a sexy tone. "Actually, can I be the chick in the video? You know ... the one who'll give you something that won't be forgotten."

"Whoa." Tremel laughed. "Sure. I don't see why not."

"Oh mama, I'm gonna be in his video," she said and giggled. "What you doing after the video shoot, though? You wanna go half on a baby?" Her laugh sounded like a donkey. I was so annoyed.

"Let me behave." She continued. "I was told to ask you this by every woman that called the station when they heard you were coming. Are you married, engaged, or in a relationship, and are you accepting booty call applications?"

"Wow." He cracked up for a while then answered. "No, no, no, and it depends on how big the booty is." I dashed to turn the station, but Nat intercepted and shot me a dirty look.

"Ladies, if you think he looks good on the CD

cover, you've got to see him live. You've gots to see what I'm seeing." She took a deep breath, sighed, then continued. "Now I feel like Nelly. It's gettin' hot in here. Lord have mercy." She changed the subject. "So, how are you enjoying the South Florida weather?"

"Well, I'm no stranger to Miami. I was living here until December. I lived here for two years."

"And you never called me?" she asked. "My booty is pretty big."

He said, "It sure is."

She giggled. "Is there anyone here in South Florida you'd like to give a shout out to?"

"Ah," he thought for about two seconds, "I'd like to give a shout out to the Marlins, world champions. Job well done, guys." There was a bunch of clapping, cheering, and shouting in the station for a few seconds. When everyone calmed down, he continued. "I'd also like to say hello to everyone at Northern Miami Middle School. Go Panthers."

"All right, Northern Miami Middle, y'all represent fa ya boy." I could do a better job than she was doing. Why wasn't I working there? "So, I hear you're going to be at Vocalize tonight doing your thing."

"Yeah, I'll be there doing some poetry." He plugged himself. "Miami, come out and get into some spoken word at Vocalize on the beach."

"What time you want me there, baby?" she asked.

He snickered again. "Doors will be opened at eight, and the first poet goes on at nine."

"All right, Miami, Y'all heard that? Give it up for Tremel, y'all. Go out and get the CD, *TreMelody*, at a music store near you. Also, get to club Vocalize on the beach tonight where Tremel will be going back to his poetry roots, so represent, Miami." She paused. "It was very nice meeting you, Tremel."

"Likewise," He added, "I look forward to seeing your face in the place."

"No doubt." She seemed to get louder. "All right, Miami. It's five o'clock, which means I'm bouncing up out of here. See ya." A commercial came on, and I felt like I wanted to feel on Christmas, New Year's Eve, and Valentine's Day. Although he wasn't speaking directly to me, hearing his voice did something for me. There was a tiny part of my heartache that didn't drift away in the Gulf of Mexico. I still missed him.

Back at my complex, I traveled alone on the elevator and allowed myself to flirt with the idea that there might be a message from Tremel on my answering machine. Best-case scenario, he'd be waiting upstairs for me, willing to take me back. Everything I thought I had given up to the ocean flooded back into me as I turned the key to my apartment and walked in to find things just as I had left them. My messages? Two. They were both from Savion. He was doing okay and was just calling to say hello.

"Damn, I can't go back into this feeling sorry for myself shit." I was seeing the strength I built over the weekend melt away like snow. "I can't stand this." I sprung up from the sofa and walked over to the mirror. "I don't even recognize you." I really felt like I wasn't myself anymore. I was a puppet, not of Tremel but of myself. I was allowing my emotions to pull my strings. "I have to get out of here." After some fast ironing, a shower, and a sit-down makeup job, I did just that. I got the hell out of my apartment.

It was 9:00 when I started driving the streets of Miami looking for a place to go. At 11:00 I still didn't have a clue what I wanted to do. The radio station made my search seem endless by choosing this hour to be their Whitney Houston hour. At the moment they were playing "Didn't We Almost Have It All." The song was a slap in my face, but I didn't change the station. I toughened up and took it like a woman. Trying to avoid where I obviously wanted to go, which was club Vocalize, I traveled in the other direction. I feared that going there would make my lonely situation even worse.

I drove around and around trying to find a place to go. I was stuck in traffic on Washington Avenue when Whitney sang that there was something on her mind. When Whitney asked where broken hearts go, I threw caution to the wind and made a U-turn. I knew where to take my broken heart. I was through denying it. I had to see Tremel in order to block the doorway to the insanity in my life.

As I walked through the doors of Vocalize, Tremel's face was the first thing I saw. He was on a poster outside the second set of doors. Seeing him made me nervous. I was trembling. I continued into the club, skipped the bar, and was glad to see the crowd of people. I wanted to see him but I didn't want him, to see me. I asked a man if Tremel had performed yet and he said no, Tremel was the last act. I smiled and surprisingly found a vacant spot on a couch. There was an older man on stage reciting a poem about sex after age sixty ... that's exactly what everybody came to hear.

A few acts later, Twalik "Leroy" Abdul came to the stage draped in clothing from the motherland. "All right, the next performer is probably the reason we don't even have standing room in here tonight. You've had the opportunity to listen to his entire CD, *TreMelody*, before the show began. It is on sale at the front door as well."

291

He grinned. "If you don't live under a rock, you've had to have heard the song "Forgotten" on the airwaves." All the ladies screamed. "He may be a stranger to America, but he's no stranger to us here at Vocalize. He's come a long way and we're extremely proud of him." My heart was beating like he had just said that Dr. Martin Luther King was found alive. "Ladies and gentlemen, sistahs and brothas, queens and kings, I present to some and introduce to others Mr. Tremel Colten." The crowd went wild, but Twalik didn't leave the stage. "That's right, y'all. Give it up. He deserves it." I clapped my hands wildly, but I was too afraid to stand.

When the crowd calmed down and took their seats again, I was staring hopelessly again at the love of my life. He looked better than I ever remembered he could. Smoother skin, goatee trimmed, hair cut very low. His upper body looked even firmer; the black fitted shirt said it all. He adjusted the microphone stand. "What's up, Miami? What's up, Vocalize?" he yelled and the crowd yelled back. "It's great to be back. I've missed you, I've missed your energy, and I've missed the love that you have for me." He looked out over the crowd. "Thank you for all the support, thank you for the support, and thank you for the support. I can't say that enough. Thank you." He smiled. "Y'all are probably tired of hearing me on the radio, so tonight I'm going back to my other love, poetry." As the crowd clapped in appreciation of whatever he wanted to do, Tremel cleared his throat and took a sip of his water.

Going Broke

Two tears in a bucket ... and fuck it.
Real women don't do things that result in an apology.
Even if they do, there is a proper methodology.
My mother said "If you make your bed hard, then lie in it."
Enough of your tears, your explanation, fuck that shit.
Lies, lies, and more lies; I don't need that shit.
Stood by you, behind you, and in front if you wanted me to.
Treated you like a queen, did things nobody else would do.
I didn't deserve what you did and how you did it to me.
Left you 'cause you were keeping secrets from me.

Left you 'cause you were sleeping with men that weren't me.
Left your ass 'cause you were making a damn fool out of me.
Once! You only get to do that one time.
Very convenient for you to confess to a crime
Everyone but me knew that you were committin'.
You didn't swallow, did you? You should've been spittin'.

Oops! Did I offend you? Ask me if I care.
Understand that I don't hate you; I just don't want you near.
Still, the thought of you makes me upset.
And I have to sing that song, so I won't soon forget.
Remember how I kissed you? Remember how we met?
And remember how I said that you I'd never regret?
I've changed my mind, and yes, this is my outlet.
Everything I feel for you is now off of my chest.
My mind is finally cleared, now my heart can rest.
Even if you don't hear me, I have just one request.
Remember that this is the way you wanted things to be.
You're the one that really walked away . . . not me.

He knew that I would show up, and once again he used the microphone and stage to humiliate me. His intention was to make me feel about as big as a mustard seed, and he had exceeded that. As the crowd roared and stood to their feet to praise Tremel, I stood too, but not to worship Mr. Colten. I walked toward the exit. Before I made it through the first set of doors I was already in tears, so I dashed through them and into the bathroom. I landed in a stall where I quietly let out my frustration.

"I hate you, Tremel." I wept and whispered to myself. He had just told about two hundred people all of my business, and I couldn't appreciate the "art" in that. I was looking for closure and I found it. I wanted nothing more than to slap the taste out of his mouth. The line between love and hate was on a diet. It got so thin that I hopped over it and ran. "I can't stand you." I wanted to punch the tile, but I'd look pretty dumb walking out of the restroom with a broken wrist. It took me fifteen minutes to count to one hundred, dry my tears, and contain myself enough to make it to my truck.

As I walked down the sidewalk, people were staring at me like Tremel showed a poster-sized picture of me and told folks to avoid of the whore. I sucked up my paranoia and almost ran to my truck when I saw it. I just wanted to get in, go home and call Nat to tell her that I wouldn't mind if she collected the $200 loved ones received for turning in someone to the insane asylum. For a moment, I wondered if they'd give me the $200 if I presented myself as I walked in. "You're so stupid," I said to myself with a laugh.

I deactivated my alarm, looked back at the club, knowing that it would probably be the last time I would ever see Tremel. I smiled and said, "It was nice knowing you." When I opened the door, there was an assorted bouquet in shades of purple flowers I saw on the driver's side seat. My hands covered my mouth, and I let out a muted cry. I picked up the arrangement and read the card. *I'd like to call a truce. Please meet me back inside to negotiate the terms. Tremel.* They were the exact same words he captured me with.

Instead of being overjoyed, I was filled with mixed emotions. A part of me wanted to run back into Vocalize and jump back into his arms. Another part of me wanted to run back into the club and jump-kick him. A part of me said that expecting him to forgive me was selfish and undeserving. And the last part said that I needed to leave well enough alone. After two minutes of thinking, I did what I thought was best. I walked over to a homeless lady sleeping on the sidewalk and placed the flowers in a bag next to her, then I got into my truck and pulled onto the street.

I rode around for an hour trying to convince myself that what I did was right, but for the life of me I couldn't understand my decision, and I didn't until I pulled into my parking spot. For the first time in a long time, I, Sarai Emery, thought not only of myself but of someone else. It didn't matter that Tremel was now floating in cash. What did matter was that Tremel did treat me like a queen, and he deserved better than what I did to him, better than anything I could probably ever do. I couldn't expect him to forgive me after I knowingly did what I did to him. I no longer felt worthy of his forgiveness. I was just happy that his dreams came true and he didn't hate me.

The End . . . Almost
(Stop here if you're not a hopeless romantic.)

"'Tis better to have loved and lost than never to have loved at all."
–Alfred Tennyson

Bank Statement # 17

Account Balance: $45,689.61

I walked into my apartment and found things just the way I left them, a mess. Newspapers, shopping bags, magazines, cups, and clothing were everywhere. Forget lying down and curling up in bed, I needed to make this place look livable. I spent twenty minutes in the living room before it actually looked like the room I was paying rent to be in. After picking things up and washing dishes, I started vacuuming and spotted a small box on the sofa. "Stuff is poppin' up from everywhere," I said to myself as I turned off the Hoover. I grabbed the box and walked to the kitchen before opening it. "Aaaaaaah," I screamed and sent the box and the live blue crab falling into the trash can.

"It took you long enough to find it." I heard a voice coming from my bedroom and stepped into the hallway to see Tremel walking out with a smile. "I come in peace." He threw his hands up as a symbol of the end of the war. "If you don't want me here, I'll go, but first I'll let him out of the trash can and then you'll be on your own," he joked.

I was in disbelief as he got closer to me. "I'm so sorry," I said, my body beginning to quiver and tears were sliding down my cheeks. "I didn't mean to—" I stopped in mid-sentence. He was close enough to touch, but I didn't know if touching him was the right thing to do. However, it was what I wanted to do most.

Seeing my hesitation, he moved first. He pulled me to him, stared into my eyes, and wrapped his firm arms around me. I breathed a sigh of relief, remembrance, relaxation and then buried my head in his chest. As though we were dancing, we stepped slowly until we backed into the sofa where he sat down and pulled me into his lap.

I gazed at him a while as though he was a ghost. I didn't want him to disappear like he did in my dreams. I pinched myself and ran my hands over his face like I was Helen Keller or Stevie Wonder. I needed confirmation that he was truly in front of me, not just a figment of my nightly imagination. I closed my eyes and embraced him. When I opened them and found that he was still there, I knew that I could die a happy woman tonight. Right there in his arms, I cried the Nile, Mississippi, and Potomac Rivers.

I knew why he was back, but even if he had only come to pick up a pair of socks, I would still feel the same way. Tremel made me love him; no other man had ever sat me down and told me why he loved me. I waited my entire lifetime to find Tremel, and being without him felt a lifetime longer. It wouldn't matter if he was still sweeping floors, bussing tables, or opening the front door of a hotel for its patrons. Real love comes but once in a lifespan, and before my eyes closed that night, I could say that love was a friend of mine.

He spoke, "I'm not going to lie. I was hurt. I didn't want to see you, want to hear your voice." He sighed. "I needed time to figure out if I was man enough to believe you, understand you, live with you, and love you." He took a deep breath. "And I came to a conclusion that I want to at least try," he said as he rubbed my back again and again. "Sarai . . . I'm back."

"I, I . . . " The other part of my soul had been found, perfect timing. "I didn't mean to hurt you. You have my word that I will never do that to you again, I'm so sorry." Although I was hyperventilating, I tried to smile. "Three months felt like forever."

"Yes," he said, "but a minute earlier would've been a minute too soon."

"I'm not that type of girl, Tremel." I felt the need to explain. The night he left he only heard what I did, but not why I did it. Not that any reason would be justifiable, but it wasn't because I didn't care for him. "Times were hard, and I saw everything that I had slipping away from me. I was going to get kicked out of here, I needed money for Daddy, my truck was about to be taken, my phone, my lights. I felt like I was in a tornado all by myself. I couldn't land a job, and it seemed like I had nowhere else to turn." I sighed. "The moment I got involved in it, I knew that it would somehow ruin my life, and the moment I started lying to you, it did ruin my life. There was nothing I wanted more than for you to come back, but I was prepared to accept and understand if you never did." I cried, "Thank you. Thank you so much for thinking enough of me, in spite of what I did, to give us another chance."

"You were always on my mind," he said. "I never stopped thinking about you."

I joked, "You mean a big time singer had time to think of me?"

He tickled me quickly. "Yes, he did.

"And enough time to write that awful poem too." I had to go there.

He fumbled in his pants pocket until he handed me a folded piece of paper. "Read it." It was a written version of the same lines he scolded me with at Vocalize earlier.

I put on a heavy, old, Deep South voice. "I don't think I could make it through another whippin,' massa'."

He laughed. "Then just stare at it and see if you get the message." He held the sheet in front of me.

I was confused. "What am I looking for?"

"Never mind." He turned to me and looked at me peculiarly. "Sarai," he paused, "you hurt me more than anyone I've ever known—"

I interrupted. "I know and I'm—"

"Shh." He silenced me. "You've hurt me more than anyone I've ever known, and I think that is because I love you more than I've ever loved anyone in my entire life." He paused. "It killed me not to call you, not to see you, and not to be with you over the past few months." He paused briefly. "When everything started happening with my music, I was happy because I thought that it would make it easier and I wouldn't think about you so much." He shook his head. "But singing those songs over and over again, knowing that you're the life behind the lyrics was hard." Then he added, "Plus, you're partially responsible for me being who I am right now. You helped to make my dreams come true, and ... I just can't see my life without you."

Thank God his shirt was black because my makeup was running a marathon down my face and onto him. "I didn't know about you being on the radio until today." I sucked back snot I felt was on the verge of draining down and embarrassing me. "Congratulations. I'm so happy for you."

"We've made it," he whispered in my ear.

I blushed. "Hearing you on the radio earlier was how I ended up at Vocalize."

300

"I announced it because I wanted you there."

"I almost didn't go, though. Then I said   In a way I wish I hadn't."

He cringed. "Why?"

"Hmmm, let's see . . . " I pretended to have to think about it. "Because you tore me a new asshole with your poem." I rolled my eyes playfully.

"A new asshole?" Tremel cracked up before he continued. "I had some steam to let out, but at the same time I wanted you back in my life. So, I dusted my feet before I came back in. I didn't want to walk back through the door with that anger." He made sense to me. "I'm not here to deal with that situation. I'm here to deal with the fact that I still love you." He smiled and held up the poem again. "Look at the first letter of every line."

I did, and read aloud the words formed by those letters. "Tremel still loves you, Sarai Emery." I looked at him. "Aw, that's so sweet."

"So, even though I was rippin' you a new one, I did it because I'm still in love with you." He moved closer to me. I felt his breath on my top lip and got nervous like we had never touched. "I love your hips, I love your thighs. I love your lips and the way you roll your eyes. I love not just what you say, but the way you say what you say. I love being with you, love coming home to you every day. I love when you're strong, but I love it when you're weak. I love when you're happy, but even when you're bleak. I love the big things, but also the simple things that we do. For you, I'd do anything, Sarai, because I love you."

"I love you too." I held him tighter and felt my mouth open, but didn't know what I was about to say. "Please don't leave me again."

"Didn't you just hear what I said?" He picked up

my chin. "I love you. I'm never leaving you. I'm never giving up on you, on me, or on us. When I saw you giving the homeless lady my flowers, I knew that I hadn't gotten through to you." He smiled. "Coming here was Plan B." Then he pointed at the kitchen. "The crab was Plan C."

"So, you forgive me?" I asked.

"Yes," he said. "Let's just promise to keep no secrets from here on out." Tremel was willing to be with me, love me, and forgive me all in the same hour. I had to be hallucinating.

"I promise." I paused. "But I have another confession." He looked concerned, so I continued. "I kept a bottle of your cologne."

"I know. I saw it on your dresser. You owe me because when I left, that thing was almost full."

"Child, please! Owe you what?" I asked.

"I'll think of something." He started tickling me and I jumped off his lap. "Come back here," he yelled, but I was already running around screaming.

"Don't tickle me! I have to pee," I joked. We played around for two or three minutes before I fell into his trap. I was dumb enough to run into the bathroom, and with nowhere else to go, I turned on the water, grabbed the removable showerhead, and pointed it at him. "Step away from me." I was still giggling. "If you tickle me, I'll be forced to shoot you."

Tremel took a few steps toward me with his hands up as though he was really in a life or death situation. "Ma'am, I am not armed, so please put down your weapon."

"Stop!" I yelled. "Don't take another step. I don't trust you." I looked him up and down. "What are you hiding?"

"I don't have anything." His hands were still up. "I

come in peace."

"I don't trust your kind." I scanned his body like he was a criminal. "Take off your shirt."

"Come on, that is ridiculous," he said.

"Obey my orders or I swear I'll pull the trigger, sir."

"Okay, okay." I watched him remove his shirt. Seeing his chest again made me ready to stop playing this little game. "Do you want my pants off too?" Tremel smiled.

I smiled back. "As a matter of fact, I do." I held the showerhead closer to him and pretended to be astonished when I saw a bulge beneath his silk boxers. "What's that?"

He joked, "That's a weapon of mass destruction." He went to reach for it and I sprayed him. "Put your hands up, sir." He obeyed, lifting his hands back over his head. "Remove your shorts slowly. Let me see this destructive missile."

"No problem." He removed his boxers, and all of the nights he had pleasured me with that weapon flooded back to my memory. It was still beautiful, pointing straight at me like it was a compass giving northern direction.

I walked over to him. "How do I know that you're not hiding something in your mouth?"

He moved closer to me. "There is only one way to find out." When our lips touched, I quickly pulled his tongue into my mouth. During our gentle oral tug-o-war, he passionately slid his tongue between my lips. It was a welcomed visitor. I forgot about the showerhead, I dropped it and sent it crashing to the ground. We were both breathing heavily.

Tremel was back! Back inside of my apartment, my arms, and back inside of my heart. He wrapped both of his hands around my waist, and during our nasty tongue tango, he didn't unbutton or unzip anything. He literally ripped the clothing from my body. At first when I heard the material tearing, I thought of the cost, but I quickly dismissed that thought. My man was back, and if he wanted to snag the skin from my bones it would be all right tonight. I felt his extension growing more and more against my stomach. "Is there a way to deactivate that missile?"

"I'm sure there is." We kissed and took baby steps all the way back into the dark bedroom. I reversed into the bed and crawled backwards into it. "Will you allow me room in your silo to prepare for the deactivation?" Tremel asked.

At this point, he was sexier than ever to me. "Yes, yes," I whispered, pulling his body down toward mine on the bed. "Make love to me." Had he asked to park it in my backyard I might've consented that night. "Make love to me, Tremel."

He continually pecked at my nipples. "May I leave my gun powder inside of your storage area?" I knew exactly what he was asking me. The week before things went berserk, Tremel and I, in Cleveland, discussed the possibility of starting a family. It was agreed upon that we both wanted a baby. I told him that when I was ready, I'd stop taking the pill, which I did a few months ago. Tremel had said that when he was ready, he'd just simply stop pulling out as he always did. Tonight was the night.

"Come on." I reached down and guided him into me. "Give me all the gun powder you've got." Before he was completely through my entrance I was trembling, grabbing hold of his back. During the first thrust we both let out loud gasps. Our bodies started vibin', they said

304

hello, began a conversation, then let loose to do pleasurable damage to one another. He plunged, thrust, and sweated while I grinded, squeezed, and squealed. He plowed his gunpowder rapidly into my silo. I was glad to be the keeper of it. His lips found mine and tears soaked me once again. He held me atop him the same way we had finished.

"I have a question to ask you," he said.

"Ask." I rested my chin on his chest to look at him.

"Can I interest you in looking for a job ... " he continued, "in Boston?"

My heart skipped a beat; this was no metaphor. "What do you mean?" I knew what he meant.

"I already have a place there, but I want *you* in that place." He smiled. "Move to Boston."

"Move to Boston?" I asked with a Bostonian accent.

"Yeah," he mocked me.

"Shore," I joked. "Sure."

I didn't truly appreciate Tremel until I had to face living my life without him. Like they say, you never miss the water until the well runs dry. Just as I couldn't appreciate having the finer things in life until I was at a point where no one liked to be, I was about to lose everything, including myself. Being back together was better than where we left off.

The End . . . Again

(That's if you're a sucker for romance. Only the bold can read on.)

* * * *

"I wish you were there when it was snowing."
Tremel pulled me closer. "It's beautiful up there. You'll love it."

I cuddled up next to him and thought of being with him, and closer to Daddy as well. "I love it already." I rubbed his chest. "Thank you."

"For what?" he asked in the darkness.

I answered, "For coming back." Suddenly then I heard noise come from the living room area. "What was that?" I asked him.

He chuckled. "It's probably just the crab, it may have crawled out of the garbage and hit the floor."

Then there was another sound, like something had fallen down in the kitchen. "Whoa." I was scared.

We both sat up and Tremel now seemed very concerned. "Did you lock the door behind you?" He sat up.

"I think so." I tried to remember, but it was too late. The bedroom door swung open, the lights came on, and in stepped Dwayne Cart/Damian Carter. "Damn, how the tables have turned," Damian said. His face was evil and full of rage. "I come home and you're in bed with someone else." He laughed.

"What the fuck?" I threw my bathrobe over Tremel then reached into my dresser drawer and grabbed my ugly and bulky green housedress. Tremel, in my robe, was pissed. He passed me on the way to Damian. "How did you get in here?"

He frowned at Tremel. "The same way that you did, motherfucker."

I didn't want problems, so I got between the two of

them and pushed Damian out into the hallway. "Damian, what are you doing here?" I was scared out of my mind, but happy that Tremel had picked this night to come back. "What do you want?"

He said, "I'm here to finish what you started."

"What in the hell are you talking about?" I asked as I backed him up into the living room. Whatever was going to happen, I didn't want it to take my place in my bedroom.

"You fucked up everything that I planned." He didn't flinch, falter, or back down. "Me fuckin' with India was part of a plan," he said. "She had exactly what I wanted—money. Her shit was supposed to be the way I started my own company. But you and your jealous ass had to find out and go ballistic. Then you sent her up to my hotel room. That was wrong, that was dumb. I almost killed that bitch that night. I put her in the hospital, and I've been in jail for almost four months. I got fired from my damn job at the firm. I've lost everything."

While Damian spoke, I saw Tremel grow angry. I watched his hands form fists and knew that that wasn't the answer. I spoke up before he did anything. I believed that I was the right one to handle the situation. "I'm sorry, Damian." I wasn't sure if I meant that. "I didn't mean to cause all of that to happen to you." I tried to calm him. "What can I do to help you?"

He reached into his jacket and pulled out a 9 millimeter. "You can start by getting this nigga the fuck out of my house."

"I'm not leaving." Tremel wasn't intimated. He stood bravely beside me and grabbed my hand. "And if I do, she's coming with me."

This was a whole new ball game. "Please put the gun down," I begged. "I'll do whatever you say. Anything you ask me to do, I'll do it. Just put the gun away, Damian."

He aimed it at Tremel. "What now, pretty boy?" "What the fuck are you gonna do now?" Damian's eyes were watery and his pupils were dilated like he was on something. "There is something that you can do for me." I had never seen him this way. His clothing was wrinkled and dirty, and he smelled like he had been rolling around in vomit. "You can suck my dick again, right here in front of your man."

"You're out of your fuckin' mind." Tremel let go of my hand and leaped toward Damian. He pushed him onto the sofa where they wrestled around a bit. I saw only hands and feet; I couldn't see the gun.

"Stop!" I screamed. "Please stop." My fear was that Tremel wouldn't walk away. I yelled, "Stop it!" as it happened. I heard the trigger click, then the gun went off. Tremel's body stopped moving, then so did Damian's. I was confused; I couldn't move. My hands rushed to my mouth. I couldn't even scream when I saw a sign of life. Both Damian and Tremel stood to their feet. They were fine.

As crazy as everything was around me, I found the strength to smile as Tremel walked over to me. I was happy that he was all right. "Sarai." Tremel looked at me. "Sarai." He called out to me again. As badly as I wanted to answer him I couldn't.

"Oh my God!" he screamed, but my eyes couldn't focus on him. I couldn't focus on anything. My sight just got dimmer and dimmer until I couldn't see, then I felt my legs fold under me. "Sarai," he called over and over again. He thought I was close to him, but in reality I was already miles away. He yelled at Damian, "Look what you did! Look what you did!"

Going Broke

He asked Damian to call 911, but Damian yelled something back and I heard the door slam. Tremel left me only for a moment to run and get the phone. He hit three buttons, then I heard him telling someone my name, address, and the entire story of what happened.

"I love you, Sarai," he cried. "Please don't leave me like this." I felt his tears hitting my face, and if I could cry I would've. If I could do anything, I would've. He ran his warm hand down the side of my cold face. "I love you. Please don't go, Sarai. You can't leave me like this." He rocked my upper body back and forth. "Please stay with me. Let me sing for you." He tried to stop crying. "I had forgotten how to live, forgotten how to give. I forgot how to trust, and how to lust. But through you I learned to care. Please forgive me if this seems rare. Now that I've found you, my life seems brand new. So, you'll never be... forgotten." It was the chorus to the song he wrote for me.

"Where are you damn guys?" he screamed, growing impatient that there was still no sign of the police. "We can't wait on them." He wept and cradled my lifeless body and walked me through my apartment; he struggled to open the front door. "Don't you leave me," he yelled at me as I heard the elevator doors open.

"I shouldn't have come here tonight." He blamed himself. "Just hold on, Sarai." His voice was starting to sound further and further away. "Don't you leave me."

I didn't know how to tell him, but I was leaving. As we made it to the ground floor I heard sirens. Tremel burst out of the elevator doors with me folded up in his arms screaming for help. Help was waiting, but I was already gone.

The Real End
(for now)

309